Power
The Year the Lights Went Out

By
Suzanne Goldring

From one powerful woman to another!

Sue

ISBN-13:
978-1523407194

ISBN-10:
1523407190

Dedication

The Elstead Writers Group
with thanks for their support and encouragement

Tuesday, October 8

The power's been off for five days now. Everyone's saying it's like this all over the country and they don't know when it will come back on again. Some people are saying the national grid has been sabotaged and we'll be without power for months. At first there were radio bulletins declaring a national state of emergency, telling everyone to stay calm. They also announced that the Government has been moved to Chequers and the Royal Family have been evacuated to Balmoral. But now we can't get any more news on the radio, apparently they were relying on backup generators which could not last forever.

The village shop sold out of fresh bread and milk the day it happened. People were anxious but not panicking, though some were struggling to understand why they couldn't pay with debit cards. Luckily, Martin had sold his record collection on eBay for cash only a week ago, so we actually had money in our pockets. We stocked up on dry goods and long-life milk and I'm now beginning to think about what else we will need if we are stuck without power for a long time. Being used to bad weather in the country I've always laid in a good stock of food for the winter, but I can't rely on the freezer now and must think carefully how to use what we have.

It is strange to live without TV and the papers, or any kind of diversion. So I've decided to keep this diary, partly to record what we learn in case we are in it for the long term and also in case, for whatever reason, I am no longer here. Life has suddenly become very different to the way it was before. There are no trains, no commuting to London, no television and no computers. We can still charge our mobile phones, but the transmitters must be down now and the landline is dead. We no longer know what it is happening in the world, let alone our own country.

Wednesday, October 9
Today we have finished a strange soup I made with the vegetables that are normally frozen. Peas, broad beans, sweetcorn and spinach all stewed together with the last of the tomatoes and diced bacon for protein. We have no bread left now, but we didn't waste a single crumb, unlike before. The last crusts, hard though they were, tasted good softened in our freezer soup.

I am annoyed with myself though for not making better use of the meat we had in the freezer. It was hard to believe that the power would not come on again in a day or two. So by the time we realised how hard things might be, we had already eaten some chicken pieces and some of the minced beef. But once we began to get a clearer idea of our predicament I decided to preserve what could be kept. So I have a belly of pork and half a leg steeped in salt, which my oldest recipe book calls 'dry cure' and which I am praying will help the meat keep. I have made a big pot of stew with the shin of beef and the rest of the mince I made into meatballs with a little onion and stale breadcrumbs, then cooked them through. They keep for a few days in a cool place and aren't too dry heated up in a little flavoured stock. I used to serve them Italian style in a tomato sauce, but I am holding back on my tinned tomatoes for now.

I don't know whether to think we are fortunate that the weather has turned colder or not. Cold means the foods normally kept in the fridge and freezer are still usable, but the drop in temperature, especially overnight, means we need to keep the fire going for warmth as well as cooking. I've never cooked in our inglenook fireplaces before, but Martin has rearranged the firedogs so we can hang pans and kettles over the heat. I wanted to keep both fires going in the house, but Martin says we should conserve our wood and use just the one room until we go to bed.

I am trying not to worry about the children, they are adults, after all. But the country must be safer than the towns and cities. Stephen last rang us four days ago and Jane has not been able to call for five days. I must try not to worry. The hens laid four eggs today.

Thursday, October 10

We spent this morning collecting barrow loads of kindling from the surrounding hedgerows and fields. We have had another dry day and the wood will burn straight away. Once the weather changes and we have long periods of rain it will be difficult to dry the wood out. We are stacking it in the greenhouse, shed and garage, as well as filling baskets in the house. We still have a supply of firelighters for the moment, but cannot rely on being able to get any more. We also have a stack of old newspapers which we retrieved from the recycling bin as the rubbish collectors have not been on their normal rounds. This paper, together with dry twigs and the fir cones

3

we've collected, will light our fires in the weeks to come.

Martin has also been splitting logs from the seasoned wood which has been drying out over the last couple of years. We were sad when some mature trees, oak, apple and pine, fell in the last bad winter, but now we are very grateful for the firewood these have produced. It's a good mix of hard and soft woods which burns well.

It's hard work gathering, splitting and stacking all this wood, but we know it's essential if we are to stay warm and be able to cook and heat water. We are stacking the logs wherever we have a sheltered corner outside, in the porch, the lean-to and the old coal bunker. But I have drawn a line, so far, at letting Martin stack logs in the hall and drawing room. This is still a house, not a wood shed, I've said. We may be cold, but there are limits and filling the alcoves provided by the inglenooks is enough.

Four eggs.

Friday, October 11

A cold day. The weather changed last night. There was a bitter wind blowing this morning and although the sun shone for a bit, it could not raise the temperature. It has made us realise just how cold we are all going to be this winter.

Stephen arrived with Anna last night. Both were cold and very frightened. They were afraid to stay in Woking any longer. People have been looting the shops and taking goods they cannot possibly use. What is the point of stealing a flat screen TV in a power cut? A bag of flour has far greater value and I would gladly welcome it. I have six 1.5 kg bags of flour, as well as pasta, rice and a large sack of potatoes, but I have not worked out just how long it will all last. Anna sensibly brought food with her to add to our stock and they also thought to bring their warmest clothes.

And then we all sat by the fire and worried about Jane. We hope she is safe for the moment, as she said she would stay inside until there was further news. Martin wants to go and fetch her from her student flat in Bournemouth. The car has plenty of petrol as we had fortunately both filled up on separate journeys the day before the power went off. Martin had also filled up the four petrol cans we normally use for the garden machinery, so we at least have fuel for the time being.

After talking it over we decided that Martin and Stephen will go together. And though none of us likes the idea, they will take Martin's air rifle. If there is looting there may be other disturbances and a car with petrol will be a target. Martin will stick to the back roads and will drive through the night in the hope of meeting no one on the journey. Anna is concerned for her parents and sisters too, but they are too far to be reached, down in Cornwall. We are all trying to reassure her that as they live in a rural coastal area they will have food and the resources to keep well.

Only two eggs today.

Saturday, October 12
They were back in one piece by midday. I have never been so anxious in my life, wondering if they got

there safely then waiting to hear the crunch of the car's wheels on the gravel. Anna and I rushed out to hug them and bring them inside to warm by the fire while I made tea.

Jane was laughing about the difficulty Stephen had in getting her out of the flat while Martin kept guard over the car, but underneath her smiles I could see she had been very frightened. It's all very well having an entry phone system, but when there's no power a block of flats becomes a prison block. Stephen had to shout up to her window then meet her round the back, where the big wheelie bins get collected and help her climb over the locked gate.

Jane hadn't left the flat at all since the power cut first happened, but she had seen people breaking into the shops across the road and realised she was safer staying where she was. She laughed too about her enforced 'diet' of the last few days, then asked me what there was to eat. She has brought warm clothes with her but no food. Students don't keep much food in store at the best of times, unless you count the mouldering tin of beans in the fridge or blackened bananas in a bowl.

I was so happy to have Jane home and so relieved that Martin and Stephen had also made it back safely that I probably indulged them with more food than I should. I extended the stew with some meatballs and made dumplings with a little of the flour and some suet. They are always a favourite and make a good filling meal. Then we had apples I had baked in foil by the hearth with the last tin of custard.

Martin made light of their journey from Bournemouth but he looked very tired. Stephen said they noticed numbers of abandoned and wrecked cars as they drove and there were bonfires in the centre of the town and on the beach.

Sunday, October 13

Martin has found a radio station working. Not in the UK, but a foreign one which is issuing bulletins and weather forecasts. So now we know there is good news and bad news in what continues to be defined as a state of emergency. The good news is that attempts are being made to restore power supplies and to keep people informed of progress. The bad news is that this situation could go on right through the winter and also that heavy rain and storms are coming. Little was said about how people are coping in towns and cities, but we are all thinking the worst.

The news about the weather means we all agreed we should collect as much kindling as possible while we can. With five of us to do the work we can achieve a lot before the weather soaks everything. I had to keep breaking off and checking our fire indoors as I have potatoes baking in the ashes. It is easier than boiling and this way we don't waste the skins, although the hens are missing the peelings I used to boil up for them with bread and layers of mash. They have to be satisfied with weeds and a handful of corn, though I have also been digging in their run to make it easier for them to find worms for themselves. I am wondering whether to let them free range, which I never used to because they made dust baths of my flower beds, but I am worried that a fox will get them during the day and the hens are too precious for us to lose any now.

Anna noticed the heavy crop of beech nuts under

the trees and said she was sure she had read somewhere they can be eaten. So we collected those too, although many husks are already empty because of the squirrels. However, many more are yet to fall and we picked those we could reach. There is a good crop of acorns this year too, many more than our pet pig needs, so we shall have to find out if those can also be put to good use.

Three eggs.

Monday, October 14

The forecast was right. It has been raining steadily all night and all morning. It is now 4.30 in the afternoon and the rain is still falling. There is just enough daylight for me to see to write this if I sit near the window, but in a short while we shall need to light a candle.

I have now realised that when I rushed to the village shop at the start of this crisis I didn't remember all the things we would need. I didn't get nearly enough candles or batteries. And I should have bought water. Who would have thought that in a rainy country where flooding is often a problem we would not have fresh water? There is no longer any mains water and Martin has been up in the loft checking how much we still have in the supply tank. We also have some in our hot water tank, which of course can no longer heat.

We luckily have two rainwater butts, which we installed the summer before last when a hosepipe ban was announced just before one of the wettest summers ever. And Martin and Stephen are now investigating the old well in the courtyard. They have removed the grille and are clearing away the moss and ferns growing inside. Then they are going to work out how to collect the water and check the quality. I'm hoping nothing is living in it and that it will be drinkable. We may have to filter it somehow and then boil it.

Maybe rainwater will be safer. I am collecting rainwater in bowls and buckets I've laid out on the lawn, just in case. Anna and Jane are beginning to fret about washing their hair. We have all managed so far to wash as best we can in cold water, but we have not yet washed clothes or hair. I'm hoping the next forecast will give us a dry sunny day for that. I've realised that without electricity our lives have jumped back a hundred years, maybe more.

Four eggs today.

Tuesday, October 15

Anna found a use for the beech nuts which made us laugh. They can be used to make a cooking oil, which I think could be very useful, or roasted and salted as a nibble to serve with drinks! We thought that very funny in the circumstances, but she is determined to make them and says if it is still like this at Christmas we should have some treats.

It is about the only thing to make me laugh today as I have been fretting over water and washing. I heated some of yesterday's rainwater to wash my hair and underwear. Late this morning it looked as if the sun was coming out, so I hung the socks and pants out on the line, then an hour later there was a heavy shower of rain. I could have cried and I know it seems so trivial, but I really miss my washing machine and tumble dryer. Everything is now hanging over the fireguard to dry, but I really think we must get used to having a second fire lit so we can dry clothes away from the one that's boiling water and cooking food.

Water is very precious now. The dirty water we've used for washing is recycled in the downstairs toilet cistern. We keep a bucket of water in the cloakroom for topping up and have made it a rule that we only flush when it's really necessary. Hard to remember that sometimes when we were so used to mains water that we took for granted.

Tomorrow I'm going to call on Robin down the lane. He knows a lot about the countryside and I want to find out which of the fungi growing in our grounds are edible. There is so much around and it looks tempting, but I am terrified I will kill us all if I pick and cook the wrong ones. From the book I have I think we've a lot of honey fungus, horn of plenty and beefsteak fungus. It would be wonderful if they are all safe to eat.

No eggs today – the hens always seem to go off laying when there has been a lot of rain.

Wednesday, October 16

Didn't collect mushrooms, we did the laundry instead. Today was sunny and breezy, chilly but good enough to start drying our washing. We carried hot water up to the bathroom so we could tackle sheets and towels in the bath and have space to wring them out. Such heavy hard work and we siphoned off the dirty water into watering cans and buckets for flushing the loo.

Stephen rigged up a second washing line in the courtyard so we could get everything pegged out. I told the girls about my grandmother's old mangle. They could hardly believe that such things were once everyday appliances in these days of tumble dryers and washing machines with their spin cycles, but now they wish we had one.

We left the washing out till 4pm, when it clouded over and brought everything inside to hang over chairs and airers. I've asked Martin to hang my laundry rack up in the hall, so we can dry washing by the fire there. He'll agree to letting me keep two fires going if it means he can have dry socks.

Three eggs today.

Thursday, October 17

Today we had heavy rain until 2.30, when it was suddenly warm and sunny, which made us all feel much more cheerful. We quickly hung out some of yesterday's washing to finish drying in the sunshine. The bedlinen is more crumpled than I'd like, but I can't think how to iron it.

In the morning I visited Robin and he came back with me to identify the fungi in the grounds and garden. To our great delight we have a number of edible ones which we collected this afternoon and fried with eggs for supper.

In exchange for Robin's help I gave him some of our soup for him and his wife. I'm beginning to realise that we are going to have to help each other in this crisis and I'm wondering what we have that's worth bartering. No one's going to need advertising at a time like this, but Martin and I have joked that we could make comical birthday and Christmas cards. A fat lot of use that will be this year!

Robin says Deidre, his wife, has dried wild fungi in the past. Perhaps, if I offer to share some of our finds with her, as we have so much growing here at the moment, she'll show me how to do it. I suppose it will be a bit like the very expensive dried porcini the farm shop sells. Fancy that, gourmet treats in a time of national disaster.

Four eggs.

Friday, October 18

What a relief to have another warm sunny day. Not only could we tackle more washing this morning and have it hanging out by 9am, but we picked loads of honey fungus and field mushrooms. We have sliced large numbers of them and they are now strung up like Christmas decorations to dry. Our once tidy house is beginning to look like a refugee camp with washing hanging everywhere and buckets of water waiting to be boiled or reused. But today was a good day with all of us cheerful because of the sun and all of us busy preparing food, splitting logs and bringing in more kindling.

Anna and Jane have been collecting acorns too. Apparently they can be dried and used to make a flour or coffee. It seems odd that one nut can be made into two such different things, but it seems a pity not to collect them while they are so thick on the ground this year and we may be glad of them later if our supplies run low. There are still plenty left for our pig. The girls also picked up fir cones which have been falling steadily, and found a few more blackberries. We have quite a lot of fruit which will have to be eaten soon, as I can't spare enough sugar for bottling or to make jam.

The pork has been in salt long enough now, so I rinsed it properly in clean rainwater. Both pieces are hanging up to smoke now. I believe they could be eaten without smoking, but I'd like to be sure it will be safe to eat.

Three eggs today.

Saturday, October 19

Today I swapped some fungi for a few lettuce seeds. Martin is thinking of risking a drive to the nearest nursery to buy vegetable seeds. We have been talking about how we must plan to grow more of our own in case this situation goes on much longer, so we have decided to clear some of the flower beds. Part of the garden is fenced to protect it from the deer, so we'll concentrate on this section and prepare it for when we have the seeds or seedlings. I'm also thinking we may have to save some potatoes and use them in the garden. We still have a sack of potatoes in a cool dark corner in the pantry, but I fully expect some of them to be sprouting eventually.

So today I asked Simon to remove the kindling from the greenhouse so I could sow winter lettuce in there and more vegetables, if we can get hold of seeds. This may be the only green stuff we get when the weather gets colder. For the moment we have dandelion leaves, sorrel and bitter cress, but this will die out in the winter.

We all worked together to clear the beds. I felt a bit sad pulling out the first phlox and delphiniums, but then I thought about cabbages and onions and set to it. Martin and Stephen worked really hard and the beds were mostly cleared by the end of the day.

Four eggs today.

Sunday, October 20

Heavy rain and thunder this morning. I had been thinking about walking to church today if it was fine, not just for the comfort of the service but to maybe hear news of the village. It's about two miles away, which is nothing, but I would be soaked in this weather and I do not want to waste petrol. Martin is not keen for me to cycle there alone as he thinks we must careful now that people in towns are suffering.

Martin and Stephen didn't finish clearing the flower beds but instead split and stacked more logs. We are consuming a huge amount of wood, so they are talking about tackling some of the dead trees on the edge of the field. Most timber can't be burnt immediately, but the dead wood will burn readily without seasoning. However, I'm concerned for their safety as neither of them is trained to do this kind of work. This made me think about our ability to deal with injuries and I decided to check our supplies. We have disinfectant and TCP and one full tube of Savlon. I'm not sure how we'll manage if anyone gets more than a minor scratch, so I spent some time ripping up a clean old sheet into bandages.

After that I decided to stew some of our fruit down into a glutinous paste and spread it out on trays. This is apparently called 'fruit leather' and I am hoping it will keep well. I sterilised a couple of large jars with boiling water and when the mix has dried out I will cut it into strips and store them in the jars. It won't be very sweet, but I'm hoping it will add some variety to our diet and still give us some nutrients in the winter months. So far, we have all been in good health, but what shall we do if one of us becomes seriously ill or is injured? We have no way of knowing how the hospital is coping.

Monday, October 21

Heavy rain again from the start and on and off all day. Martin decided as it was so wet out he could safely drive around the area and check whether the local pharmacy was open, as well as the doctor's surgery. He came back to report that the chemist be will open on Mondays and Thursdays until further notice and that the doctor will be offering flu jabs tomorrow.

Martin also went as far as the dual carriageway, which he said was completely empty of moving traffic but he could see some abandoned cars at the roadside in the distance. He visited the nursery last of all and returned in triumph with cabbage, onion, pea and bean seeds.

And mid-morning Joe, our regular gardener, arrived in his truck. We had not been expecting to see him at all during this crisis, but he has turned up with all his tools and some warm clothes, asking if he may camp out in one of the outhouses. He is thin and tired, with dark circles under his eyes. He says Aldershot is chaotic and that people have run out of food and water and the weakest are dying. Joe lives alone and his mother is more than thirty miles away. He wants to reach her as she too is in a rural area and may be able to cope, but he needs rest and food first. We said he should sleep in the house as there are plenty of rooms and he has promised to help with felling the trees before he leaves us.

Four eggs.

Tuesday, October 22

We all walked to the surgery in the village today, leaving Joe working on one of the dead trees. He's not registered with our doctor so he said he will take his chances. When we got there, the queue stretched back almost to the green, but it was good natured, with people talking about how resourceful they were being and showing concern for their neighbours. It must be our isolation that makes us so resilient as many people remember the long power cuts of the eighties and have coped with heavy snowfalls in recent years. Everyone seemed to think the power must come back on again very soon.

When it was our turn for the jabs, Martin and I were accepted, because of our age, but the girls and Stephen were told they were not considered to be a priority. Two of our regular doctors and the nurse were on duty, all administering the vaccine quickly and efficiently, and also answering our concerns for staying healthy at this time. As I thought, we are being advised to boil the water from the well and to continue washing as much as possible.

After we left, we called at the village shop, which is also working restricted hours these days. It has little edible stock left now, unless you count cake decorations like hundreds and thousands and baking powder. But I thought it would be sensible to pick up more cooking oil, toilet paper, soap and washing- up liquid, all of which are being rationed by Ken, the manager. He said he wishes he'd got more stock, but there is no way he can get any supplies. The last normal delivery was the day after the power went down and he daren't drive to the nearest cash and carry as that is nearly twenty miles away and he could be risking his vehicle and his life, only to find an empty warehouse.

It was sunny this afternoon, so the boys finished raking and clearing the vegetable bed, while the girls collected more acorns to dry. I filled some seed trays in the greenhouse and sowed more winter lettuce.

Wednesday, October 23

Today started chilly, but as the sun came through it became quite warm and we all worked outside without coats. After picking the last of the apples, which we'll lay out on trays in a cool, dry place, I decided I simply had to tidy the flower garden. I know it is vitally important for us to grow our own food at this time, but I cannot bear to see my once flourishing garden deteriorate. The lawns are still growing and we cannot spare the petrol to mow the grass, so I must accept that they will be shaggy carpets from now on, but I can at least weed the beds and mulch and rake up leaves. The cosmos and michaelmas are still flowering and looked so lovely in the sun that I felt quite cheerful.

Martin and Stephen heaved barrow loads of compost from the heap to dig into the new vegetable beds, then decided to clean out the hen shed and add the poultry manure to the heap. They think it would be a good idea to collect some of the sheep and pig manure as well, but this too will have to be mixed and allowed to break down before it can be used. In the past we've usually had composted manure delivered by the sackful, but we can make our own just as well for now.

As it was so fine today, we had our main meal in the middle of the day and were able to cook outside on the barbecue. It was hardly the kind of food we used to have before this all happened and we did find ourselves reminiscing about steaks and pieces of chicken, but we enjoyed our bacon, eggs and mushrooms very much. And as we have so many apples, we had some stewed with raisins and honey.

All the hens laid well today and I collected six eggs.

Thursday, October 24

A cold start to the day, almost frosty, with a haze of mist on the fields. I couldn't get warm until midday, when the sun came out. It made me think about how we can keep warm as winter comes on, so I've been airing blankets we haven't used in years and finding all our old hot water bottles, which were never needed while we had electric blankets. I've also suggested that we all start wearing more layers and have found old gloves which I will cut down to make mittens for all of us to wear indoors as it gets colder.

Now that the dining room is functioning as the main room in the house, serving as kitchen and meeting room for all of us, we have rearranged the furniture slightly, taking the occasional tables away and replacing them with armchairs. I've moved the best china out of the oak sideboard too, so this can now house all the everyday pans and plates I need for open fire cooking.

We are all missing bread terribly. Such a basic foodstuff we normally take for granted, but how we long now for a hunk of fresh crusty bread to slaver with butter and jam. I have no way of making an oven for baking, so I'm experimenting with a batter similar to that for drop scones and cooking it on a flat baking sheet. The first ones were soggy, rather than brown, so I've done some more in a large frying pan, which works better. They can't really replace a crusty loaf which smells of yeast and has a satisfying bite to it, but they are something to dip in soup and fill our stomachs.

Four eggs today.

Friday, October 25

Mild weather today, but much more windy. Martin noticed that it is a south-westerly and says that means more rain is on the way. So it was a good day for drying our washing and there is the likelihood that more dead wood will fall.

The wind will also bring more acorns, which may turn out to be a blessing. We've collected loads so far and the girls have been soaking them to remove the tannin. This will take several days and then they will have to shell them before roasting and grinding them to make coffee. Goodness knows how all this will taste and what it will do to us, but they are kept busy and more cheerful and I know we shall be grateful if they are successful when our present supplies run out. If this goes on for a long time, I feel sure we can be resourceful and manage for meat, eggs, vegetables and fruit, though limited in variety, but our stocks of flour, sugar, tea, coffee and milk cannot last. And although I still have some butter, dairy spread, cheese and cooking oil, I must use these sparingly as I have six of us to feed, including Joe, who is still with us. Bread thickly spread with butter now seems a luxury.

Our kindling stocks are falling rapidly, so we all gather sticks whenever we go outside as a matter of habit and stack them under cover when we return to the house. Jane was in a bit of dream this afternoon and wandered back empty handed, but Martin noticed and shouted "Firewood" at her and she laughed and ran off to collect her share.

Five eggs today.

Saturday, October 26

Tonight the clocks go back. We all had a debate about it this morning, trying to remember which way round it was until Anna said, "Fall back, spring forward", which settled it. But what it didn't settle is whether we need bother. We are guided more by the daylight than clocks now, but Martin, who has always been a stickler for routine, says he will change all our clocks anyway, the windup ones that is, so we are in step with the rest of the country when the power returns.

I can't see what difference it makes as we are woken by the light, not by alarm clocks now as none of us needs to be up early for work, deliveries or appointments. We used to be woken by the paper boy and the milkman, but that seems so long ago now.

But I do like to be the first up to coax the fires and set the water to boil. I still like my morning tea, though I am having to get used to drinking it without milk. We have some long-life milk, but I want to save it for more important things than tea.

Today was very mild for the time of year and the wind was getting stronger. All the conkers have fallen now and Martin has collected them to throw on the fire when they are dry. It's a boy thing, I suppose, enjoying the explosions they make as they burst. The wind is stripping the leaves from the trees and normally I would want to clear them from the lawns, but it's too big a task without a petrol powered mower, so I'm only concerned with keeping the paths near the house clear, so we don't slip and fall.

Joe left us today and we wished him well on the journey. We will have no way of knowing if he arrives safely, so could only send him with our prayers and thanks, along with a little bacon and hard-boiled eggs to eat on the way.

Four eggs today.

Sunday, October 27

There was more rain in the night, so we shan't be short of clean water. It was breezy this morning and quite bright, so I hung out some washing and nearly managed to get it dry before it started to look grey just before lunch.

I woke with the first light, just as I thought I would, in spite of Martin changing the clocks. The hens don't know we've changed the time either and were ready to be let out and fed at 7am. They are still laying well, but will soon go off as the days shorten. I collected four eggs again today and wondered if I could work out how to preserve eggs but I don't think I can get hold of the right ingredients... isinglass, is it?

Our food is becoming somewhat dull I think, partly because of the lack of variety and partly because of the means of cooking available to us. If the weather is poor I have to cook over the fire inside and I haven't yet worked out how to roast. Today we could have used the barbecue again but we have no meat, other than bacon so we had to have another thick soup, which is what we are having most days. It was quite filling though, because I served it with some little dumplings I'd simmered in the soup, flavoured with rosemary. And I also had an idea because of all the apples we've collected and decided to make apple fritters with a thin watery batter, made with cornflour, then dusted them with a little cinnamon and sugar. They were really quite good and we all enjoyed them.

Martin thinks he can probably bag us some pheasant with his air rifle, so maybe we'll have meat again very soon. He is a good shot, but doesn't think the pellets will be powerful enough to get one of the deer that we see regularly in the garden. I saw three in the courtyard first thing this morning, nibbling away at the roses and really wouldn't mind if they got their comeuppance and ended up on our table.

Monday, October 28
Terrible wind and rain all last night. Martin joked

this morning that it was the sort of weather we used to dread bringing on a power cut. Now the worst fear is running out of water and food. We checked the outside of the house once we were dressed, but there was no damage despite the awful noises we heard in the night. Then we went round the grounds to see how much the storm had brought down. Our fences are still standing, so the sheep won't escape onto the lawns, nor can the deer penetrate the new vegetable garden. We found branches scattered everywhere and the large willow has two huge limbs dangling which we kept clear of while the wind was still blowing this morning. Willow is not very good for burning, but it can be cleared when the winds drop. A tree has been uprooted in a neighbouring field but there was no damage to the fence.

The acorns are still falling and are so plentiful that it's like walking on a pebble beach in places. Anna and Jane have soaked and dried the ones they've gathered and have shelled a large number too. They are going to try grinding some today to make acorn flour, then they'll roast others and grind them to make the acorn coffee. I have my doubts about both ideas, but as we shall run out of flour and coffee eventually it is worth trying.

After collecting more fallen kindling, I found a few more blackberries which are quite plump from a few days of mild weather and rain. And then I had my first row with Stephen because I came back inside the house and found him eating the berries straight from the basket. I told him they weren't meant for him, they were for all of us, and they would go much further mixed with apple. He looked at me in amazement and said he'd only had two. But we can't help ourselves to food whenever we feel like it now. We have to think about all of us as a group and we all have to stay healthy if we are to come through this difficult time. Then Stephen tried to make amends by digging over the hen run so the chickens could find more worms and I felt rather mean. He gave them weeds too and found four eggs.

Tuesday, October 29

Deidre called by with apples, saying she has far too many to use for just the two of them. She also had other good news for us, as she'd heard that a farm only a couple of miles from here was giving away cabbages, leeks, onions and pumpkins to local families. They normally grow produce for the supermarkets and the vegetables will go to waste now they can't be delivered. We agreed that it would be worth using some of our precious petrol to go there and collect as much as we can, so in return for the apples we gave Deidre a lift with us, returning with huge boxes of lovely fresh veg. We decided not to take too many cabbages and leeks as they won't keep well, but the onions and pumpkins will be very useful.

The people at the farm were very kind and said we could take as much as we liked, but we thought it was only right to take a reasonable amount. I was surprised to see two men loading boxes and boxes of veg into their van and asked them if they had a lot of people to feed. They just laughed and said they'd find a use for it alright. When I told Martin he said I was lucky to get away with just a laugh from them. He said they were probably going to sell it on the street and that there must be a black market developing all over the country.

Anna and Jane were excited by the pumpkins and decided they wanted to carve lanterns for Halloween. I really don't like this tradition, but as it will amuse them I'll let them get on with it, as long as every scrap of pumpkin flesh is saved to be eaten. I am more excited by the leeks and onions as they add such a lot of flavour to food and we had completely run out. I'm trying hard to think how best to use the pumpkin as we can't have pies and think I'll use some for soup and may try making a sauce for pasta. Martin and Stephen say they are getting sick of soup, so I'm trying to think of something more substantial I can cook. But without an oven or more meat we don't have much choice.

Wednesday, October 30

I feel quite pleased with myself. Last night's meal was a great success and put us all in a good mood. I found a recipe in an old book for a steamed onion and leek pudding. It is so simple and so filling. You line a basin with a suet crust, then fill it with seasoned layers of onion and leek. To make it more satisfying I added some mushrooms and diced bacon, then steamed it for three hours. So it is not a quick dish to make, but it was very well received and well worth the effort. I would like to make steamed puddings more often, but the fat will be a problem. Not our fat, but the fat that mixes with the flour. I have another couple of boxes of shredded suet in the larder, but doubt I will be able to get more. Maybe I can try making a pastry with oil? After all, some cakes are made with oil, aren't they and I can remember making a wonderful flourless chocolate cake with olive oil.

We woke this morning to the first real frost. We have been lucky so far, but it will be much colder from now on. Our bedroom windows were misted on the inside and I expect they will be iced over this winter.

Anna and Jane have scooped out four pumpkins and were talking of giving the seeds to the hens, when I remembered that they could be dried for us to eat. We have no breakfast cereal, but I can make a kind of muesli with porridge oats, grated apple and seeds. I'm not sure how to dry the seeds to make them edible, so we'll try toasting a few of them in a pan.

Martin was in a better mood today because he ate well yesterday, so I'm going to try hard to think how to feed us today.

Thursday, October 31

Today is Halloween and Stephen and the girls say they are going to sit by the fire tonight and tell ghost stories. I think life is frightening enough at the moment, without trying to scare each other with silly tales, but it may do them good to have some amusement. With no prospect of power returning soon, their lives are in limbo, unable to work, study or meet friends and, in Jane's case, a partner. Anna is a lovely girl and I can see that she and Stephen are well suited. I couldn't wish for a nicer girl for him.

It was raining this morning, but much milder than yesterday, so I felt able to shed some clothes for a really thorough strip wash and also washed my hair. The girls were quite envious when they realised I had managed to clean myself from top to bottom, as it were, and decided they would follow suit, which I am quite happy for them to do if they fetched and boiled the water for themselves. It is hard work when water is no longer on tap, so we find ourselves thinking carefully about every drop and are no longer careless with our resources.

Last night's meal did not go down well with Martin, though the others laughed and said it reminded them of happier times. I found some packs of Pot Noodles and Super Noodles lurking in the back of the larder. I think they had been there since Jane and her friends went to Glastonbury last summer. So I cooked some bacon and mushrooms in a wok with shredded cabbage, then threw in the softened noodles. I thought it worked very well and was quite tasty, but Martin grumbled so much that I was quite cross and told him we have to be thankful for anything we can get right now and that there must be people in desperate need who would be more grateful. But I don't want him in a bad mood, especially now he and Stephen are working so hard, fetching heavy loads of wood and water. So I am going to try making pasta with the machine that he gave me for Christmas two years ago which has sat in the back of a cupboard ever since. I will need to use a few eggs, but the hens laid well again yesterday and I collected five eggs, so I think I can spare enough for the dough.

Friday, November 1

Today we were greatly surprised by the arrival of
Neil, our tenant, who keeps sheep on three of our
fields. He has been used to coming and going
without any involvement from us for a couple of
years, but today he and his wife Linda turned up in
their scratched old Land Rover, towing a caravan
and asked if we would mind if they parked it in the
field nearest to the house.

When Martin asked why, Neil told him he is
concerned about sheep rustling. He says he has
heard on the shepherd grapevine that there have
been a number of incidents now that the
supermarkets are out of supplies and he would like
to stay on site to protect his flock. Of course we
agreed, especially as he is about to put the ram in
with the ewes. He always does that about this time –
tupp on Bonfire Night he says, for Easter lambs. And
we also agreed because Neil pays his rent in kind
and that will seem very welcome this year.

He soon got to work separating some of the older
ewes from those born this spring, with the help of his
dogs, Meg and Molly. He has to make another
journey to fetch the two rams he is using this year
and Martin offered to go with him, but Neil said
unless he was prepared to see off intruders he would
rather take his chances with the dogs. He has to drive
almost to Alton, but most of the run is on isolated
country roads so he thinks he will be safe. Martin
gave him one of our precious cans of petrol in case he
has to make a diversion and runs short of fuel.

The pasta I made yesterday was much tastier than
the dried, which I still have stored in the larder. I

made a savoury pumpkin sauce, scattered over toasted seeds and also wilted dandelion leaves as these are still easy to find. My recipe made plenty, so we are having it again today and Neil and Linda will join us to welcome them to our family for the foreseeable future.

Saturday, November 2

Such changeable weather I can't risk putting any laundry outside today. There is breezy sunshine one minute and dark clouds and rain the next. But it is mild, so we must be grateful and I woke easily at 6.30am with the light. The days are getting noticeably shorter now, making it very difficult to do anything indoors once the daylight has faded.

We are trying to manage with one candle at night, to ration our supplies. The fires give a fair bit of light and once I have cooked and we've eaten, we can manage fairly well. Martin's eyes are not good in the dark, so he has to have a candle to take upstairs to bed. The youngsters can cope and I find my eyes adjust quite well. I have always been used to shutting up the hens in total darkness, while Martin relied on a torch. A candle or nightlight set in front of a mirror is quite effective, so we are trying to do that wherever possible.

Neil returned safely by midday with his rams in a small trailer. He is going to cull one of the older ewes and butcher it himself. He has promised us some cuts and asked if we would like some of the offal right away. I've only ever had lamb's kidneys and liver before, so I don't know how good this will be from an older animal. The joints will be mutton of course, which will require longer cooking. We've agreed that it can hang in our big garage, to keep it safe from the foxes and vermin. As there is no refrigeration, Neil will estimate the hanging time according to the ambient temperature and thinks it should be ready in no more than a week. The thought of a good piece of meat is very exciting and as Neil has a twelve-bore shotgun, he is willing to help Martin try for a deer soon.

Four eggs today.

Sunday, November 3
We had a long discussion with Neil and Linda by the fire last night. He has always paid us in kind in return for grazing our fields and we have always appreciated the cuts he has given us. But now we and he wanted to come to an agreement over how we could help each other.

Whilst they are happy to live in the caravan, they would appreciate sometimes being able to warm themselves by our fire, have access to the well water and to join us for food cooked over the fire a couple of times a week. They will make do with a campfire most of the time, but we have the ability to cook bigger and better dishes with our great inglenooks. We also have hens and can share our eggs when we have some to spare.

After practising their shooting, the men have also agreed that Martin is the better shot and that he stands more chance of bagging us game. And in fact he has already done so, bringing back two pheasant today, which I'll teach the girls to pluck and draw. Then we can make a casserole of sorts to share.

And the final bonus was Neil pointing out that he can still get milk from the six ewes that lambed late this year. They will soon dry off, but he thinks they may be productive for another two or three weeks. This will be a great boost to our supplies and we all agreed that it would be best used as cheese, which will keep well and be a wonderful addition to our diet through the winter. We all tried to remember which cheeses are made with sheep's milk as Stephen was pulling a face and saying he didn't think he'd like to try it. But when Anna came back with a recipe book to check and found that feta, Roquefort and Manchego are all made with milk from ewes, he had to change his tune.

Today is colder and windy, but it is bright and sunny and we have kept warm outside gathering more kindling and acorns. The first batch is drying off so we shall try grinding them down into flour tomorrow.

Monday, November 4

I've decided I must make more of an effort to be up with the first light, at around 6, as the days feel much shorter now. I set the alarm for this morning and had the fires lit and water heating by the time everyone else was stirring. I've realised I must also make more of an effort to do most of our food preparation in daylight hours, as it is so difficult to see properly once the light fades and it is dark indoors at 4.30 in the afternoon. As we get further into winter, it may be easier to have our main meal in the middle of the day and eat something simple in the evenings.

Last night's pheasant was really quite good,

although we all wished we could have Brussels sprouts and roast potatoes with it. But it was very tasty and we ate it with cabbage and apple sauce. We stripped the two carcasses pretty thoroughly, but I've picked them over today and managed to scrape together a few bits, which will enhance the soup I've made from the bones for tonight. I've made it much like the soup my mother used to make from the Christmas turkey, with some vegetables and split peas. It will be very thick and filling.

Anna and Jane made their first batch of acorn flour today. It took them ages, grinding the nuts in a pestle and mortar, after first breaking the nuts in a bag with a rolling pin. They tried grinding the acorns down in my old hand mincer, but it still left large lumps, so the mortar seems to be the best method. I've suggested that they shouldn't make any more until we have tried this lot first. It is yellower and coarser than normal flour, but it smells fresh and nutty.

There was a very cold wind blowing today and the hens only gave us two eggs.

Tuesday, November 5

Martin cycled to the village this morning to see if he could get any batteries for our radio and torches. He came back with one pack and said the village bonfire and firework display would still be going ahead tonight. The girls and Stephen are very excited at the thought of having a social life again, so we've all agreed to go, leaving Neil and Linda to enjoy the fire at home. The bonfire will be lit at 7pm and apparently there will also be a hog roast, which should be very popular.

Today I used some of the acorn flour to make a kind of polenta. It occurred to me that as the flour is quite grainy this might work rather well. I boiled it up with seasoning then let it set in a baking tray. I then cut it into chunks which I fried up with bacon and onions and rosemary. It would be better with cheese, but we haven't made that yet. And then I served this with the remains of the thick pea soup from yesterday. I thought it was tasty but Martin gave it some funny looks. Oh well, he can tuck into the hog tonight and maybe that will satisfy him.

Only three eggs today.

Wednesday, November 6

There was a very strange atmosphere at the bonfire last night, so we all left early. This has always been such a friendly village with many families that have been here for generations, but yesterday I recognised hardly anyone.

We arrived at 6.30 so we wouldn't miss the food and found there was already a crowd waiting for their share. It was good, tasty meat, though yet again we missed bread to go with it. And we were all standing around on the green and eating when we noticed a large group with burning flares coming along the road towards us. That's never happened in these parts before, though I know some Sussex villages have a tradition of torch lit processions.

And as they came closer we could hear chanting, which we couldn't make out at first. They were mostly young men, in their teens maybe or a little older, and they were shouting, "Light, light, light, bring back the light." They marched right through the crowd standing on the green, pushing past older people and children regardless, then circled round the great unlit bonfire, still chanting. Then finally, one of them held his torch up high and shouted, "Bring us light" and at that point they all thrust their torches into the bonfire and it burst into flame. They stood back for a moment then they all cried out, "The light is here" and began to dance wildly around the heap.

I remember looking at Martin and he had his worried expression on and both the girls were holding onto each other and Stephen. We didn't know any of these people. I'm not sure they were even from the village. Then Martin bent down to me and whispered that we should make a move, so we all slipped to the back of the crowd and left. It was very unsettling and we walked back along the dark lane in silence until we were nearly home.

Thursday, November 7

We are all still feeling very disturbed by the scene at the bonfire the other night. Anna and Jane are worried that the torch bearers may spread out around the village and come over here. Martin has decided to keep his gun by the bed and Neil says he will be watchful too. They are both nervous about intruders but seem to think that the type of troublemaker we saw on the village green are more likely to head for small towns and the centre of villages, where they will hope to find tinned food, alcohol and cigarettes. I guess they are right, but it has made me think a lot about how fortunate we are here with access to water, heat and regular, though sometimes strange, hot food.

I'm trying not to worry about it now and concentrate on what we might eat today. As the acorn flour polenta was well received I think we could have that regularly so the girls are grinding more of the nuts. There are so many, we should have a good supply for quite some time. However, we are not sure how well it will keep, so we think we should prepare it a couple of times a week and leave the whole acorns in a dry place until they are needed. Anna and Jane keep coming across more in the fields and grounds and go out to collect them whenever they can, along with any fresh greens they can find. They have persuaded me we really should try making the acorn coffee next, so we may have a go tomorrow.

The hens laid four eggs today, but for the third time in a week our young cockerel was very aggressive and flew at me when I bent down to collect the eggs. If he carries on like this, we may not be able to keep him.

Friday, November 8

The most extraordinary piece of luck! A deer has suddenly dropped dead in the garden and we didn't even have to shoot it. The last time this happened was a few years ago when I found a deer sprawled outside the front door one Sunday morning, just as I was collecting the papers. That time we hauled it into a wheelbarrow and trundled it down to the wood then left it for the foxes to deal with.

But now, we are all delighted with this windfall

and certainly won't be throwing it away, although Jane is still a little apprehensive, because she thinks the deer are so pretty. However, I think even she will not baulk at eating Bambi if we can deal with the butchering out of her sight.

We told Neil straight away because he has had more experience of dealing with carcasses and used to shoot deer for venison on a local estate. We'll share our find with him of course, because it is far more than we could all manage to eat before it starts to go off. And I suggested to Martin that he might think about taking some of it up the road to a neighbour who is a keen angler. Then we might be able to exchange it for fish as there are trout and pike around here. I could also badly use some carrots and may suggest we visit the allotment holders in the village and barter with them too.

Neil thinks the venison will be all the better for hanging for a while, so we shan't have any of it just yet, but hanging will tenderise it and may improve the flavour. Most of the innards were eagerly received by Neil's dogs. In the meantime Martin will have to see if he can bag some more pheasant.

The hens did well today with five eggs, but the cockerel was very difficult again and I think he is becoming quite dangerous.

Saturday, November 9

Martin and Stephen decided to drive round the village to see if there were any signs of the rough crowd from bonfire night. I didn't really want them to go, but Martin said if we have a bad winter we may need the help of local craftsmen, so we must know what is going on in the locality. When they returned they said there was no sign of any disturbance, other than a scorched patch on the green where the fire had burnt out. But they had been down to the allotments to see who was around and whether anyone was prepared to barter and found two very disgruntled locals whose crops had been ruined by the vandals. However, they also had onions to spare and Martin agreed to return with some cuts of venison next week once the deer has been butchered.

The allotment holders said some of the older villagers are finding it very difficult to manage. Some have moved in with neighbours who have open fires or wood burning stoves. And they've heard that some of the larger houses in the area are empty, apart from caretakers, as their owners left the country in the first week of the power cut. They must have escaped by private plane or boat I suppose.

I feel quite concerned about vulnerable people in the area. Although we are not near enough to our neighbours to chat over the garden fence, we know quite a few families in the village socially and through church. Martin says we cannot be concerned about everyone as it is hard enough to look after ourselves, but it bothers me. I think if we have a surplus we should make an effort to share it.

Tomorrow is Remembrance Sunday, so I am insisting that we should all go to church. I have no idea if the service will be at its usual time, but I am assuming that the most faithful members of the congregation will be doing their best to show up and demonstrate that if we can win two wars we can come through our present difficulties.

Sunday, November 10

We walked to church in chilly sunshine this morning for the Remembrance Service and although it was not as full as it has been in past years, there was a good turnout. At the door we were each offered a homemade red poppy, a simpler version of the ones that are normally sold on the streets. It was very touching to see this tradition being maintained.

Although this is always a serious service, this year we could all feel an air of quiet resilience. There were families present whose predecessors names are recorded on the village war memorial; they are determined their names will continue, despite the current hardships.

After the service we walked to the memorial for the silence and the bugle call, which always touches me deeply. And then we stayed to talk to some of the people gathered there and heard that the village pub, The Golden Lion, was open for business, so we all walked across.

The publican, Mick, apologised for not being able to offer beers and lagers on tap, but he still had some bottled beers and wines which were most welcome after our enforced abstinence. He had lit open fires too so there was quite a cheering atmosphere.

Our vicar, James Dyer, joined us and said that a number of people are concerned about vulnerable villagers. So far, there have not been any unexpected deaths, but some of the elderly are finding life very hard. James and Mick have suggested that the pub could act as a central distribution point for surplus produce. After some discussion we all agreed to try making Saturdays a bring and barter day. Donors will bring in foods and exchange them for other goods or services. But it was also agreed that anyone who is unable to make a donation for reason of age or ill health, may receive supplies. And Mick is willing to trade his drinks for produce if people no longer have any cash.

I suppose we will just have to see whether people can be reasonable and fair, but we shall certainly have a surplus of meat in the near future, particularly if our cockerel continues to misbehave.

Monday, November 11

We are all feeling most encouraged after yesterday's service and our chats with other villagers. Realising how hard everyone is working to keep themselves in good health and spirits, makes us feel that we can all survive these hardships.

Of course we have all been worrying about family members in other regions and we realise that people in towns and cities will not have as much access to food and water as we do in the country, but we keep telling ourselves that we are no worse off than people in many parts of the world. When Martin tuned into the radio again today, we heard a report from Dublin about a disaster in the Philippines, which reminds us how fortunate we are here. We may be in the dark, but we haven't lost our homes or our loved ones. We do wonder though, what is being done to restore power and order here.

We also heard yesterday that the village school will try to stay open throughout this crisis. It will not be staffed by its regular teachers and head, but by local parents and a couple of teachers who worked at schools elsewhere before the power cut. They have simplified the curriculum and will teach younger children three days a week and coach senior school children the other two days. This way they hope that all the little ones will continue to become proficient in the Three R's and the older ones won't fall too far behind.

It is still rather cold today, but I warmed up sweeping leaves from the paths again. There are still many more leaves yet to fall, although the stormy winds of two weeks ago did their best to strip the trees before they achieved their best autumn colours. However, our little acer, which I planted twenty years ago, is putting on a brave front with glowing auburn foliage and it cheers me every time I look at it. But the cockerel is not cheering me. I defended myself with the big leaf rake when I went to feed the hens today and he still tried to attack me.

Tuesday, November 12

The cockerel has been plucked and dressed for the pot. When I tried to collect the eggs today he flew at me and almost caught me in the head and face with his vicious talons. I kicked him away and he still came for me, so I had to back out of the run with the rake and ran to Martin, telling him to get rid of him. He got him in the head with one shot.

I'm sorry he had to go for he was a magnificent bird with long glossy tail feathers, but he was too dangerous and while I had been willing to take my chances, I would not have liked anyone else to risk entering the hen run. So now he is simmering for our dinner, with some onion and carrot. I showed everyone how to prepare him and Anna finished the plucking, which is best done while the bird is still warm. I always think the hardest part with an active bird is removing the guts, which needs to be done with a twisting action of the hand. Stephen had a go, as I thought he should learn how to prepare poultry as well as the girls, but I finished dressing the bird by myself in the end.

Martin said how much he fancied roast chicken, but I thought it would be best to cook him slowly in a pot as, although he was a young bird, he was very active. All that showing off and wing flapping will mean a lot of muscle which could be tough if cooked any other way. And even though he was young and active, there was quite a lot of fat, which I shall render down as it may be useful.

Jane wasn't keen to help with the plucking and dressing, but fancies some of the long feathers for an old hat she has taken to wearing.

Wednesday, November 13

This morning I decided to thoroughly tidy my larder, to check how long I can make our stores last. When the power first went off, over a month ago, I never thought we'd have to manage on our own for so long. I imagined emergency reserves being distributed, but so far no news has come out this way. I suppose international aid is being directed at disasters far worse than ours.

At the back of the top shelf I found an old pack of dried yeast, dated best before March 2004 and a bag of bread mix, to be used by April 2007. My family have always been sticklers for dates on packaging, but I can't believe any harm will come to them from these products. I know I can't actually do any baking, without a working oven, but I am going to try making flatbread with some of these ingredients. I've read that naan bread can be made with a little oil in a griddle pan. I think my only problem will be finding somewhere warm for the dough to prove.

I've also been checking my old cookery books for potted meat recipes. We are soon likely to have a surplus of meat and I am determined not to waste any. Although the weather is chilly and parts of the house are very cold, I worry about how well the meat will keep. And potting it may also be a good way of taking extra supplies to the pub on Saturdays to barter. I have sorted out all my old kilner jars and raided Martin's store of jars which he always says 'might come in useful'. I will scrub them first then sterilise them in boiling water ready for use. I'm going to use the remains of the cockerel for my first attempt, sealing the meat with its own melted fat. The bird was very tasty last night and I'm making sure we don't waste a scrap by removing every sliver of meat from the bones for potting and then boiling the bones again for soup stock.

Anna and Jane are shelling more dried acorns to grind into flour. We are finding this a quite acceptable substitute for regular white flour, but then we aren't making delicate sponges these days. It will be interesting to see how the acorn flour works with the dried yeast. I must also see if I can find out how to make a yeast starter – a sort of 'mother yeast', like those friendship cakes that were so popular in my mother's day.

Thursday, November 14

Neil came over this morning and announced that the deer was ready, so he's cut it into joints. As I'm not used to cooking venison I asked Linda, his wife, the best way to prepare it. We consulted my copy of *Jane Grigson's English Food* and decided to marinade the haunches and saddle for three days, with some vinegar, oil and herbs, then they will be suitable for roasting. The other cuts are better slowly stewed so we can cook those immediately. Linda has taken some shoulder across to the caravan to cook on her fire for tonight and she and Neil will join us for a meal on Sunday. If it is fine we hope to be able to cook a joint over a fire outside.

As we have such a quantity of fresh meat for the time being, Neil has decided to postpone culling the ewe for a day or so. This is very sensible, but it is odd to think that we will now have a whole week of eating venison followed by maybe a week of mutton. So different to the varied diet we had before when we could order all we wanted online and have it delivered to our door.

Neil asked if I'd like to help him with the ewe, as I have been used to handling sheep, but I said I have not been used to killing them. However, I may help once he has performed the deed, as he said we could collect the blood if I'm interested.

We all agree that we may be able to take some of the venison to the pub for the first bring and barter session on Saturday. I think we need potatoes and more root vegetables, but the men may disagree. I am looking forward to going and hope there may be news of government action. Martin heard a faint report on the radio saying that supplies are coming from Europe, but we still have not seen any signs out here.

The weather has been very chilly for the last two days. The only warm room in the house is the dining room which now doubles as kitchen. We are keeping the fire lit in the hall as well, but it does not heat the room as well as the one on which I am constantly cooking and heating water.

Friday, November 15

Today is cold again, but it's bright and dry, for which I am thankful. Martin cycled into the village and brought back aspirin, vinegar and news. It seems that help may be on the way. Apparently a young soldier cycled through the village yesterday and handed posters out to the shop, the chemist, the pub, the surgery and the rectory, saying that every effort is being made to restore the power and that foreign aid will soon bring supplies. Of course there is no clear indication of when this will come and what form this aid will take.

We all began to speculate on what should be brought into the country. Martin said petrol is the most important commodity, so generators could keep running and then we might have regular broadcasts on radio stations we could actually hear clearly. I think supplies of staples like rice, flour, oil and potatoes are the most important, along with fresh vegetables. I had sent Martin to get Vitamin C tablets from the chemist but we had forgotten that they are not open on Friday and he could only get aspirin from the village shop, which is hardly the same thing.

The thought of official news travelling by bike amused us all, but presumably even the army, which surely must have secret reserves of fuel, needs to conserve its supplies. And I am not placing any great faith in rations of any kind spreading beyond the cities and reaching us out here in the sticks. I think we should continue to manage our own supplies carefully, until we have confirmation that help really is coming our way. We are eating quite well and although I think we have all lost some weight since this began, I don't think any of us are less healthy so far. We enjoyed our venison stew last night and I extended the stock to make a good soup for us today.

Saturday, November 16

When I went outside last night to shut up the hens, the grass around the henhouse was silvery with the moon. But this morning the grass was silvered with frost rather than moonlight and it has been bitter all day. However, walking to the pub with our goods warmed us up and we were welcomed by a cheerful crowd and a good fire.

Martin negotiated with Mick to run a tab for our drinks over the next few weeks, so that we can settle up with a joint of meat in due course. Then Mick called for attention and told everyone about the soldier who came by yesterday. Mick had grilled him for more information, as the posters he was distributing said so little. Mick says there is still no immediate prospect of power being restored as the fault appears to be a form of computer sabotage. He also learnt that, as we suspected, whatever supplies do reach the country will be distributed in the cities, in an attempt to restore law and order.

This made us all mutter crossly about it being a disgrace, but then we got on with inspecting the supplies that other people had brought in to exchange. We had come with four large pieces of venison flank, which is a good cut for stewing. One lady offered pots of jam for our meat, but I didn't want that as I still have plenty of jam made from the plums I picked from our tree in mid-September. Martin was keen to have a couple of flagons of homemade beer, but I said I thought one would do and then we could have Jerusalem artichokes, a cabbage and some carrots, which would be very useful. In the end he agreed, as he does like his food and realised he would end up drinking the beer rather quickly with Stephen's help. Several people had brought acorn flour but we have plenty of our own and still have a good supply of nuts yet to be ground. I would have been glad of more suet though and Mick said he will ask the farm shop to come next week as they have a butcher there.

There were four eggs today, but I think one hen has gone off laying as her comb is pale.

Sunday, November 17
Although today has been less cold there is a heavy greyness in the sky which makes me think of snow. But surely it can't come yet, can it? In mid-November? My feet have frozen in the last few days and I have chilblains again. They developed last year even with central heating, so this winter with only open fires and hot water bottles to warm my toes

they will swell and throb painfully. I have a little ointment left over but must see if the chemist has more when he opens on his two days a week.

I used to blame Martin for the condition of my feet as he always rationed our heating and would not allow it to go on before November 1st and then insisted on it going off at Easter, no matter when it fell. But I cannot blame him this year.

However, we have had words about personal hygiene and I think this is the first time I have been really cross with him since this crisis began. I know it is difficult for all of us to keep clean when we have no mains supply and all our water must be heated on the fire, but I realised last night that he had not washed all day and when I asked when he last had a strip wash, he said he wasn't stripping off for anyone in this cold house. And I said if that was the way he felt then I wouldn't be stripping off for him either at any time in the near future, unless he had a jolly good wash with soap and water, as I had thought I detected a sour smell and it was definitely him. He grudgingly agreed when I said that if he fetched the water I would heat it for him on the fire. He moaned about taking it upstairs to our bathroom but I said he could have his wash at the kitchen sink if he doesn't mind everyone seeing his bits and pieces. That soon shut him up and we are friends again now after a good hot meal of stewed venison and some of the Jerusalem artichokes. I must say, I never imagined we could eat so well during a national emergency.

I collected only two eggs today. As they are brown I know they are from the Rhode Island Reds. I do hope the Legbars don't all go off lay.

Monday, November 18

For some time we have been worrying over the whereabouts of our nearest neighbours, Tony and Gail. We had not seen them since just before the power failed, but today Tony turned up, knocking on our kitchen door. He was even thinner than usual, dishevelled and unshaven.

He said they'd been visiting their married daughter in London and became stranded, without enough petrol to make the journey home. But now they are all here, with Zelda, their daughter, her husband Brad and their young son Alfie. Their son Flynn has also come back with them.

Tony quickly told us how terrifying it had been, hiding in the house in south London, venturing out when the streets were quiet for what little could be found. He said he'll tell us more when the family have rested, but they are in need of food, water and warmth right now. He has managed to light their wood burning stove but has very little wood stacked for the winter, so Martin will take them dry logs and kindling. I gave Tony eggs and soup and promised them stew and vegetables later. Stephen will fill any containers they can find with water.

They are also in need of milk for the child, who is about eighteen months old and we shall see if he can tolerate fresh sheep's milk. Neil has been bringing some up recently, but we were waiting until we had enough to make cheese. However, this is a greater need and we must share what we have.

In a few days, when Tony feels stronger, he will join Martin and Stephen in splitting logs and gathering more timber. They may eventually use some of our precious petrol to tackle a fallen oak in the field with a chainsaw. We are so glad to see our neighbours again as they have become good friends in the time we have lived here. But as we must all work together to survive this difficult time, we are also thankful for Tony's practical skills in building and repairing as that could prove invaluable.

Only two eggs today.

Tuesday, November 19

There was a white frost this morning, but the day was bright. After I restarted the fires I thought if it stayed fine we could roast some of the venison outside. So I took Martin a mug of tea and told him my plan. We started the fire early on the kitchen lawn and roasted the remaining haunch and the saddle. Both joints cook well this way, but as venison has so little fat I had to keep basting it with a marinade of oil, wine vinegar and herbs.

As the meat can be dry I made a version of Cumberland sauce, using apples, to have on the side. I also thought I could spare potatoes and as I cannot roast them, I boiled them first then sautéed them in a little fat with poppy seeds.

We invited Neil and Linda and our neighbours to share the meal as there was plenty to go round. Tony and Gail came with their family, but all ate quietly and still looked very tired and drawn, though the little child was lively. I gave them some meat to take away and we shall do our best to help them until they have recovered.

We have all been wondering about their recent ordeal, but won't press them for details. I am sure they will tell us when they are ready. When I took some food up to their house yesterday I saw their car in the drive. The paintwork was badly scratched, one of the side windows was smashed and the windscreen was crazed, as if a large stone had hit it with force.

Neil and Linda filled the silence while we ate, telling stories of escaping sheep and fending off foxes from newborn lambs. Neil plans to cull the old ewe tomorrow.

Four eggs today.

Wednesday, November 20

I wasn't there when Neil killed the old ewe, but I was present when he drained the blood. I didn't think I would be able to do this, but as I know it will be good food for us, I decided I should witness the whole process of gutting the carcass and cleaning the intestines. Neil thinks sheep casings are not as good as pig, but as they will hold the filling together, I was willing to try.

Linda, Neil's wife, has made sausages before so I was glad of her help and advice. We diced onion, softened it in sheep fat, then added the blood and cooked it with seasoned oatmeal till it thickened. The task of cleaning the casings was very time consuming without the help of mains water. We washed the skins with salt water, then turned them inside out, scraped them clean and rinsed them again in clean salt water. We used a funnel to fill them and made a coil of sausages to share. The rest of the family did not want to be involved in the preparations, but I know they won't be so squeamish when they can have something different for their breakfasts.

There was also a lot of hard fat around the sheep's kidneys, which we have finely chopped into shredded suet. This will be most useful as we are very short of fat for dishes. We are going to cook the liver and kidneys today as they will not keep well. Neil says the heart and lungs are also perfectly edible, but I'm not sure I could persuade any of my family to eat them. Neil just laughed and said his dogs would not turn their noses up at it and as they are hardworking animals, they deserve a good meal too.

I am going to cook our share of the offal with onions and potatoes, maybe with the addition of some smoked paprika. I'll do my cooking early while there is still some light then take a pan up to our neighbours for their supper.

There were four eggs today.

Thursday, November 21

The black pudding Linda and I made yesterday was delicious. I had saved enough eggs for us all to have a couple of slices fried with an egg for breakfast. All that was missing was toast, so we had to make do with acorn flatbread. We missed milk in our tea as well, but we have become used to drinking black tea over the last few weeks and the sheep milk is being kept for Tony and Gail's grandson Alfie.

I was very glad that everyone ate the black pudding, as it is very nutritious, being full of iron. Martin said it could do with more seasoning, especially pepper, but then he always smothers his food in condiments so I won't have my cooking judged by his standards. Stephen said it was very tasty but he wasn't sure if he'd still want it once we have run out of ketchup, which is likely to be soon. After that, he'll have to use whatever is left in my larder – mint sauce, horseradish, Tabasco or any of the other old bottles and jars at the back of the shelf.

I took a portion of the sausage up to our neighbours and told Gail how we'd made it and how best to use it. She seemed a little uncertain, but I think she is still shaken by their experiences in London. Her son and son-in-law were bringing in wood while we were talking and I noticed that Brad had a fading black eye and Flynn's cheek was cut and bruised. I don't think they have been fighting each other, so I can't help wondering what they ran into before they managed to get away.

The mutton will be cut up into joints tomorrow and we shall be able to use some straight away. We have agreed with Neil that we should take some of the smaller cuts to the pub on Saturday in the hope of exchanging them for vegetables and extra eggs. I'm planning to boil a leg of mutton as that is a good way to cook old meat and suggested to Gail that they might all like to join us as there will be plenty.

Only two eggs today and we could use more.

Friday, November 22

The mutton is simmering nicely. My recipe describes it as 'boiled' but really although it must come to the boil at first, it just bubbles slightly for the next two or three hours. It's bathing in my largest jam pan with carrots and onions and I skim off the fat now and then as it rises. I'm going to try and make a caper sauce on the side, though as I don't have any butter I'm not sure whether I'll succeed. If it doesn't work out there's an unopened jar of red currant jelly.

I'm not sure if all of Gail and Tony's family are coming for supper, but I want the meal to be good and comforting for them. Anna and Jane are helping to clear the dining table of their acorn grinding and have peeled potatoes which we'll mash later. As I don't yet know how many of us will be eating, I think I'll make some little dumplings and cook them in the mutton stock, so I can be sure we have enough for everyone.

We'll eat at 6pm, when it's dark, so I'm going to sacrifice some of my precious tea lights for the table, so we can see what we're eating. And Martin thinks he will open one of the bottles of claret which he's been saving for Christmas.

We won't be able to have cheese and port at the end of the meal, but I will make some kind of dessert from our apple store. Apple fritters would be nice and are so easy to do.

Three eggs today. Two brown and one blue.

Saturday, November 23

We shared our food with everyone last night, although Zelda, Brad and their son didn't actually come to supper. They wanted to bath their little boy by the fire at home, then settle him down to sleep, so I saved a portion to be taken back for them.

The mutton was very good and the apple fritters appreciated. And as they ate the food and drank the wine, Tony, Gail and Flynn seemed more relaxed and began to tell us a little about how they had coped in London.

The day the power failed they realised they didn't have enough petrol to get home. Tony said they kicked themselves for not keeping a spare can of petrol in the car. If they'd had a couple of cans they could have come home much sooner, but neither he nor Brad had enough to make the journey. So, as Zelda's house is near a large cash and carry, Brad and Tony immediately went off to collect bumper packs of nappies, bottled water, toilet paper, tins and dried pasta.

After several days they ventured out again to see if any shops were still open. They returned, shaken by what they found. Shop windows had been smashed, all were looted and some were burnt out. There were abandoned cars on the roads and bodies in shop doorways, presumably crushed or beaten to death in the scramble for supplies.

At this point in the story, Gail began to cry and Tony said he wouldn't talk about it any more. Flynn was quiet too, so we still don't know how he and Brad came by their injuries. We all agreed it was enough just to know they are safe here and together and then Gail was able to smile a little and say thank God, they were all in one piece.

I think they will tell us more little by little, but now is too soon. I suggested they might like to come with us to the pub today, but they would rather not leave the house just yet. So if I can get more eggs, I will bring some back for them.

Only two eggs from our hens today.

Sunday, November 24

Today is 'Stir-up Sunday', the day when Christmas puddings are traditionally made. Most years I have made several of different sizes and have always put one by to keep for the following year, but this year I don't have a pudding and I don't have all the ingredients. I gave away the extra puddings I made last year and now I'm really regretting it. I've collected together all the ingredients left in my larder that might possibly make a pudding and have been staring at them wondering whether it will be worth it.

I don't have the right mix of dried fruits for a start. I have raisins, but no currants or sultanas. I have some flour, but no breadcrumbs. I have apples but no mixed peel. I have a little shredded Atora suet, but I will have to add some of the fresh suet we made the other day.

I looked and looked at the recipe in my school exercise book, which I have been using to make the puddings ever since I was sixteen and which my grandmother said (and said it to my sister too, when she made her first pudding) were as good as her mother used to make. And then I thought damn it, I'll make a pudding of sorts come what may. Even if it doesn't taste as good as usual, at least we shall all have had the pleasure of making a wish by stirring the mixture and of seeing it come to the table flaming.

So I set to and the girls helped with peeling apples and chopping them finely. We replaced the breadcrumbs with coarse acorn flour and added half a pack of ground almonds, which I found hiding behind some old mincemeat. In place of brandy we used Armagnac and the girls promised not to tell Martin. There wasn't enough of anything to make a batch of puddings, like I normally would, but we have made one and set it to steam by the fire all afternoon. And I have nagged everyone to keep an eye on the water level, as I could not bear to waste it after all this effort.

I don't know what everyone else wished for when it was their turn to stir, but I wished for the power to be restored and for us to have a mild winter. I expect they wished the same.

Only two eggs again today, so I'm glad I was able to get some at the pub yesterday.

Monday, November 25

It is a struggle to leave a warm bed in the mornings and face a cold house, cold water and cold fires. But once I have begun work and the fires are crackling and water is boiling, I am too busy to think about what we lack. At least we have the open fires and many don't. Gail is using a camp stove, but the gas canisters won't last forever.

We are trying to remember to set a kettle of fresh water by the fire when we go to bed, so that it might be less than stone cold in the morning and will soon be ready for tea. First thing, I splash my face with cold water and brush my teeth. I have a warm wash mid-morning, once everything is organised.

Today Tony has joined Martin and Stephen in the field, working on the old oak. He looks less tired and I think it is probably good for him to be out there, working together and developing a daily routine to put the bad times behind them. Flynn joined them and when I took hot drinks out late morning I could hear good natured banter and they all seemed pleased with their work.

I took some mutton broth up to Gail to heat for lunch and found her digging their vegetable patch which still had onions and carrots. She too has sown winter lettuce to give them some green stuff with their meals.

We took some mutton chops to the pub on Saturday to exchange for turnips, parsnips and potatoes. It will become quite a little farmers market soon, as the egg farm and the farm butcher have said they will both be there next week. Quite how we are all going to pay for their produce we aren't too sure, but it will be good to know there is going to be a constant supply of nourishing food this winter.

Only two eggs today and one of the hens has gone into moult, which is always a ridiculous thing to do when the weather is cold. So she won't be laying for a while.

Tuesday, November 26

Last night we sat by the fire for quite a bit after we'd eaten. Martin said Tony had told him more while they were working in the field. I suppose it was easier for him to talk openly without fear of female tears.

Apparently, after about three weeks of hiding in the house, Brad and Flynn went out one night to see if they could siphon fuel from abandoned cars into old water bottles. Most vehicles had already been drained, but they had some success and were returning when they were confronted by a couple of thugs in a truck, who wanted to know what they were carrying. The boys split up and ran for it then zigzagged back to the house, once they were sure they'd thrown off their pursuers. A day or so later, they tried again and for several nights after that as well, slowly managing to gather enough fuel to make the journey home. Every time they went out, the family was terrified they would not return. But each night they came back with a little more fuel, breathless, sometimes shaken and sometimes bruised.

It was clearly very dangerous out there and eventually they all decided they shouldn't wait any longer. Some houses down the road were on fire, dogs were roaming the streets and menacing cars of men drove through from time to time. They left in the early hours of the morning, hoping not to meet anyone, but as they came up to Tolworth on the A3, they had to slow down because a wrecked car half blocked the road. As they edged past, a couple of men with iron bars leapt onto the car and smashed the windows. But Tony accelerated and they escaped.

I told Martin I think we've got off very lightly. So far it's been inconvenient, but our lives have not been threatened. But Martin said we should all be on our guard, because if the towns and cities cannot sustain life then the strongest will gradually move out. I know I shouldn't think this, because it must be terrible trying to survive without the resources we are lucky to have here, but I imagined a slowly creeping horde of locusts coming ever nearer. And my hens only laid two brown eggs today.

Wednesday, November 27

Anna doesn't seem very well. I hope it isn't the food. I was a bit worried that our meal last night of steamed mutton pudding could be a little indigestible. All that suet and fatty meat was tasty and filling but I dread to think what it is doing to our bad cholesterol levels. Martin said bugger the cholesterol, when I mentioned this. He said he'd gladly eat pure cholesterol if it keeps him warm and stops his stomach from grumbling. I don't think there's any danger of that happening, but I do hope this unbalanced diet doesn't have long term consequences for all of us.

We are going to have mutton again tonight, but I'm going to cook it as a Lancashire hot pot with vegetables. I'll slice the potatoes and put them on the top about half-way through and though I know I won't be able to brown them as I would if it were cooking in an oven, I think it will be quite satisfying and tasty.

Martin said the wild ducks have started coming to the pond and there may be more down by the river, so he is going to try and bag some soon. That will make a nice change and I'm keen to have them for their fat as well, as that would be very useful for cooking and for potting meat.

Four eggs today, two brown and two blue.

Thursday, November 28

I think Anna is missing her family. They are so far away, in Cornwall, and however much we tell her we're sure they'll be coping just as well as we are, I quite understand how worried she must be when she can't speak to them. We're all fretting about friends and family elsewhere, especially those who living in cities. After Tony's recent account of the horrors in London, we dread to think what is happening elsewhere. In the country we have better resources and Anna's father can get fish from the sea and there are nearby farms which are sure to still have meat and milk. I'm sure they will be managing.

Communication is also something we are all missing terribly. It's not like being abroad on holiday, when it's quite a relief to be far away from the daily blather of constant news. Lying in the sun or sightseeing, you know you can always ring family members or be contacted if there is a problem back home. Now, we can't even get in touch with friends in the nearest town. In fact our main points of contact are the pub and the church.

And it's also very frustrating not being able to Google answers to questions, like the one that occurred to me this morning – how can we use our central heating oil? We had filled up the tank early in the autumn when the prices were low and here we are, in the freezing cold, not using a single drop. Martin thinks it might be possible to use it in one of the cars and I think we could use some for lighting the house and filling the two old paraffin heaters we have. They might make a bit of a smell, but it would be wonderful to have more heat. Martin's going to see what Tony thinks, as he's very practical and knows the answers to a lot of things.

I dug over the hen run today, hoping a diet of worms will help them lay more. Only two eggs.

Friday, November 29

Martin shot half a dozen duck yesterday, which we've plucked and dressed today for today's supper. They are much smaller than the commercial Aylesbury ducks and, as everyone knows, no duck has a lot of meat. However, it will make a welcome change so I'm planning to pan fry the breasts, then confit the legs in the fat that frying releases. The birds are not as fat as I'm used to either, but I think if I render down the whole carcass after jointing them there will be enough fat to cook the legs this way, which has the advantage of ensuring that the meat will keep well for some time.

I think a couple of confit legs, set in their fat in jars, will be good for bartering at the pub tomorrow. It's no good us going if all we achieve is more on the tab because Martin and Stephen can't resist having a beer. We need more vegetables as we've eaten all our first crop of winter lettuce and soon there will be no wild greens to pick.

The girls helped pluck the birds. That is, Jane helped and Anna started but then said it made her feel ill. In fact I think she actually went outside to be sick. It's not a job everyone can do I suppose. So she ground some acorns instead as we have a constant need for the flour and we've become used to the background noise of the grinder going round and round.

We'll have apple sauce with the duck and maybe some fried potatoes. The weather has become a little milder, though still very grey, but the hens did better for me and laid four eggs.

Saturday, November 30

We all came back from our visit to the pub feeling quite jolly. Not because we'd over indulged, although Martin did have a second drink, but because there was a good selection of produce there and Robert Proud, our farm butcher, had come with cuts of beef. He is not demanding goods in return, but is taking note of what everyone has and says we will put it right when life gets back to normal. We think it's very decent of him and all agreed to honour what is owed.

No one took very much, as everyone worries about meat going off, but I came away with minced beef, several pounds of chuck and skirt and, as a real treat, some steaks. The vegetables were good too, with carrots, cabbages and potatoes available, so we shall do very well this week. I exchanged my confit duck legs for two dozen eggs as my hens are doing so badly at present.

Yet in spite of the cheerful atmosphere and the plentiful supplies, there were frowns as well as smiles. We learnt that there had been a terrible fire in a house in the village. It seems the owner had tried to use paraffin in an old oil lamp and it had exploded. The occupants escaped, but the house is burnt out. And Mick, our publican, said some of the younger residents are struggling to fend for themselves as they simply don't have the know-how. It really seems that the older villagers are managing very well, as long as they can get hold of supplies, because they were brought up to cook properly as well as make do and mend.

I overheard a few mutterings about scavengers

too. I'm not sure if that means people local to the village or from outside, but I suppose it is inevitable.

When I was feeding the hens and collecting eggs (four today) I thought I heard rustling in the woods nearby, but I expect it was just a deer.

Sunday, December 1

I had the strongest urge for church today and tried to get everyone to come with me. Martin said he wouldn't as he wanted to go out with his gun again and Stephen said he would help him. Anna didn't feel well, but Jane came and Linda joined us.

It took a good half hour to walk there, but it was just as well we walked briskly as the church is very cold now there is no heating. There is no organ either as that relies on electricity too, so we sang accompanied by piano. There wasn't a huge turnout, but I think fifty plus is quite good when it's so cold.

They used to serve coffee after Sunday services, but that's not possible now. So we mingled for a while afterwards until the cold began to seep through our layers. James, our rector, said he is hoping to hold all the services he would normally have during Advent and that gives us hope. If there is no earthly help for us, apart from what we can manage for ourselves, we need to pray. I would like to go to the beautiful evening Compline services he has organised in previous years, when the church is silent and lit only by candles, but Martin won't be keen on any of us walking that far in the dark.

When we got back home, we were rosy and warm, which was just as well as no one had minded the fires in my absence and I had to start all over again.

But I wasn't too cross as the service and singing the first verse of 'Oh Come Oh Come Immanuel', which we shall add to week, by week, made me feel hopeful and able to anticipate Christmas with some joy.

In the past, even though the children have been grown up for some time, I have refilled the drawers of our little cardboard Advent calendar in the shape of a Christmas tree every year. So I went up to the attic to find it and decided that even though I cannot buy gifts to fill it this year, we should maintain the tradition. The drawers now contain miniature Christmas cards, messages of hope and useful things like safety pins and buttons. Tonight we shall decide who opens the first drawer.

Today was so grey and dull the hens have been less inclined to lay well and I only found two eggs.

Monday, December 2

Deirdre came up to see us this morning, full of excitement, and announced that there are sweet chestnuts for the taking in the grounds of the big house along the lane. The house is owned by a big company and is only used for corporate functions and international visitors, but no one has been there for some time. The caretaker has told Deirdre we can all take as many chestnuts as we like, before the squirrels and other wild animals finish them off, so I set off with the girls immediately.

There was such a heavy crop we quickly filled our basket with the shiny nuts, most of which had split from their spiny casings. After a bit I left the girls to carry on sifting through the leaves and spines so I could get back and check the fires and heat our soup.

When they came back they said they will have to go again tomorrow, as there is so much to find. The chestnut trees grow all along the drive and have cropped well this year, like the oak trees with their acorns.

We shall have to think how best to use this windfall as it could be useful for our Saturday bartering. I voted for chestnut flour, but the girls are less keen as they are getting tired of grinding the acorns. We'll start by blanching the nuts with boiling water, then we can peel them once they are cool enough to handle. I might start with a chestnut soup which is very simple to make with stock and onion. I don't think we'll bother with marrons glacés as none of us are keen on them, but we might roast a few in a pan over the fire tonight after we've had our beef stew and dumplings. We all agreed Anna should open the first drawer in the Advent calendar last night, as she is missing her family.

Two more eggs today.

Tuesday, December 3

Martin bagged a couple of rabbits on Sunday. We hung them in the garage and will eat them later in the week or maybe take them along to the pub on Saturday, as we have plenty of beef for the moment. The rabbits remind me of my childhood when we stayed with my great-aunt Hilda and uncle Will in their pub near Midhurst at Christmas, where the cellar was filled with well hung game as well as barrels of beer and cider. The hares and pheasants were given by locals in lieu of payment, which fed us well over Christmas, but didn't pay the bills, my aunt would complain.

I think Martin's enjoying his role of hunter-gatherer and Stephen is going out with him and learning to shoot, which he must do in case Martin is indisposed in future. An accurate shot with an air rifle can bring down the smaller creatures, but if they go after deer they will have to borrow Neil's gun.

Yesterday Jane opened the second drawer of the Advent calendar and Anna presented us with a homemade Advent candle. I had been saying how sorry I was that we didn't have one this year and now we do. She had marked a tall white candle with evenly spaced scratches, engraved numbers with a pin, then painted the etched marks with red nail varnish. We shall burn one section every night, just as we normally would and it will seem as if Christmas, and life, is more like it should be.

Only two eggs again today, so I hope there will be eggs on Saturday.

Wednesday, December 4

A momentous day in which one piece of good news was eclipsed by another, of even greater significance. Firstly, Martin and Tony have worked out a way of using the kerosene from our oil tank and from Tony's. I don't really understand how they are obtaining it or adapting it, but this will mean each home will have a paraffin heater and a lantern, as long as the fuel lasts. They think it should be possible to eke it out through the winter, which will be a great bonus.

But even more important news was delivered by Anna, who came to see me with Stephen to tell me she is pregnant. I should have guessed she wasn't ill at all, it was just morning sickness, which she is still experiencing. Stephen cycled to the chemist at the beginning of the week for a testing kit to be sure and they told me with excitement, but also fear.

I am afraid too, but I won't let it show. We have a doctor in the village and I am sure there must be some trained nurses or even a midwife living nearby. All over the world women have babies without medical intervention, so I keep telling myself it will be alright. I'm hoping the surgery and the chemist will still have stocks of vitamins or iron if they are needed and that, as Anna is young and generally very healthy, she will have a good pregnancy.

Martin was shocked when I told him. I don't think he fully appreciates the risks, he just said, "You mean I'm going to be a grandfather? I don't feel old enough." I said we must do our best to look after Anna. Girls need their mothers nearby, especially in first pregnancies, so we must ensure she eats well and make her feel safe, so that she can look forward to the birth.

With all this happening I nearly forgot to shut the hens up and only remembered late in the evening, long after it was dark. They'd only laid two eggs again and as I closed the henhouse door an owl was calling in the trees on the edge of the field.

Thursday, December 5

The paraffin heater makes a popping noise, but by lighting it in the dining room in the evening we have one really warm room now. Elsewhere in the house it is very cold, but I'm sure we can survive with hot water bottles and extra blankets. I remember frost on the inside of windows in my childhood and misty breath in unheated bedrooms and think we shall have this cold snap for a while now.

Martin was being unreasonable today when I asked if I could have some of the old jars he has been saving for nails and screws. I am desperate for jars to make confit and potted meat and he has a whole box of spare jars, as well as the full ones that already line the tool cupboard. In the end he grudgingly said I could take a few, when I pointed out that he was hardly likely in the current circumstances to come across a new supply of nails or screws to fill his wretched jars. I've sterilised them with boiling water and will hide them from him in the larder.

I also need some jars for the chestnuts. Even though none of us like marrons glacés, Deirdre pointed out that they could be a very good thing to take to the barter market, as we are beginning to call it. Some people might be very glad of a few sweet things nearing Christmas, so we are both making a sugar syrup to preserve the cooked chestnuts. I am a little concerned at using up so much sugar, but Deirdre has given me some of her surplus, as she didn't make all the jam she had planned to prepare this autumn. Anyway, sugar is not an essential food, so we are better off without it.

I only got two eggs again today. I'm wondering if they have enough food. I used to give them mixed corn and layers pellets, which we can't get now and there are very few scraps to spare for them.

Friday, December 6

The young are so optimistic, and I must be too. Stephen and Anna want to get married. They told us last night after supper, while we all sat by the fire, enjoying the extra heat of our kerosene fired heater. They sat holding hands, and told us they know they are meant to be together and that they feel they can be more hopeful about the future and the coming of their baby if they marry very soon.

I can't believe I had tears in my eyes and I think they may have had them too. But we all laughed and kissed and hugged and said of course they should go ahead if they really want to. We aren't quite sure how to arrange a wedding in these times, but I said they should come to the pub tomorrow as the Rector is sure to be there and he will know how to proceed.

Then Martin said we should have a toast and found the half full bottle of sloe gin at the back of the sideboard, leftover from last Christmas. We all had a very small glass, though Anna only took a small sip, and toasted the health of the happy couple.

A wedding and a baby are signs of hope, surely. And everyone deserves to have a happy, memorable wedding, so we must all do our best to make sure it is a day to remember, whenever it is. First Christmas, then a wedding, that must be something to celebrate.

I dug over the hen run again today and the hens were frantic for the worms, standing on my fork as I turned over the soil. But there were only two eggs.

Saturday, December 7

I can hardly believe I have been able to order a goose for Christmas dinner! Our farm butcher, who fattens his own birds, had his order book out in the pub and will have the birds ready for us to collect on December 21. How I'm going to cook it, I can't quite think, so perhaps Martin will have to help me work out a way of roasting indoors at last. The birds won't be quite as big and fat as previous years, because they are free ranging and their grain is being rationed, but they should be all the tastier for that. Martin was a bit sniffy about having goose as he says he only likes turkey. But the fact is, he's never actually eaten goose and I said if it's a question of having goose for Christmas dinner or having nothing at all, what would he rather have. Then he said as long as there's plenty of stuffing he might be able to manage it. Without bread for that and bread sauce, I'm not too sure how I'll cope, but I'm sure I can devise something to keep him happy. But even more important than the goose, was speaking to James our lovely Rector, who said he can certainly marry Stephen and Anna. He will start calling banns of marriage from tomorrow and will read them out on the following two Sundays, in accordance with the requirements for church weddings. This means that they could be married any day after that, assuming that there are no 'lawful impediments', which made us laugh. As they would like to be married as soon as possible, they decided to hold the ceremony on New Year's Day. We all agreed that would be a wonderfully hopeful way to start the year. My marrons glacés were well received and I exchanged them and some confit for cabbage, carrots, swede and eggs. I noticed Martin frowning when he saw his jars being given away though. We only took two rabbits to barter, as we weren't sure how many people would be keen to have them. The younger customers were very unsure about them and I think if we do it again we should skin and joint them first and then they may find them less daunting.

The hens did a little better today, laying three eggs.

Sunday, December 8

We all went to church today to hear James announce the banns of marriage. It made us feel very happy and gave us hope. It's also given us a lot to think about and to do, as even in these difficult times we want the day to be special.

As we walked home we talked with excitement of our plans for Christmas and for the wedding, but Anna was quiet, walking slowly, and didn't seem as happy as the rest of us. When I asked her what she was thinking, she said she wished her parents could be here. I hugged her and said we should think of them often and pray for them, although I am sure they are being brave and resourceful. I also said they would be proud of her and glad that she was safe. Then I asked her if she'd like to add her family traditions to our Christmas preparations, as then her family wouldn't feel so far away, and she brightened.

When we got home, Jane took Anna up to the attic to find all our old Christmas decorations, which go back to when the children were tiny and include everything they made at nursery; gilded walnut shells, plaster stars and felt bells. We've never had a tasteful, colour coordinated tree and I don't suppose we ever will. Stephen decided he wanted to find out if the local farm would have its usual stock of home-grown trees and cycled off to the other side of the village to check. Martin had some soup and then went out with his gun.

I'm glad everyone is busy and each of us has an important job to do. In these days without the distractions of phones, the internet and television, we need to be occupied. If we are kept busy fetching water and wood and performing other chores, we cannot dwell on how difficult life has become, we just have to get on with it.

I gave the hens some fatty scraps yesterday and I think they have benefited from it already, as they gave me four eggs today.

Monday, December 9

We had the last of the beef stew last night and as Martin bagged another couple of rabbits yesterday, we shall have them casseroled tonight. He says there are a lot of pheasant around in the surrounding woods and fields as there obviously aren't any organised shoots on the estates this year. So he plans to go out again tomorrow, once he and Stephen have stocked up our wood supplies and drawn water.

Stephen found another source of trees yesterday, only a mile or so down the lane. He has put our name down for one and as it is not too far away, he and Martin will be able to carry it back between them later this week. The price for a good sized tree of about seven foot is a brace of pheasants, which seems a bargain.

All of this is making me feel optimistic, but Stephen also quietly told me and Martin that when he cycled to the farm on the outskirts of the village yesterday, he thought he heard cars in the distance so he cycled up to the A3 junction to check. Very few locals are using their cars. We're all saving any fuel we have for emergencies, so it's very unusual to hear traffic now. And Stephen said when he got to the bridge across the road he saw two pickup trucks racing each other, each on opposite sides of the dual carriageway. There was a couple of men in each vehicle and they were waving banners out of the open windows and screaming.

Stephen says he kept out of sight and didn't say anything to Anna, as she is nervous enough as it is. I don't like the sound of this at all and said how could people waste petrol like that. But Martin said there's fuel enough for those who want it. He said he expects some people have worked out how to access the reserves in the petrol stations, or they're using central heating oil, like ours. Apparently diesel vehicles can run on kerosene. That's as may be, I thought, but these people weren't using their vehicles for emergencies, these were men set on causing mayhem.

I stopped to listen when I shut up the hens last night. Before the power cut we could hear the faint drone of traffic on the A3 as well as the rumble of the trains between London and Portsmouth. But last night all was still and quiet. And all was well this morning, though my hens laid only two eggs.

Tuesday, December 10

It was lovely to see the girls happy and laughing after they had fetched and boiled water this morning. They had decided to collect fir cones and greenery to make garlands to decorate the old beams in the house and for a wreath for the front door. Anna says her mother always uses natural materials, so I can see this is making her feel more cheerful.

They came back indoors from the cold, breathless and rosy, with lots of cones from the grounds. After Christmas they can be used to stoke the fires, so the labour won't be wasted. Anna asked if she could use an old tin of white emulsion from under the stairs, to give the cones a snowy coating once they are strung together.

And while she was busy, Jane told me that she wants to help Anna make a dress for her wedding. I suppose Anna was too shy to ask, but I've told Jane we shall all help her if she wants us to and that she can use anything she feels will be suitable. We are fortunately a family of hoarders and there are old clothes galore in the wardrobes and lace curtains and remnants of fabric in cupboards and trunks upstairs.

Seeing them busy and happy is helping me to put aside the horrible thoughts I keep having about raiders on the road. I hope they were racing back to London as they were both going in that direction.

The hens only gave us two eggs today, but then the days are so short now.

Wednesday, December 11

Jane and Anna found some thick old rope in the garage and are using lengths of this for their garlands. They've laid the rope out on the floor of the sitting room which we never use to sit in now, as we don't light the fire in there. When they are not grinding acorns, boiling water or washing, they are fixing the cones onto the rope with strands of garden wire. Anna says it reminds her of the great garland that is always made to decorate the Great Hall at Cotehele in Cornwall, though that one contains dried flowers and this will be full of berried ivy when it's finished.

The wreath for the front door will be made last of all, using a twiggy base saved from last year, with the addition of cones and greenery.

The girls have also assembled a pile of materials they want to sort through for the wedding. They've found lace and ribbons, petticoats and old fur coats and are spending a lot of time talking with great excitement about their design. I'm content to leave them to plan as they are happier being busy.

Martin decided today to drain off some of the heating oil and hide it away, in case marauders come to steal it. As our petrol cans are still full, I'm not sure what he imagines he can store it in, but he says he will hide it in the inspection pit which is beneath the concrete floor of the garage. I have to admit that is a really good idea, although generally the pit is very damp and waterlogged.

Later, when I went to collect the eggs, I found him rummaging in the recycling wheelie bin for containers. He found several plastic juice and milk bottles and I found two eggs.

Thursday, December 12

Another happy day, as Martin and Stephen came back triumphant bearing a tree. The pheasants paid the price and the boys carried the tree over a mile and a half down the lane. They laid it outside while they found the heavy pot to hold it, then trimmed some of the straggly branches and left them for the girls to use in their decorations.

And now it is standing in our hall, making the house smell like Christmas. Although we have a fire lit in the hall most of the time, it is not a very warm room, so I think the tree will last well and won't drop very soon. In recent years we have bought our tree quite late and for the last two years it has not even been decorated until Christmas Eve, when Jane and Stephen were finally home for the holidays. But this year I'm glad to have it here early. It feels like another sign of normality, an indication that we can keep going, even if there is chaos elsewhere.

And the hens keep on laying, even if their production sometimes declines a little. The days are short and dark, so three eggs is quite good.

Friday, December 13

Martin started moaning this morning that today truly is Friday the 13th. When I asked why, he said the juice cartons were useless and were leaking kerosene everywhere. That's when I realised he'd used the cardboard ones, from the recycling bin. He's very cross with himself, but I said it's no use crying over spilt milk – or spilt oil – and he should use wine bottles instead as we have a collection of corks which will make good stoppers. There are certainly enough bottles in the recycling, at the rate he used to drink every week.

He went off to sort through the bin and I heard him tipping it out all over the gravel. I hope he clears it up properly as we don't need broken glass to add to his Friday the 13th problems.

Jane and Anna decided they wanted to walk into the village to the school, to ask if anyone has an old-fashioned sewing machine. Obviously they can't use the electric one nowadays and they seem to be hatching a plan which is going to require a lot of sewing. I'm not keen on them walking anywhere on their own, if undesirable characters are racing around in trucks, but in the end I made them promise to be back by lunchtime and we agreed on one o'clock. I said I would send Martin or Stephen out on the bike if they weren't back on time. I feel like I shouldn't have to do this, as they are adults, but I can't help worrying about who or what may come into the village.

They eventually came back with big smiles, saying that one of the volunteer teachers has said they can borrow her machine. She will bring it along to the pub tomorrow, which will be best as it is heavy and then we can all help to carry it home.

A fox has been digging around the hen run and I hope the wire is buried deeply enough. There weren't any eggs today, but then it is Friday the 13th.

Saturday, December 14

As we walked to the pub this morning, the lane echoed with laughter. The girls had decided to take the wheelbarrow, to bring back the heavy sewing machine they are borrowing, but on the way there they insisted Martin and Stephen should take it in turns to give them a ride. With lots of shrieks and yelps first Anna then Jane each had a go, collapsing into the barrow, their legs sticking out, looking most ungainly. But I declined, as I was carrying a basket with potted meat and two pheasants.

When it's dry we can cut across the fields and hop over the stiles, but we couldn't very well do that with a wheelbarrow, so we walked up the lane to the main road, noticing how heavy with berries the holly is this year. That means a hard winter, Martin said, but I think it's another sign that it was a good summer as everything fruited well in the end.

We exchanged our goods for eggs and vegetables at the pub and also trout. I was surprised to find them at this time of year, but they've come from the well-stocked fish ponds the other side of the village. It will make a welcome change for our supper tonight and will be easy to cook.

But there was less happy news too. David Henderson, chairman of the Parish Council, told us that he and his wife Stella now have a lodger, a young friend from Guildford, who arrived during the week. He cycled all the way, bringing only a few possessions but no food at all. He told them the town is no longer safe. He has not seen his neighbours for some time and suspects they may have perished, waiting in their homes for the crisis to be resolved. The only people he's seen were those breaking into houses and shops searching for anything to eat. Stephen was with us when we heard this, but Jane and Anna were being shown how to use the sewing machine and I don't want them to know.

And now, the girls have set up a sewing table in the sitting room and are happily learning how to use it. My hens tried harder today and laid three eggs.

Sunday, December 15

On our way home from church today, after hearing the banns read for the second time, we bumped into Mick, our publican. He said his stocks are running very low, even though he is only open on Saturdays now. But he says he has no objection to using the pub as a meeting place once a week, as it is in the centre of the village, so long as he can be supplied with wood for the fires. Martin and Stephen promised to take a barrow of logs and kindling along early next week, as we have wood to spare.

Jane and Anna were keen to get home to carry on sewing, so we sent them on ahead with Stephen. That meant Martin and I could ask Mick if there was any more news from Guildford or elsewhere. Mick said the village plans to send a search party to the town to see for themselves. The Parish Council has been talking to local farmers, the Scouts and the Rangers on the common and a group of the ablest and fittest plans to set out during the week. They will travel in a Land Rover and all have shotguns.

We talked about it all the way home. Is it wise I wonder, if there is bedlam in the town, to advertise the fact that we still have petrol and supplies in this area? Martin thinks it's important to determine how vulnerable we are out here and that requires reconnaissance. He then started talking about strategic planning and preliminary surveys, so I could tell he wishes he was younger and could go with them.

When we got home he vented his frustration on the pheasants in the field, so now we have more for the pot. And I collected two brown eggs after throwing the hens some vegetable peelings boiled up with a little of the acorn husks.

Monday, December 16
I couldn't sleep last night. I keep telling myself I'm being silly, but I feel as if we have been safely hidden away so far in our little village. And now, just because they like an adventure, the men are going off to advertise our presence and our resources.

It's stupid, I'm sure, and I won't let the girls know about my fears, but Martin listened to me wittering on this morning and told me to shut up. He's right, but I think even he is worried, despite all his talk of strategic planning yesterday. So he's going into the village today to find out how this expedition is being handled.

In the meantime, I'm trying not to think about what is happening elsewhere and am concentrating on how much there is to do every day. The weather is mild but wet, so we aren't too cold but there is no chance of drying any washing outside and everything has to be wrung out tightly then hung up indoors. Our clothes smell of smoke if they dry properly and of fusty mildew if they don't. Oh for a mangle!

Martin thinks there must be a way of using the kerosene to run a generator. Which is all very well, but we don't have a generator and if there were any to be had, I'm sure they will all have been bought or looted by now.

The hens looked bedraggled this afternoon when I fed them, but they'd laid two eggs. If stragglers come out from the town, I wonder if they will ask for help or take what they need? I'm frightened, but I won't show it.

Tuesday, December 17

I'm absolutely furious with Martin. He went into the village yesterday to find out about the expedition into Guildford and now I find out he's joined it! I said he had to be joking. He's not young and he's not fit, but he said he's a good shot and they could use him. He suggested taking Stephen as well, but I put my foot down. I'm not having my son, about to be married, going off on this crazy escapade. And now Martin's gone and we've no way of knowing when he'll be back, so I'm trying to calm down by keeping busy here.

Anna and Jane don't know he's gone and they're enjoying decorating the tree with all the old baubles they brought down from the attic last week. It almost looks like a normal Christmas here, now the tree is decked with tinsel and glitter.

And Neil had to move the sheep as the river field flooded after all the rain yesterday. Three of the stupid things were nearly trapped on an island of grass near the road, but he chased them through the gate onto drier ground. Geese and ducks colonised the flooded field immediately, so maybe when Martin gets back he can put his gun to good use in a real wild goose chase, instead of showing off with the boys.

While the girls were doing the tree, I shut myself in their sewing room to make some little presents. Usually, by this time of year, I would have bags of gifts wrapped or ready to wrap, but this year we only have what we can make ourselves, so some imagination is called for.

Pheasant casserole for supper, as it will keep till Martin is back. And my hens produced two eggs today, but I am concerned about the weak shells and watery whites. I have run out of oyster shell to mix with their food, so I'll have to substitute crushed egg shells and hope this will improve their eggs.

Wednesday, December 18

I can't write this. I can't settle down to anything today. I'm not just cross, I'm worried sick. Martin hasn't come back yet and now I've found out he took Tony with him. Gail just came up to see me and asked if I knew about this and who else had gone. The trouble is, I know absolutely nothing and have no way of contacting them. Stupid, stupid men.

Gail went back home feeling very upset and so she should be. Tony isn't even a good shot. He's handy with a screwdriver and is very clever with all sorts of DIY jobs, but neither he nor Martin should be at the front line.

I'm not going to be able to rest until they are safely back, so I'm going to take out my frustration on the hen run and dig it over for them to find more worms.

Thursday, December 19

I'm still furious with Martin, even though he got back here late yesterday afternoon, just after sunset. He told me not to make a fuss and said they'd had problems with the Land Rover. He wouldn't say any more, but I was sure something had happened.

This morning, once Stephen was outside fetching wood and the girls were busy with their sewing, I tackled Martin again. I said he couldn't go taking risks and leaving us to fend for ourselves, just for the thrill of it. He was quiet at first, but then he told me how shocked he and the others were by the quietness of the town. They hardly saw anyone at all. The High Street was empty, the shop windows were broken and there was no sign of police or the army. Then they drove through some of the residential areas, which also seemed to be deserted, apart from a few dogs prowling around bins. I couldn't believe everyone had left, but Martin said no, they hadn't gone, most of them had died in their homes. But how, I wondered, how could a town of people die when we are fit and healthy out here? Then Martin said they'd come across a man digging one of the allotments off the road near the old Farnham Hospital. He told them that most of his neighbours had stayed in their homes, convinced that help would come eventually. Some of them had walked into the town to find food, but most had died of thirst or cold. He said he and his wife were the only ones left alive in their road, as far as he knew, because they were self-sufficient and grew their own food.

Then Martin and the others drove across the A3 to the big supermarket near the hospital. The store was still standing, but the shelves were empty, there was rubbish everywhere and a couple of dogs were sniffing around the freezers.

And that was where they got into trouble. Suddenly, as they were getting back into the Land Rover, another car came into the car park and two men yelled at them, demanding to know what they'd found. So they drove off at top speed, but they were followed. Martin said they couldn't risk being chased back to the village, so they shot off southwards down the A3. They didn't dare drive as far as the Hindhead tunnel, in case that was blocked, so they turned off and tried to shake off their pursuers. They didn't lose them till they'd gone beyond Haslemere and had to spend the night high up in the woods on Black Down.

I was even crosser when I heard this. They could have run out of petrol, been ambushed, anything could have happened. Then Martin said he'd brought me a present. There was an unloaded pallet of toilet rolls at the supermarket, so they packed up the Land Rover and now we have a fresh supply. I must say, that is very welcome as we were getting very low indeed. It doesn't mean he is forgiven though.

Friday, December 20

We have agreed not to talk about it. Last night Martin promised he would not take any more risks and I said I would not raise the subject again. He is back home and we are all safe, for the moment. And next week it will be Christmas and we must all try to make it more of a Christmas than Christmas has ever been.

Usually by this time of year I would have had heavy groceries brought by the helpful Tesco man, a delivery of wines for a party, mince pies baked and cards and invitations to open every day. This year is so very different, but it is still special in its own way. Jane and Anna made a wreath with fresh ivy and holly for the front door and their green garland drapes the hall chimney piece. They have made paper angels from thin printer paper to stand on the windowsills, where numerous Christmas cards would normally be displayed.

And I have made cards stamped with a star-shaped potato cut. They will be hand-delivered on our way to the pub tomorrow and I'll leave some there and in the church for other local friends. We can't send cards further afield this year, but we can send thoughts and prayers.

I've also made mincemeat from the last of the dried fruit, some of the mutton suet and a few apples. I can't bake pastry without an oven, but I'll think of some way to use it to give us all a taste of Christmas.

There was a hard frost this morning and it may be cold again tonight, so I've given the hens warm boiled scraps and peelings. In return they produced four eggs today.

Saturday, December 21

We walked to the pub this morning, even though it rained all the way there and all the way back. One of my wellies has started leaking and my sock was soaked by the time we got home. Martin thinks he may be able to repair the hole in the welt with a puncture repair kit, once the boot has dried out. In the meantime I shall have to borrow his boots when I go outside.

There was much talk at the pub of the devastation in the town, following the return of the expedition. Those who are used to growing produce and handling livestock are shocked that the townspeople stayed put awaiting their fate. We are all so accustomed here to solving our own problems and have a strong survival instinct. But some said we mustn't assume that everyone in the surrounding towns has perished and that there are likely to be stragglers, both good and bad, finding their way to areas like ours eventually.

We then talked with Mick, Reverend James and others about how we should react if outsiders come into the village. Some were adamant they would not welcome strangers and wouldn't share their hard won supplies with them. But our vicar said that, while we must be naturally cautious, we are well stocked here and should be able to share a little of our stores. Finally we agreed that there should be a refugee committee, consisting of Mick, James and David from the Parish Council, to vet incomers and assess their needs. Then they could be accommodated in the village hall and given rations. I felt happy with that compromise, as while I hate to think of people starving, I am very anxious about our safety after hearing Martin's account of his adventure.

Today it was dark by three o'clock but my hens gave me four more eggs, two blue and two brown.

Sunday, December 22

Yesterday was the shortest day of the year and it felt really short, being so damp and dark. But today we are in good spirits, having walked to church to hear the banns read for the third and last time. And as we sang 'Angels From the Realms of Glory' I think we all felt the magic of Christmas was close by.

We came out to clear skies and crisp sunshine and the walk home was warming. I was very glad it was no longer raining as my boots are no longer waterproof. Martin has tried mending them, but the patch he's applied from the puncture kit needs to dry out properly before I can try wearing them again.

I'm writing this while our meal cooks on the fire. Steak and kidney pudding, which must be watched so it doesn't boil dry. I picked up meat at the pub yesterday and decided to make this for our dinner today. Normally I would casserole the meat first, before encasing it in suet pastry in a large basin and steaming for about three hours, but now I can't use the oven I have had to revert to the old-fashioned way of preparing it, by letting the meat cook in its own juices inside the pastry. That takes twice as long, but it will taste really good. Martin has donated a bottle of cheap cabernet shiraz so we can have a treat of mulled wine, which is filling the air with the scent of cinnamon and cloves. I used to make it with oranges, but we haven't seen any citrus fruit, not even a lemon, since the power failed. I've thrown in some candied peel and hope this might give a hint of orangey flavour.

I feel calmer than I did a couple of days ago, now the house is warm and happy with the smells of the season and everyone is safely home. The hens are happier with the drier weather, but they only laid two eggs today.

Monday, December 23
When I went out after dark last night to shut up the

hens, the sky was clear with stars, but such a change today. It was still dark with rain and wind at 8am this morning and the winds have increased, bringing down a tree in the wood and several branches off the old willow tree.

It is the sort of weather that normally brings power cuts, but now we are used to this permanent loss of power we are only worried about trees, chimneys and tiles. We cannot travel far so we have no concerns about highways and cancelled trains. The furthest we went today was into the village to collect the goose. Martin then decided he had to set out for some essential tool by bike, so he was gone for another hour, but he promised me he was not going near any towns.

With the rain lashing and wind howling, the hens are wisely staying in their house and I fed them inside and bolted the door early for once. There were four eggs, one very freshly laid as I saw her jump down from the nest as soon as she saw me tipping out their food.

Tuesday, December 24

Wind thundered around the chimney stacks all night and rain lashed the windows. I was awake before dawn this morning, but could not see how much damage there was until first light. Three huge trees have come down, one of them straddling and crushing the fence to the middle field.

But the worst news was the rising water. The river has burst its banks and has already flooded the nearest field and is edging across the second and third. Neil was worried about the sheep, but with water rushing across the road, there was no prospect of moving them and he hopes they will still have a corner of dry land where they will be safe.

In the morning Martin and I went to see how fast the water was rising. One of the wood bunkers nearest the field is full of wood ready to burn and I said we should bring some back to the house in case it flooded. I should have done it then and there as by mid-afternoon the logs were floating out of their dry shelter.

During the morning Tony came to tell us that our road is blocked by a huge fallen tree, which narrowly missed crashing into Robin and Deidre's house but landed in their driveway. The men spent a couple of hours cutting away the branches which filled the garden, but the trunk is far too big to tackle and the road remains impassable there. And at the other end of the lane there is a deep flood, so now we cannot leave. Thank goodness we collected our goose yesterday and have food for some time, though we have no eggs as the hens are sulking in their house, after the heavy downpours of yesterday.

Wednesday, December 25
As we could not walk to church today, because of the flood, we sang carols while we prepared our Christmas dinner. Martin rigged up a kind of spit close to the fire to cook the goose. I have coated the bird with honey and set a pan underneath to catch the fat, which will be wonderful for cooking later on.

We have potatoes and cabbage which I picked up on Saturday, but no Brussels sprouts, which I shan't miss. We have a stuffing made with chestnuts, but no bread sauce, we have apple sauce but no pigs in blankets, we have a pudding but no custard or cream. However, I have made a brandy butter of sorts and have hidden the silver charms inside the pudding.

And despite the lack of electricity, central heating, Christmas TV or drinks parties, we are all cheerful. We have no crackers but Stephen has planned party games, we have not shopped for presents for weeks, but there are still gifts under the tree. Neil and Linda will join us for dinner, once they have checked the sheep and the broken fence. The floods are receding and we are all here, safe, warm and together and that is all that matters.

Thursday, December 26

It is Boxing Day and no one can go to the sales. None of us miss the frenetic pressure to buy, buy, buy. And today is fine and sunny, almost warm in the sunshine.

Yesterday we all agreed was a very special, memorable Christmas Day. There was a lot of laughter during Stephen's games of 'What am I Humming?' and 'Animal Charades'. There was a lot of appreciative noises when the goose and the pudding were served and there were toasts to absent friends with one of Martin's precious bottles of Merlot.

There were presents too, despite the fact that none of us had been able to shop online or traipse round crowded stores. I had made lavender bags, which were appreciated more by the girls than the men, I must admit. Anna had done delicate pen and ink drawings of the house and garden, Jane had made fur headbands for us all, even the men, from scraps of fake fur she had found in the attic. Stephen gave us fans of pheasant feathers and goose quills for our hats. But my best present was from Martin. He gave me a new pair of wellington boots. So that is where he had been, just before the storm. He had cycled to the garden centre to see if they still had boots in stock and he was lucky to find the last pair in my size. So now, despite the floods, I shall have dry feet in my own boots. I wore them today, to walk across the mud to feed the hens and collect four eggs.

Friday, December 27

There were high winds and rain again last night, which we all cursed, as we have had enough of floods and fallen trees for now. But this morning, the water level was no worse, in fact it has gone down considerably and we can easily walk into the village again. There is mud and debris on all the roads and the river washed some plastic drums and garden furniture up against the bridge, as well as branches.

There are scores of ducks and Canada geese on the swampy fields, so Martin will go out with his gun again today. Stephen is attempting to cut through the tree blocking the road, with Tony and Robin, but their chainsaws aren't really up to the job. Robin said he has been telling Surrey Highways for years that the tree was dangerous and they never heeded his warnings.

Anna and Jane are busy with their sewing again. I am happy they are busy and occupied once they have helped to heat water and grind the acorns every day. I have not yet seen what they are making as they have now banned everyone from the sewing room while they assemble Anna's dress, or whatever outfit it is they have created, for the wedding.

I took a long hard look at myself in the mirror this morning. My face is pale, with dark circles under my eyes. I have run out of my favourite Estée Lauder foundation, and my hair is lank. I would never want to look 'mother of the bride' or mother-in-law of the bride, in this case, in peach dress and coat with matching hat, but I do want to look presentable for Stephen and Anna's special day. I have new wellingtons but nothing else new to wear. But at least there won't be photographs to record my pitiful appearance. I wore my new boots to feed the hens and collect their eggs. Four again today and the hen which had gone off lay has a better colour again now. She must think spring is on the way.

Saturday, December 28

There was frost this morning, but the day is bright and clear, although there are ominous clouds looming in the south. I hope that doesn't mean more rain as we are struggling to clear up after the downpours just before Christmas. Martin and Stephen are moving most of the wood to the garage which will stay dry if there is more flooding. Two of the old gun emplacements used as wood sheds were flooded and the neat stacks of logs were strewn everywhere.

We walked to the pub this morning and were greeted by the welcome scent of mulled wine. Mick said his supplies of bottled beer are nearly gone and so he is now using his wine cellar. We had brought a barrow load of logs, which though wet will soon dry out and help to keep his fires going. Martin exchanged duck and pheasant for swede, kale and parsnips, so we shall have good meals this week. I modelled my new wellies for Mick and he laughed when Martin said they'd cost him two pheasants.

The girls didn't come with us as they are frantically sewing and Stephen wanted to finish transferring the logs to their new shelter. Counting today, there are now only four days to the wedding and we have a lot to think about. Mick has said we can have a gathering – we can hardly call it a reception – in the pub, which Anna and Stephen said they would like to do as it would be a social occasion for everyone in the village who knows them. If the day is dry he plans to set up a barbecue so we can cook and we plan to take him our game birds on Tuesday on our way to decorate the church.

Before I fed the hens this afternoon I picked up fallen branches around the formal garden to use as kindling and I noticed the first hellebores emerging. The flowers are white speckled with pink, almost like a bird's egg. And then I collected an egg for every hen, a full half dozen.

Sunday, December 29

We woke to such a frost today. Our cars were so white they looked as if there had been snow. Martin went outside to turn the engines over and said it was minus one degree Centigrade at 9.30 this morning. So we walked briskly to church with collars up and scarves over our noses in the frosty sunshine. Every pew had lighted candles, which had been used for the Christmas day service we had not been able to attend because of the flooding. Reverend James says they will be lit for the wedding on Wednesday as well, so the church will look very beautiful. We sang 'O Little Town of Bethlehem' to start and ended with 'God Rest Ye Merry Gentlemen' which everyone sang with gusto. Then Martin and I left Stephen and Anna to discuss their hymns for the wedding with David the organist, who plays the piano now there is no power.

When we got home I stoked the fires, then went out around the grounds collecting fir tree branches brought down by the storms. These will give us a base when we're decorating the church on Tuesday. And Neil came across and said he had just slaughtered a hogget, that is a lamb born earlier this year, as a wedding present for the happy couple and will take it up to the pub for the barbecue. I thanked him for this on their behalf and then he gave me the kidneys and liver as well, which we'll have tonight. He has collected the blood again and so Linda will come over tomorrow to make more black pudding. I don't have many oats left, so we shall have to mix it with some coarse acorn flour and maybe ground chestnuts too.

Although today was very cold it was really quite pleasant in the sun and the hens seemed happy too, with four eggs today.

Monday, December 30
Such a change in the weather today. When my alarm went off at seven it was very dark, but it was still

dark at 8 o'clock because of the heavy rain. I went outside to feed the hens after breakfast and they were reluctant to come out of their house, so I expect tomorrow there will be fewer eggs.

It rained all morning and we started watching the fields with some anxiety hoping it will not flood again and make the road impassable this week. Then I decided I should take the greenery to the church and the food to the pub today, just in case we have trouble getting through to the village if there is much more rain. He agreed to me using the car and its precious petrol, just so long as I went straight there and back.

Jane and Stephen came with me and we spent a very enjoyable couple of hours in the church arranging our Scots pine fronds, cones, holly and ivy strands around the church pews and windowsills. Stephen even managed to tie a bunch of foliage with red berries to the porch as well, so it looks very welcoming.

Then we went to the pub and dropped off pheasants and ducks. We shall make a kind of flatbread to serve with the meat and bring that with us on the day.

Once home, it was straight to work with Linda who had made a start on the black pudding mix. And now we have a good supply of sausage again to serve with our own eggs. There were four today, two blue and two brown.

Tuesday, December 31

I'm pleased we decorated the church yesterday and delivered food to the pub, as the weather is not so good again today. I have begun to worry how we shall get to the church tomorrow if it is very wet. Anna had wanted to arrive on horseback, but that won't be practical if it is raining. Martin is meant to be giving her away, in the absence of her own father, but he may have to drive us all there as well.

I still have not seen what the girls have been sewing in secret, but I have my own fashion and beauty problems to worry me. In these powerless days, warmth and comfort have been the greatest priority rather than style, but I feel I must make an effort to look presentable. So after breakfast I boiled as much water as I could for hair washing and a strip wash, so I would have a clean canvas as it were to work on. Then I used some of my dwindling stock of moisturiser and body lotion to improve the condition of my red nose and cracked hands.

But I cannot endure even a wedding if I am cold, so I have decided to wear leggings under a long velvet skirt, which will hide my new boots and knee length socks. With this, I will wear the cashmere and mink cardigan Martin and Jane brought back for me from a vintage dress shop in San Francisco several years ago. It is so warm it can only be used in very cold weather, and over this I'm wearing a long black velvet coat with a big fur collar. I know black is not usually considered appropriate for a wedding, but I shall brighten it all up with raspberry gloves and a matching velvet hat, which I shan't take off, even in the pub, as my hair is so grey now.

I felt much happier once I was clean and had sorted my wardrobe. I hope Anna and Jane are making themselves feel attractive too. It doesn't matter for the men and Martin has grumbled about having to wear his suit and smart coat tomorrow, but I've insisted.

Tomorrow is New Year's Day, the start of a new year, the start of their married life.

Wednesday, January 1

I am ready, but the bride is late. We have to leave very soon, the rain is pouring and by the time we return it will be too dark to write. Yesterday was a flurry of activity with Anna and Jane deciding that they too needed to have clean hair. In the end they carried bucket after bucket of hot water up to the bathroom so they could wash properly, though they shared the water. They asked to borrow the paraffin heater to make the bathroom bearable. I couldn't blame them, especially Anna, for wanting to look their best for her wedding day. I took them breakfast on a tray and left it outside the sewing room, which is full of their laughter and excitement. And now we must go.

Thursday, January 2

I didn't think I would cry, as it was not my own daughter who was getting married, but I did. I cried when I saw her emerge in her dress and I cried again when they said their vows. The church had an ethereal air because of the shadowy candlelight and the natural foliage we had draped everywhere. And Anna was dressed in the colours of Christmas, white, green and red.

She was a winter princess in a remodelled evening gown of dark green velvet, slashed and draped to reveal a white underskirt and bodice, adorned with red silk roses. A heavy velvet cape of dark red, lined with thick fur from a very old coat kept her warm and Jane had made a garland of silver wire strung with red and green beads, like the leaves and berries of the holly tree, for her hair.

Jane's dress of dark red and gold brocade, complemented the bride's and she was warmly wrapped in a burgundy cape lined with bright green artificial fur. I was full of admiration for their ingenuity, but was also highly amused by their resourcefulness in adapting clothes from the spare room wardrobe, the old dressing up box and in seizing the moth-eaten velvet curtains which had been tossed into the attic. And if the service was quietly magical and romantic, then the reception was loud and lively. There was music, singing and dancing, all energetic, undignified and noisy, from Martin and Stephen's ukulele duet of 'Why Don't Women Like Me', to Mick the publican's rock band belting out 'Devil Woman' as vigorously as they could without amplification. We ate roasted lamb, pheasant and duck, wrapped in flatbreads that I and many other ladies from the village had brought, spiced with pickled plums and redcurrant jelly. We drank mulled wine and hot cider and although I had not been able to make or order a wedding cake for lack of sugar and a working oven, dear friends with a solid fuel Aga had made a rich fruit cake, which was cut with great ceremony by the happy couple, despite the lack of marzipan and royal icing.

It wasn't a lavish, expensive wedding that had taken months and months to plan and years to save for, it was simply a beautiful wedding that made all of us very happy and proud.

Friday, January 3

There is no let up to the rain. We have never seen the fields flooded for so long in all our twenty years here. An elderly villager told us on Wednesday that it has not been this bad since 1964, when he had to carry his wife into the village on his back. The water was that deep.

Neil has been fretting about the sheep. A group of a dozen or so became confined to a small dry corner of one of the fields, both before Christmas and again yesterday. But today, as the waters receded they cleverly joined the rest of the flock in a slightly higher and therefore slightly drier field. They may still get some foot rot but at least they won't drown now. Neil is also concerned about the lack of grazing and says he will have to go off in search of hay and feed tomorrow.

Early today there was bright sun, but it soon clouded over again and there were several heavy showers. Stephen and Martin are moving wet logs out of the flooded bunkers and into the garage. It is heavy tiring work, but if they don't do it now and there is a whole winter of rain, the logs won't have a chance to dry off. Where there were once neat stacks of wood on pallets, labelled according to how long they had been seasoned, now there is debris and the logs have been tossed together like matchsticks by the force of the water.

The girls have 'undressed' the Christmas tree today and put away the decorations. Tomorrow Martin will cut it into small pieces and the dry branches will make good firelighters to kindle our fires. And I am cooking a curry to keep us all warm, using the remains of the lamb from the other day. It was so good, there is little left, but I have scraped the bones clean and am simmering them for stock.

My hens all have rosy red combs and should all be in lay, but they don't like rain and so there were only two eggs today.

Saturday, January 4

Linda has just been in to see me. She is concerned at how long Neil is taking to find fodder for the sheep. He left early this morning and has been gone nearly seven hours. It's now mid-afternoon and will be dark in another hour. He is a capable man and he went off in the Land Rover with his trailer, but she didn't think he would go very far afield, although he was determined to come back with bales of hay and sacks of ewe nuts. I've tried to reassure her that he knows how to look after himself, but knowing what happened when Martin and the others went off to Guildford, I'm very aware that there are undesirable characters around and I share her concern. At times like these the lack of phone contact really matters.

Martin has cut up the Christmas tree and left piles of dry twigs and branches indoors to light our fires. It's so dry now it catches instantly and flames shoot up the chimney, which is a great help with other wood being still damp from all the rain.

We've had more rain again today, though not so heavy as to swell the floods. But the ground is still sodden and even the highest lawn is puddled with water. I forgot to shut up the hens last night and wondered this morning if the fox had paid them a visit, as there was no sign when I went outside this morning. But they were huddled inside the house sheltering from the rain and I fed them under cover. They only gave me two eggs.

Sunday, January 5

There has been good news and bad news on all fronts today. Neil eventually returned after dark yesterday, which was good, but the floods have risen again. He managed to find fodder but had to go almost as far as Petersfield before he had any luck. He said he was very wary of confrontation as he drove through the countryside but he encountered no opposition. In fact, he said the good thing about his expedition was finding that the small towns and villages are coping well, like us.

Midhurst was quiet, but he saw people who looked healthy and well fed. Nearby villages like Lickfold and Lurgashall seemed as well ordered as here, which is good news. He picked up his supplies in Rogate, where he heard that they've had some contact with Petersfield, which hasn't coped so well and which has had marauders from as far away as Southampton. That was the bad news and made us think that it's only time before we see some unwelcome incomers around here.

However, Neil also said that most of the country roads, particularly the back lanes, are difficult to drive through. The Christmas storms have felled many trees which are blocking access and there are also many flooded roads. One of the reasons his search took so long was because he had to keep diverting and finding other routes. He thinks these impediments will discourage motorised raiders to some extent, so that is also good news. And when we asked how he had paid for his feed, he said he had taken a pregnant ewe with him in the trailer. She and her lamb, or possibly twins, have covered the cost of keeping the flock fed. Neil has also offered me some of the hay and ewe nuts for our old pet pig, as he is looking very thin. I had thought it was mainly due to old age, but I have not been able to feed him much this winter and he has probably eaten the last of the acorn crop now.

And the last piece of bad news today was the lack of eggs. Well, there was a crushed shell in the nest. The shells are still very thin, but I don't know what else I can give them.

Monday, January 6

When I shut up the hens last night the air was really mild, almost warm. But of course that signalled rain and I was kept awake all night by the sound of water glugging down the drainpipe that runs beside our bedroom window. I haven't walked up the lane today but I expect it is flooded again.

My sleep was also disturbed by an annoying cough. I won't waste scarce medicine on something so trivial, so I am hoping a spoonful of honey will soothe my throat and it won't develop into anything more serious. In these difficult times we are all anxious to stay healthy.

At least Anna is blooming and in the best of health. Her pregnancy is progressing well so far and our doctor estimates she will be due mid to late July. He told her to get iron tablets and vitamins from the chemist now, just in case supplies run out later on when she really needs them, so we hope she will continue to thrive.

Martin and Stephen have been clearing up more of the trees felled by the storms. It is so important to have dry kindling to keep the fires going that I have given up trying to stop them piling branches and fir tree fronds inside the house. It is so wet outside and so damp in the shelters, that the house is the only dry place.

I think the chickens are feeling the effect of the weather too. There were three eggs today, but the blue one laid by one of the Legbars broke as I tried to pick it up, so I tossed it to the hens and they ate it immediately.

Tuesday, January 7

I struggled to wake this morning when my alarm went, partly because it was so dark and also because I had slept so badly. The cough is worse, though not yet bad enough to make me trek to the doctor. However, it is slowing me down, particularly early in the day. I wish I had lemons for a hot drink but have made do with hot water with honey, ginger and a sprig of thyme instead. It is only a cough, I keep telling myself. It isn't flu. Everyone else is in good health so far.

Once the winds and rain died down this morning, Martin went outside to help Neil mend the fences, which have either rotted over the years or been damaged by the storms. Neil picked up some new fence posts on his travels the other day, along with a roll of stock fencing. Robert Frost said good fences make good neighbours, but in our experience good fences keep these naughty sheep in their place.

Half the fields are flooded again from the latest bout of rain and our road is swamped once more. If there was any traffic about it would have to avoid our lane and the main road into Farnham. In the past, whenever there was flooding, we were always astonished at the number of town drivers who would drive at speed through the water, ignoring signs that the roads were closed. But now, instead of the sounds of revving cars and angry cries, we only hear the ducks and geese and the occasional screech of heron.

I've spent little time outside. I want to stay warm and long to be resting. Only two eggs today, both brown.

Wednesday, January 8

I've given in. My head hurts, my chest hurts and my back hurts from coughing. I've swept the floors, made the fires, fed the hens and can do no more. I'm going to bed with a hot water bottle and more honey, ginger and thyme. Maybe tomorrow I'll feel stronger. For now, Martin, Stephen, Anna and Jane can cope. It will be chaos downstairs I know, when I emerge tomorrow, but I don't care. I'm taking to my bed. If there was power I would watch reruns of *Lovejoy*, but as there is none I shall re-read *Rebecca*, my favourite 'ill in bed' book of all time.

Thursday, January 9

I'm sure I'll be back to normal tomorrow. I rarely give in to illness, but this bug is exhausting. Martin has managed to light the fire in the bedroom, so the room is warm for once, which makes it a bearable sanctuary with hot water bottles, steaming tea and a crafty cat asleep on top of me. If life was normal, not just healthy, but with power as well, I would be at the hairdresser today. My grey hairs would be disguised, the layers would be sharp, I'd be reading fashion magazines all afternoon. How life has changed in three months.

Friday, January 10

It was inevitable of course. Just as I start to feel better, Martin announces that he has a tickly throat. He's complained that there is no more echinacea so I've told him to have a spoonful of honey. I can't be a malingerer any longer and shall force myself to work today. The girls have done a good job keeping the water boiling and the floors swept, but I like things done my way and I've been moving cups here and pans there, wiping tabletops and scrubbing sinks.

I've realised, over the last couple of days, just how much we normally take for granted and that includes paper tissues. There are none to be had now and I'm reluctant to use our precious store of toilet paper, so I'm cutting up an old sheet into squares for handkerchiefs. The centre was threadbare and it would have torn the next time it was on the bed, so I'd saved it meaning to put sides to middle, but I never got around to it. So now, my fine Egyptian cotton sheet, for which I can't remember the thread count, is going to blow noses. If Martin and the others get this bug, the hankies will get plenty of use.

The hens didn't lay too well while I was indisposed and today they gave us three eggs. Just as well, since while I was malingering all the other eggs were eaten.

Saturday, January 11

I decided I felt well enough today to walk to the pub. It's a bright sunny day and not at all cold, so I thought it would do me good. Martin didn't come as he wanted to finish propping up more fences before he gets 'the cough' and can't work for a few days.

So I walked there with Stephen and the girls. To our surprise, not only were there the usual offerings of vegetables and meat from the farm, but there was a pile of mineral water in flagons and also large bags of flour.

While we were all pleased to see these new supplies, our hopes that help is at last coming were dashed when Mick said this was probably all we'd be getting. He told everyone that an army truck had driven through the village yesterday and had briefly stopped to drop off the goods but had little more information. They said aid is coming into the country from abroad but the power problem still cannot be resolved. Mick said he told them some generators would be more use, but they just shook their heads and then drove off towards Tilford.

Every household in the village was allocated one flagon of water and a 1.5kg bag of flour. While I am glad to have the flour and will use it, I wish they had given us fat or oil to put with it. And more than that I wish for an oven. When we refurbished the kitchen many years we debated having an Aga and now I so wish we'd had one. I miss baking pastry and cakes.

As we left to go home, I noticed a couple sitting

on the bench under the oak tree on the green. Mick noticed me looking and said they were the first of many. I was confused at first, then realised he meant the first of the refugees from the cities. They just looked tired and old, not at all menacing, so maybe I shouldn't be so worried. After all, we are eating well enough and helping each other. A few more wouldn't hurt, would it? And we have eggs again. Four today from our own hens and some from the pub.

Sunday, January 12

Martin is very ill. He came in from stacking wood this morning complaining he was hot and now, mid-afternoon he is wearing layers of clothes, is sitting on top of the fire and says he is freezing.

It is certainly colder today and this morning there was a hard frost which had even iced the waterlogged lawns, so they crackled as I walked. But then there was sun, followed by chilly and misty rain, so Martin is right in saying it is cold. However, I can't help thinking that the first day I began to feel ill I still cooked our meal and kept the fires going, while he can't even keep the water topped up in the kettle on the fire. I suspect his illness is going to be much worse than mine. Thank goodness the power cut means he can't consult his symptoms on the internet. I still remember the time he had a rash and scared himself thinking it could be meningitis.

Stephen has taken over the log splitting and stacking as we are in great need of dry wood. The logs that were soaked in the flooded bunkers and restacked in the garage are still very damp and although we are trying hard to have one side of the inglenooks filled with wood that is ready to use and the other with logs drying out, we consume such a quantity of wood now we no longer have central heating that it's hard to keep pace.

Stephen will need help if Martin is indisposed for long, as they'd planned to clear some of the dead wood out of the copse where the trees fell in the storm. The newly fallen trees can't be burnt for at least a year, but they have exposed other branches and trunks that are ready to use, so we should then have enough wood to see us through the winter. I suggested he ask Neil for some help or maybe Tony in return for some of the logs.

And I have gone back to my old habit of collecting kindling every time I walk around the grounds and came back with an armful from feeding the hens, plus two eggs in my pocket.

Monday, January 13

Stephen has made a really good job of restacking the wood in the bunkers on pallets so they have a chance to dry off. If there are more floods as bad as we had over Christmas, they will still get soaked, but if we are lucky enough to just have normal winter rainfall, they should be safe. Today, he started work on the copse with Tony, but they have said they will have to be careful working there as one of the tall Scots pines has splits all around the trunk and could topple with the next high wind.

The vegetable plots at the bottom of the garden, which used to be flower beds, still look very waterlogged. Although there is a lot of gravel in the beds for drainage, the roots will be in water if we get much more rain. Today started bright and sunny but suddenly, in the middle of the day, we had three or four very heavy showers of hail and rain.

I know we have maybe three cold months of bad weather ahead of us, but there are signs of spring. I can see the tips of daffodils piercing the grass along the drive. The hellebores are bursting open with pale pink and deep burgundy flowers. And the snowdrops cannot be far behind.

But all of these signs of hope have not stopped me thinking about the people who have suffered more than we have. That couple on the bench on the green looked so lost and alone. There must be more out there.

And now the rain has stopped and I can see a gap in the clouds before another shower. So it is time to dig over the hen run and make those hens work hard. I want a full clutch of eggs today.

Tuesday, January 14

Such a cold day with ice on the puddles and frost on the grass. But we could have colder still. I've not yet seen frost inside the windows, but I expect we shall before the winter is out.

Martin took a while to get up this morning because he is feeling thick-headed and tired. But I was up at 6.30 to rekindle the fires and boil water. My morning routine has changed so much in three months. Before the power cut I would still wake early but could quickly make tea in a warm kitchen heated by radiators, then, after reading the papers which were delivered early, I'd have a hot shower, unless it was a day for swimming when I'd shower at the pool. Then, after dressing, I'd empty the dishwasher which had been on overnight and finish reading the papers over breakfast before checking my emails or doing shopping online.

Now, especially since it has grown colder, I pull layers on over my pyjamas, stuff my feet, already encased in socks, into even thicker socks and boots, drag a brush through my hair, splash my face with cold water and brush my teeth. It's too cold to strip first thing before there's hot water, so I wash mid-morning after I've made sure the fires are stoked and everyone has eaten a hot breakfast. That has changed too. None of us wants yoghurt and muesli these days. We happily eat eggs, bacon, sausage or black pudding every day. There are no mushrooms at present, but we still have a good breakfast, despite the lack of toast. Oh I'd love a thick piece of toast made from fresh tiger bread, with that crackly brown crust, the crumb singed a little in the toaster. Then I'd pile on real unsalted butter and thick cut marmalade. We've got marmalade, but no butter, no bread.

Maybe the hens are missing the bread too. I used to give them the stale crusts. They managed to lay four eggs today though. Two blue and two brown.

Wednesday, January 15

Today is Martin's birthday and he is feeling much better. We are all trying to make it a special day for him, although it is a very different kind of celebration in comparison to previous years. No birthday cards and parcels have been delivered because there is no longer a postal service since the power cut started. There will be no funny email cards or messages, because there is no internet. And he can't listen to renditions of 'happy birthday' over the phone because the phone lines no longer function. I can't even make him his favourite birthday dinner of roast turkey followed by a fresh cream Victoria sponge.

But we can still make him laugh and have a happy time. Jane has made her father a crown of ivy, so he can be 'king for a day'. Stephen has tied bundles of twigs and cones into handy firelighters, Anna has made him a warm scarf and I have given him a fragment of a Victorian clay pipe that our pig unearthed in his paddock, which must have been dropped by a local farm worker over 100 years ago. We have all made Martin cards from scraps of paper and shall play charades by candlelight after supper. In some ways, because we are all making an effort and we are all here together, this must be a better and happier birthday than many people are having in these difficult times or indeed, have ever had.

The weather is drizzly and grey, but there is a sunny atmosphere here today. We are all relatively well, we are surviving and our hens are laying. Three eggs today.

Thursday, January 16

Stephen and Anna went to the doctor today and came back with worrying news. No, Anna is fine and all is well with the baby so far, but there is illness in the village and it's spreading. The newcomers we saw at the weekend, plus a handful more who have arrived seeking refuge in the last couple of days, have brought flu with them.

I thought we were safe here, because Martin and I had flu jabs in the autumn, soon after the power cut started. And I wouldn't have thought that flu could spread so quickly. But the doctor says that the incubation period can be as little as twenty-four hours. We didn't actually speak to the couple on the bench on Saturday but others did, so the infection is spreading fast.

The doctor has advised Anna to stay away from the village and his surgery unless there is an emergency. The rest of us can't avoid the village completely, as we have become reliant on the Saturday market at the pub for supplies, but I suppose it would be better if it is just Martin and I who go there until this epidemic calms down. We can just about manage for eggs and meat on our own, but it is our best source of vegetables for the time being, until our own crops start growing.

It is dry and mild today and as I walked across to the hen run I noticed the first snowdrops are just opening. That gives me such a feeling of hope, despite the news from the village. Spring will be here before long and the hens keep on laying, with three eggs today.

Friday, January 17

Signs of hope in the garden yesterday, but reminders today of the threats that we may be facing. Not only have we heard via Neil that this flu is racing through the local population, but we've also had more rain which will affect the health of the sheep and the success of our crops.

When I went outside early this morning to unlock the hens I noticed that the sheep were behaving strangely, all huddled together and staring hard in the same direction. Then I saw a large, very healthy looking fox, deep auburn with a magnificent tail, slink away and across the field. Neil says foxes won't attack healthy adult sheep so I think they were just on guard. He then went on to tell some horrific story about badgers gnawing an old sheep's leg to the bone. He does love these gruesome details, but I'm not in the mood for horror stories when we may yet face trials of our own.

When we picked up the supplies dumped at the pub by the army, there was no information about when and if more rations would be distributed. So I've decided that we shall keep both the bottled water and the flour for emergencies. For the moment we are still managing very well with our acorn and chestnut flours, coarse though they are. Once our stock has dwindled we shall be glad of plain white flour. We also have more than enough water for drinking and washing for now, but come the summer, we may be short of fresh water if there's no rain then.

I'll make sure I shut the hens up as soon as they go in to roost in case that fox is keeping an eye on them. Only two eggs today.

Saturday, January 18

Heavy rain overnight has flooded our lane again and we had to walk slowly through the flood on our way into the village for our Saturday bartering. I exchanged some of the mushrooms we dried in the autumn for dark green kale, as I think we need the vitamins. We picked up potatoes as well, but there were no more emergency supplies delivered this week.

Everyone was grumbling about the water and flour left last week, saying it would have been more use to have candles and petrol. I agreed about the candles, as we are very low and are using tea lights sparingly too, but I am not so concerned about the petrol. I don't want to travel any further than the village at present, with all the uncertainty about disease and looting.

There were fewer people at the pub than usual, because of the flu I expect. Mick said the doctor is running low on antibiotics and is being very strict about prescribing them. Medicines would also have been a useful addition to our supplies.

When we came home I went out to the caravan to tell Neil that I had noticed something odd with the sheep this morning. A few of his flock are quite friendly, because when they lambed last year I gave them oats regularly so I could take a close look at the lambs. They still come up to the fence when I call and this morning I noticed that a couple had clouded eyes and could not immediately see where I was standing. Neil said he has noticed it too and is going to check the whole flock when he can round them up. The wet weather has been making it difficult for him to do all the routine maintenance.

But the hens are fine, though not very productive. There was only one egg today. Just as well I got more at the pub.

Sunday, January 19

The roads were wet but the day was dry, so we walked to church in good spirits. There was a reasonably large congregation today, because the service was dedicated to the life of one of the oldest parishioners, Dotty Evans, who died recently at the age of 102.

Hearing the readings and singing the hymns, made me think how much she must have seen and how much she must have survived during her lifetime. Born just before the First World War, a nurse in the Second, she would have experienced feelings of despair and hope, yet I remember her as ever cheerful and smiling. If she could live so long despite such traumatic times, then surely we can too.

But as we left, we heard that some of those suffering from flu are deteriorating and there is bronchitis and pneumonia amongst the sick. I hope they will all recover, but I fear this village will see several more funerals before this winter is out.

Back home, Neil came across to say he is very concerned about the sheep and will have to consult a vet, if he can find one. The nearest practice for farm animals is beyond Cranleigh and if that is no longer open he will have to go the other side of Horsham. He needs to take one of the affected animals with him in a trailer, which will slow him down considerably. Linda is very concerned about him travelling any distance on his own, especially as he won't be able to make a quick escape this time, so Neil has asked Martin if he will go with him. I'm not at all happy about it, but we need both Neil and the flock in good health, so I can't stop him from going.

They'll set off early in the morning.

Four eggs today, so I'll hard-boil some for the journey tomorrow and give the men a Thermos of tea.

Monday, January 20

Cranleigh isn't very far and under normal circumstances it would only be a thirty minute drive, but Neil has allowed more time, both for reduced speed with the trailer and for diverting if there are problems. He'd like to stick to the back lanes, but they may be flooded or blocked by trees so he said he'd have to use the main roads.

They left at 7.30am and it's now 4pm and the light is starting to go. I'm trying not to worry, but I can't stop myself. Every time anyone leaves the village they seem to find trouble. I told Martin he was not to take any risks and that I'd never forgive him if they went any further than Horsham in their search for a vet. He may be a good shot, but that doesn't mean they can outrun determined marauders.

I've tried to keep busy and managed to get some washing out on the line as the day started bright with fairly warm sunshine. It hasn't dried completely, so it's now strung up on the airer indoors and I've stoked the fire some more.

Gail came up to see if she could use the sewing machine, which we borrowed to make Anna's wedding dress. She is making Alfie some trousers out of old denim and she agreed with me that we'd feel a lot calmer if the men didn't like going off on such expeditions. She is glad Tony didn't know about this trip, as she's certain he would have jumped at the chance of another adventure too.

I'm sure she's even more relieved now that the light is fading and they haven't returned. I'll shut up the hens soon so at least they'll be safe. There were four eggs today.

Tuesday, January 21

They were home just as it finally got dark yesterday. I couldn't be cross with Martin, as it was important for Neil to have company and travel in safety. The Cranleigh vet is still operating, but when they got there he'd had to go out to a calving and they had to wait for him to return. Farms in the area are coping like ours are round here, but everyone is finding the work harder than usual.

When the vet finally returned, he examined the ewe Neil had brought with him and decided the blindness was caused by contaminated feed. It will clear up slowly if left untreated, but he injected the sheep and gave Neil more medication for the rest of the flock. They need to be treated as soon as possible as a number of ewes are in lamb and need to be well nourished. The big bale silage they were eating will have to be destroyed as well. Neil will need help holding the sheep when they are injected, so Martin and I will give him a hand tomorrow.

Our pig doesn't seem to have been affected by the feed, but maybe it was from a different batch. However, he is still losing weight and I wouldn't be surprised if he didn't last the winter. He is eighteen after all and his brother went last year. But the hens are fine although there were only two eggs today.

Wednesday, January 22

Today has been exhausting but as it was the driest day we've had for ages, it was important to help Neil with the sheep. I asked the girls to take over the washing as there was a chance of getting most of it dry today, while I went across with Martin.

We started by carrying some spare hurdles over to the corner of the first field that Neil wanted to use. It was the driest patch available, so we linked the hurdles to form a holding pen with a narrow race leading out. Then Neil rounded up the first flock with his dogs and we penned them up.

I was meant to inject while Neil manhandled the sheep and Martin set them free one at a time, but I had such trouble parting the thick fleece of these woolly devils and stabbing them in the right place, that Neil had to take over. I then had the job of holding them under the chin to keep them still while he treated them. He also turned them over and trimmed their feet at the same time to save rounding them up another time.

Once we'd dealt with the first batch we broke for lunch. Linda heated a thick soup with dumplings over her campfire and we sat outside enjoying the spring-like sunshine. But we didn't stop for long and were soon carrying hurdles across to the second field. I then came back home, leaving Linda to take over my job while I prepared supper for all of us tonight. We're having potatoes and apples baked in the ashes and a meaty stew, to which I'll add kale towards the end.

Thank goodness the hens don't have to be treated. They seem very healthy and laid four eggs today.

Thursday, January 23

Martin has been complaining about his back all day. I think he overdid it yesterday when we helped Neil with the sheep. It was a lot of work, lifting hurdles over fences and dragging them across the rutted fields. He often has back problems and we can no longer get the heat pads from the chemist that used to help. I've reminded him that he hasn't done his Pilates exercises, which are meant to strengthen his muscles, since Christmas, but he just keeps saying he'd rather have a massage.

But despite the pain today, I know he rather enjoyed the work yesterday. In fact, I think all the men are finding the physical work they are having to do very satisfying. I always thought when we were first renovating our house and had to employ builders and workmen, how happy most of them looked. I particularly remember the man who came with a small digger to dredge the drainage ditches and think I've never seen a happier worker driving his machine all day.

I don't think I can say the same about the women though as our chores have increased and are harder without electricity. I miss my oven, electric kettle, washing machine and tumble dryer especially. I can live without central heating, but cooking and laundry have become enormous tasks without the appliances we are all so used to. And of course I miss clean running water. We are managing to collect enough water and the well is very full since the heavy rain, but it may not be so easy if this carries on into summer and the supply dries up. To think we used to take tap water for granted.

Friday, January 24

After I fed the hens this morning I took a few scraps and some ewe nuts across to Itchy, our pet pig, but he was not very interested. Normally he comes running back to his pen, if he is grazing the paddock, as soon as any of us goes over there. He loves his food as well as the grass but today he was still in his shelter. I called to him and he grunted, then came tottering out unsteadily. He came over to his feed bowl and sniffed it then walked away and back to his bed.

I have never seen him behave like this before. The expression 'eat like a pig' was created for our pig, just as 'behaving like sheep' describes perfectly the way the sheep all stick together. But today our pig is not being a pig, he seems tired and uninterested. I've been out to see him every couple of hours during the day and he just wants to lie in his bed. He is not grinding his teeth in pain, which I know from past experience is the way to tell if a pig is in distress. And he is still talkative, uttering soft little chattering grunts, but he simply doesn't want to be active or hungry today. I have tried taking him some boiled potato peel and even tried to feed him a mash of acorn flour, which I was sure he would love, but he just grunts and says he doesn't want anything today, thank you.

If I could phone the vet I would, but as I can't I'm not going to distress him in any way by transporting him all the way to Cranleigh. He is old and he is tired. Maybe he has simply had enough of life, this life that he has spent foraging for acorns, grazing the grassy paddocks, fighting his brother for the best scraps and sometimes chasing stray sheep. So I have tucked a thick covering of straw around him and stroked him on the soft part of his snout and hope he may feel better tomorrow.

The hens happily ate the mash he didn't want and they were very grateful, giving us four eggs again today.

Saturday, January 25

I waited until I had fed the hens, before I checked on the pig. He was not in his paddock, he was still in his bed and he was cold and dead. But he looked very peaceful, tucked up in the deep straw, just the way he was when I left him yesterday afternoon. His bedding was not disturbed and his eyes were closed, so I think he passed away quietly in his sleep, the way anyone would wish to go.

I told Martin the news at breakfast and he was as sad as I am. Itchy had been part of our lives for eighteen years. Then Neil called by and when he heard the news he asked if we were going to butcher him. Martin and I looked at each other in shock. We hadn't even thought about it. Then I said we couldn't because Itchy was a pet pig, not a bacon pig. Neil said he was probably too old to be good eating anyway.

But then we had to decide what to do with the body. In the past we have had to arrange for the bodies of sheep and the last pig to die to be taken away by the knacker man for incineration. But in these powerless times we can't arrange for that to happen. And the water table is still very high so we can't dig a deep grave without it filling with water.

Every time we bury any pets we have to entomb them in stones to prevent the foxes finding the bodies.

So then I told Martin I'd rather the foxes had a fresh corpse than a rotting one and why didn't we take the pig into the wood and leave it there. So we did. He was still extremely heavy, despite the recent weight loss, but we managed to get him into the wheelbarrow, then we trundled it across to the back of the copse and tipped him out. Given our past experience with dead deer, it will only take a couple of days for the foxes to find him and invite their friends over for dinner. If the weather was very cold it might take longer, but I expect most of him will be gone in a week.

Sunday, January 26

When I shut up the hens at about 8.30 last night, the sky was the clearest and blackest it has been for weeks. That heavy grey blanket of rain cloud had cleared, leaving the brightest sharpest stars I think I have ever seen. The Plough and Mars were shining above the house and the air was crisp.

But this morning the rain returned. I wanted to go to church, but I didn't want a soaking, so I decided to stay here to cook the pigeons Martin bagged yesterday. To make it seem like a normal pre-power cut Sunday, I thought we should eat our main meal at lunchtime for a change. I boiled potatoes and finished them in a pan in a little dripping, which made them taste just like real roast potatoes. I cut the pigeon breasts into strips and stir-fried them with curly kale, black pudding and onion, all spiced with some soy sauce and smoked paprika. I used to do this dish with chorizo, but the black pudding and paprika gave a similar result. Maybe the next time Linda and I make the sausage we could add spice to make it taste more like chorizo.

It was quite an elegant lunch I think, for people sitting round a smoky fire in layer upon layer of grubby warm clothing, looking less than sophisticated and certainly less fragrant than we used to. I wasn't wearing wellingtons, but I'm not sure if Martin and Stephen had even removed their muddy boots before they ate. Everyone enjoyed the meal and Martin will try to get more pigeons as we are seeing so many around and they will be a nuisance once the veg start growing.

The rain had passed over by this afternoon so Martin dug over the hen run and the chickens scrabbled over the earth for the worms. And they gave us four eggs.

Monday, January 27

The bright sunshine this morning was heartening, but it also revealed dust, dirt and cobwebs throughout the house. On grey days without electric light I don't notice how much my standards have lapsed, but a bit of sun reveals grimy windows, mud strewn floors and molten wax on the windowsills, worktops and the dining table.

So once we had taken advantage of the fine weather and hung out the washing, the girls and I set about with brooms and dusters to restore order. It's slow work without a hoover, but we managed to clean the hall and the dining room by lunchtime and the window panes sparkled and the rooms smelt fresh.

However the wax is defeating us. Jane took a blunt knife to the drips and spatters but after a couple of scrapes decided it was marking the wood. If there wasn't a power cut I'd tackle the wax with a hot iron and kitchen paper. I think I'll have to ask around the village for a flat iron. I'm sure I remember someone having a collection on display.

When Martin and Stephen came in from their fence mending for lunch, I ordered them to remove their boots. We have all become careless about wiping our feet and leaving boots by the back door, but I think I'm instituting a new regime from now on. Thankfully the floors from the kitchen door through to the dining room where we eat and sit most of the time, are brick or quarry tiles and are easy to clean once the mud dries.

But this afternoon turned grey and cloudy again and it was back to the mud outside when I fed the hens, who produced three eggs today.

Tuesday, January 28

Today I insisted that everyone helped me collect dry kindling. Martin and Stephen had been bringing in unseasoned twigs salvaged from their tree cutting, which though they burn eventually on a hot fire, do little to really get a fire blazing. I suppose because I am the one who starts the day earlier than everyone else and gets the fires going again, I have become a connoisseur of good kindling and am very choosy about what I use to start my fires.

Since the storms brought down many dead and

rotten branches, there are masses of good material around the grounds and in the fields. And the fronds of pine trees will work well once they are dry too. So we went outside in between showers to collect as much as we could. Not only will it help to keep us warm but it is making the gardens look tidier again too.

The wind was cold, but the sun came shone a couple of times. The snowdrops are really bursting out in great clusters now and most of the hellebores are in bud as well. But I was annoyed to see that the mole which Martin has been trying to catch has invaded a second flower bed. This wet weather has driven them onto higher ground this year and this particular mole is proving hard to catch. We used to be able to phone or text for the mole catcher, but he lives the other side of Chiddingfold so we can't reach him without driving all the way there. Martin had always tried to work out how to set the traps but is not having any success so far. And if he does succeed, he won't lift the trap himself but will send me out to check whether it has caught the culprit. I think anyone capable of shooting birds ought to be able to deal with smaller creatures too, but he says they are too like rats for him to handle them. I don't think they are rat-like at all, with their black velvet coats and spade-like paws. But I don't like them, all the same, if they dig up my flower beds.

Wednesday, January 29

It is colder and wetter today and every time any of us comes in from outside, we head straight for the fire to warm our hands and faces. It is only a soft rain, but it still won't help to dry out our waterlogged grounds and fields.

Stephen has been complaining that his boots have started to leak and his feet are very cold and wet. As a temporary measure he is using old plastic carrier bags to line the boots, but he plans to cycle to the garden centre soon for new ones. I think if they still have stock he should get pairs for Anna and Martin as they are vital to all of us in these wet conditions.

We are also almost out of candles and tea lights. The fires give us some light at night, but not enough to see us to bed. We had a good stock at the beginning of this power cut and I doubt that we shall find any supplies nearby. It would have been a darned sight more useful if the emergency supplies that were left in the village the other week had included candles instead of bottled water.

Jane very sweetly found two scented candles that were decorating her bedroom and said we could use them. I think they've been gathering dust, unlit for at least five years. And Martin said he's sure we can find a way to use the kerosene. We've been using some in an old hurricane lamp for a while, but one lamp can't light every room in the house, so more lights of some kind would be welcome.

The hens weren't very productive today. There was only one brown egg in the nest. I think the rain is depressing them too.

Thursday, January 30
More rain again today, but I made myself go up to the copse to see if the foxes had discovered their meal yet. Martin wouldn't come and look for himself,

126

but he kept asking if I would check. I didn't go too close, only a couple of yards away from the body, but there was no sign yet that they had found their dinner. I suppose with this cold damp weather it simply doesn't whet their appetites. If it was drier and warmer they would pick up the scent in no time, I'm sure.

One year an adult deer was lying in long grass on the edge of the big lawn. I became aware of it because of the awful smell – a composite of rotting cabbage and ripe Stilton – but it attracted the foxes, who tore the carcass apart over a period of days until there was nothing left but a dainty hoof and some gingery tufts of hair.

It's often struck me that we could have our own *Midsomer Murders* here, with the foxes as enthusiastic accomplices. A body of any kind would quickly disappear if laid out in overgrown areas where nobody goes. Whenever the hens died I used to throw them in the field for the foxes as well, but now, if the hen looked fairly healthy, we wouldn't waste it on them but would cook it and eat it ourselves. I shall tell the hens that if they don't start being good layers soon. They aren't earning their keep.

Friday, January 31

We have been experimenting with ways to light the house. Martin favours using a bottle or jar with a metal screw cap. He has cut a slot in the cap and fed through a length of wick material which dips into the heating oil, leaving an inch or so protruding. We're trying twisted lengths of cotton string and have realised we have to let the wick soak up the oil first.

This works quite well and will last a long time because of the reservoir of oil.

However I'm a little worried about moving containers of flammable oil around the house and am not sure these will be the safest lights for carrying upstairs at night. Then Anna said she remembered reading about a kind of homemade lamp using a saucer, fabric and an old button, in one of the *Little House on the Prairie* books. She said it was called a button lamp and it appeared in a story about the family being snowed in one long hard winter.

Jane raided my button box and found a couple of old saucers in the kitchen, then cut some cotton into squares. Anna put the button in the centre of the square and pulled the cloth around the button. She then tied some thread tight around the corners so they stood upright in a stiff bunch. We then set the button in a little pool of kerosene in the saucer and let the material soak up the oil. When the wick was charged we lit it and it burned steadily and safely, without the risk of spillage.

We have decided that the button lamps will be used in the bedrooms and the bottle and jar lamps will be safest on the table where we eat and prepare food. Martin agreed with me that we can't risk causing a fire in the house, now that we can't call the fire brigade.

Still not much luck with the hens. Only one egg today.

Saturday, February 1

When I was feeding the hens this morning I heard a pathetic bleat from the field. I was surprised as the sheep all seemed to be gathered at the southern end in the sunshine, near the field shelter. Then I heard it again and went round the back of the henhouse to look and saw a small black sheep standing alone in a dark wet part of the field.

This seemed strange so I climbed over the fence and walked towards it slowly. The sheep made to run away, but then I saw it was caught fast in brambles. When I came closer it tried to run again but fell onto its side in a pool of water. One thick strand was twined around its middle, embedded deep in its woolly fleece and a second string was caught around a back leg, effectively hobbling the poor thing. I had to pull hard on the brambles to set it free and then it stood unsteadily and stumbled away to join the flock. I walked up to find Neil and he was checking the sheep in the second field, after another dose of medication. Their eyes are quite clear now and he is convinced it was caused by liver fluke and not the feed.

Before going off to the pub for the Saturday market I checked on the dead pig. There are signs that the foxes have begun the task of dealing with the body as it has moved from where we placed it last week and the abdomen has been torn open and emptied. They will return every night from now on until every part, even the squeal, as they say, has gone.

Sunday, February 2
Today is Candlemas, an ancient church festival in which the candles the church would be using for the year were blessed. In previous years, we've had a

candle-lit procession with every member of the congregation being given a candle to take home. But today, candles are too precious, so just one solitary candle was passed from hand to hand as we prayed for an end to this power cut.

Candlemas also marks the midway point between winter and spring, and today, although there may well be two more months of wintry weather to come, the garden seems to think spring is already here. As well as the hellebores, mahonia and snowdrops, which are truly winter flowers, I've noticed the shoots of narcissus and daffodils. Some are several inches tall and a few are already showing slender flower buds.

But the hens have gone on strike again and don't seem to realise that spring is coming. Only the Rhode Island Reds, which lay brown eggs, have been productive in the last few days. The Legbars are not being at all helpful, just when we could really do with their eggs.

I was able to get extra eggs at the pub yesterday, where one of the village old boys was holding forth about chitting potatoes. He tends to go on a bit, but we listened with interest because we are going to have to grow our own for the first time this year. He and the other experienced vegetable growers said it was best to use seed potatoes, but this year we are all going to have to try with potatoes we have left over from the winter. We need to start preparing them soon if we are to plant in about six weeks' time.

The other main topic of conversation was the flu which has left several people with bad bronchitis and worse. Two very elderly people have died recently but no one else has succumbed before their time, thank goodness. We seem to have got away very lightly.

Monday, February 3

Today I sorted out potatoes that will hopefully sprout and be ready to plant in a few weeks. The old boys at the pub were shaking their heads at the prospect of using what they called 'shop bought potatoes' for chitting. But it seems to me that human beings managed to grow potatoes long before so-called 'seed potatoes' were sold separately, so I assume we shall have some degree of success.

I fetched some old egg boxes from the back of the larder for the potatoes to sit in. I've always saved egg boxes when we've had shop bought eggs, in case I have a surplus of our own, which is unlikely at the moment with the hens on strike. There wasn't a single egg today. I put some small whole potatoes in two boxes, making sure that they all had eyes uppermost. Then I cut a couple of larger potatoes into chunks, with each piece having two or three eyes and put them in boxes as well.

Nowhere is especially warm so I've put the boxes on the dining room windowsill as that room gets sunlight and is warmed by the fire. I know I need to have pinkish green sprouts from each potato before they can be planted. Martin noticed that one of the potatoes in the sack was sprouting, but long white shoots are not the ones we need, apparently.

I felt quite excited making these preparations. Of course it will be months before we have new potatoes, but it is something to look forward to. That and the baby, of course. Anna is rosy with health and she is looking a little plumper, but only just.

Tuesday, February 4

After a sharp early shower of rain and hail, the sun
has been shining brightly along with a good breeze,
so I rushed to hang washing outside. Even a short
period on the line helps it to smell so much fresher
than when we have to dry it inside, where the smoke
from the fire permeates every fibre. I've always
preferred drying laundry outside in the fresh air,
which makes it smell of sun and dried grass, even in
pre-power cut days.

As it was fine, I then walked round to the copse to
check on the foxes' progress with the pig. They look
to have had a good feed on him, though I haven't
heard any screams after dark, and I expect the
remains won't be there much longer. At least this
abundance of pork will stop them taking too close an
interest in my hens, although if they carry on being
unproductive I might be glad of an excuse to replace
them.

And Martin took advantage of the break in the
weather to cycle off to the garden centre at Milford
and came back with boots for himself and Stephen.
He will try to get across to Frensham, the other side
of Tilford, very soon to see if they still have any
stock, as Jane and Anna also need boots.

When he came back, he said he'd seen an army
truck on the A3 as he'd crossed over the bridge. It
was heading towards London. He fiddled with the
radio this afternoon to see if there was any news of
developments, but the only bulletin we heard said
overseas aid has provided some generators and fuel

in the cities to operate relief centres. Perhaps the powers that be think villages and small towns are able to cope.

Wednesday, February 5

Tomorrow is Jane's birthday and she will be twenty-one. If this powerless crisis hadn't happened, she would be having a big party with her student friends, dancing, clubbing and celebrating. We would maybe have given her a car and taken her out for dinner. But times have changed so enormously and although she isn't complaining, I know there must be a part of her that is thinking 'what if'. So we are trying to plan some surprises for her to make her day special.

I checked again this morning on the pig corpse and could not see any sign of him. The foxes may have torn pieces from the body or it may have been pulled further into the undergrowth in the copse out of sight. They really do such a good job of clearing bodies, but I did wonder whether the urban foxes are performing a similar service in the cities and bigger towns where people have perished. There are likely to be good pickings there for the animals that were bold even before the power cut began.

As I came back towards the front of the house I was startled by a female duck flying out of the ivy over the porch. Last year a duck nested twice in the ivy that covers the front of the house. Both nests were right under Stephen and Anna's bedroom window. Then one day we saw her on the front lawn with a troupe of tiny ducklings as she led them to the front pond. It seems too early for her to be thinking about nesting again, but maybe she was just checking on the possibilities. And the hens have been making nests in the deep litter of woodchip and straw in their house, but have still not laid well. Two eggs today.

Thursday, February 6

We blamed Jane for the way her birthday was celebrated. She'd said if these were normal times and she could travel, she would have gone to Paris for the day, so that was it. We went French. It was probably a bit more *'Allo 'Allo* than Parisian, but it still made her and us all laugh.

At breakfast Stephen presented her with a Barrow Star ticket, which he said was leaving at 11am. He then wheeled her round the grounds in the wheelbarrow several times, pretending the avenue of whitebeam trees was the Channel Tunnel. By the time he brought her back to the house, helpless with laughter, Martin and I were dressed in black with white aprons as café owners, serving some of the disgusting acorn coffee we've been making. Then Stephen disappeared for a few minutes, returning on the bicycle with a string of onions round his neck. Well, not exactly a string, it was in fact just a string with an onion at each end, but it did the trick. And Anna modelled the latest Paris fashions by raiding the dressing up box and the spare room wardrobe. Her Flea Market ensemble, with a green feather boa, was the hit of the show.

For lunch I served onion soup, followed by coq au vin made with a plump farm chicken, which was marinated in some elderberry wine I picked up at the pub at the weekend. Then to finish we had crêpes, flamed with a tiny drop of Armagnac I'd found hidden at the back of the kitchen cupboard. In the afternoon we all had to behave normally for a little while and perform our regular chores, fetching water, stacking wood and so on. But after that we gave Jane home-made presents and she blew out the little birthday cake candles I always save from year to year, on her unusual cake, which was a kind of steamed jam pudding. I think she had a happy day.

Friday, February 7

Breezy sunshine today, so that meant washing and drying. The weather dictates my chores much more than it used to when I could just throw everything into the washing machine and tumble dryer. So I persuaded Stephen to help fetch water and the girls to heat it so we could wash sheets. It would be easier to rinse them in the bath upstairs, but that would mean carrying heavy pails of water further, so we used the two deep butler sinks in the kitchen.

I still wish we had a mangle, as large items like sheets are difficult to wring out, but we managed between us to wash two sets of sheets. I was determined to get the bed linen changed as it has been on the beds since before Christmas. But it was such a struggle and even on a sunny blustery day it will be hard to get the sheets dry before the day ends.

Everything felt spring-like today and I've even spotted a couple of primroses emerging beside the path around the henhouse pond. This morning a drake was on the grass outside the front door looking up at the ivy growing up the house. He didn't move away when I stepped outside, so I think he was waiting for his mate to come down from investigating her nesting site.

The hens looked happier as it was a drier day, but the soil in their run is still too damp for them to have a refreshing dust bath. Maybe they'll be more content and lay better when we've had a few more dry days. There were two eggs today, both brown ones.

Saturday, February 8

Thank goodness for wellingtons. We waded through deep water in the lane to get to the village for the Saturday barter and market. After yesterday's sunshine, the weather reverted to wind and rain and the roads are flooded once more.

The water has risen over the fields again too and the sheeps' grazing is still restricted. I walked across to see how they looked after their recent treatment and noticed Neil was waving his stick at one of them. I climbed over the fence and realised it was Stalk, the last of my own sheep, standing in a very flooded corner of the field, with the water up to his chest. Neil yelled that he couldn't get him out, so he was going to fetch a rope from his trailer. As he strode off, I called to Stalk in the way I used to when I brought him food. His head swivelled, his ears pricked up and he trotted out of the flood. That made Neil laugh when he returned with his rope, to see Stalk standing there, wondering where I'd hidden his treat.

At the pub, the old gardeners were dispensing advice again, but this time it was mainly the incomers who have fled the towns who were listening. The village hall, where they are billeted, doesn't have any ground for cultivation, but there are a couple of spare allotments a few hundred yards away which can provide them with a good crop of vegetables if they get to work.

Martin and I chatted to a couple who had come here from Guildford. They said that although life in the village is basic, it is far safer and healthier than staying in the town. The town's sewers are overflowing with the recent rain and presumably because there is no power pumping waste. They had seen rats, dogs and foxes in the streets and felt intimidated in the early weeks by looters raiding shops and then moving on to filch from private homes. We felt fortunate as we pushed our wheelbarrow back home, laden with kale, potatoes and cuts of beef. All we have to worry about here is the flood water and whether the hens are laying.

Sunday, February 9

I was woken several times in the night by the sound of the wind buffeting the chimney stacks. It sounded as if it howled and rained all night long. But after breakfast there was bright sun, so I asked the girls to hang out washing while Martin and I waded and walked to church.

At this time of year, the church holds a Christingle service, in which the children make a representation of the world using an orange. As we haven't seen an orange in these parts for months, the tributes were created with apples, some a little wizened, admittedly, but still round enough to represent the world. Red ribbon wrapped around the middle represents the love and blood of Christ and then dried fruits and sweets on four cocktail sticks, symbolise the seasons and the countries of the world. Because of the crisis sweets were in short supply, but everyone had rallied together and found some candied peel, a few currants, pieces of fruit leather and cubes of carrot. But there were no candles to spare this year to insert in the top of the fruit. So instead we used rolled white paper, with the end inked red to look like a flame. The children enjoyed the service all the same, even though they couldn't light candles.

It was still sunny when we came home, so I allowed myself a little time to wander around the garden. I was enjoying the spring flowers until I noticed that the mole is still disrupting my flower beds. There are several huge new hills around the beautiful hellebores, so I had to go straight off and tell Martin to get trapping again. That quite spoilt my mood and then there was a heavy shower of hail so I had to rush off and bring in the washing.

Monday, February 10

The ducks definitely think it is nearly spring. This morning I saw the drake on guard on the front lawn again. And this afternoon, just after feeding the hens and looking at the sheep, I noticed an egg on the platform of the duck house in our largest pond. Whether it has been laid there deliberately or has floated out of a nest in the recent rains, I'm not sure. But it was definitely an egg and only the ducks use that pond, so they are already one duckling down before they've even started sitting.

However, today hasn't been all spring sunshine and primroses. We noticed a smell around the kitchen this morning and after lifting the manhole cover beyond the beech hedge, found that the drains are backing up. Normally, in pre power cut days, we would have had our cess pit emptied at the beginning of the year, but, of course, we can't call out the septic tank man now. It may also be because there has been such a lot of rain that our soakaways are sodden and can't cope.

So Martin and Stephen had the unpleasant job of baling out the tank with buckets on ropes. They emptied the liquid into the ditch. The tank is located in the hen run, so the hens were very interested and kept rushing across to see what was in the bucket. Then Martin found some long rods to probe the drains leading to the cess pit and cleared the blockage. I made sure there was plenty of hot water for when they came indoors, so they could both have a good strip wash.

The hens laid four eggs today which is a little better than of late, so maybe they too realise spring is around the corner.

Tuesday, February 11

Martin was trying to get some news on the radio and finally heard a bulletin which said that many parts of the country are badly flooded. It sounds much worse than what we've had around here, with towns and villages awash with water. If there are still residents in those areas, they are having to leave their homes. No wonder little aid is coming out this way. By comparison the pool at the top of our road, which today only came half way up our boots, is a mere puddle.

There was a little more rain this morning but by lunchtime there was breezy sunshine, which meant we could hang out washing on the line again for a couple of hours. And the drains seem to be running freely after yesterday's efforts. Thank goodness, as this means we can continue using the downstairs toilet, as long as we keep topping up the cistern with recycled water. I don't fancy having to go outside until the weather improves.

Martin noticed today that the recent high winds have caused another couple of trees to lean alarmingly. One of the pines in the copse has vertical splits in the trunk which means it may well go down after another couple of storms. Martin thinks we should stay well clear of it on windy days. But this afternoon I took a quick look and realised that the cracks have opened up considerably and I could see bright sunlight shining right through the trunk from side to side.

I thought the sun might have encouraged the hens to lay well, but there were only two brown eggs today. I won't buy Legbars again. We need a regular supply of eggs, not just a show of pretty feathers.

Wednesday, February 12

We've had such extremes of weather in twenty-four hours. After the warm sunshine of yesterday it was chilly last night, with an almost clear sky. When I went out after dark to shut up the henhouse, there was a misty moon overhead, encircled in an areola of pewter and bronze.

Then today heavy showers and high winds, with brief bursts of sun and a huge rainbow over the fields. No more trees have fallen yet but there are torn branches to collect for kindling. As so much more rain has fallen, we checked all the drains and gutters to make sure the water is flowing away from the house. Luckily the soil here is very sandy, so it drains quickly. On the worst day the duck house was barely visible apart from the ridge of the roof, but the next revealed the whole structure.

But despite the continuing bad weather, today brought good news to brighten us all and give us hope for the future. Anna felt the first flutterings of movement, which we hope means she is carrying a healthy baby. After the initial excitement I saw a shadow cross her face and she said she wished she could share this wonderful experience with her parents. So we sat for a while by the fire and talked about them and how they will be coping well as resourceful country people. I completely understand how much she must long to see them but Cornwall is too far to travel in these times and her priority must be to stay here, stay well and give them a healthy grandchild who they will be able to meet when the country gets back to normal one day.

Thursday, February 13

A day without rain meant we could hang washing on the line. There was breezy sun, which helped, then Neil came across with good news and bad news about the sheep. They are losing condition and he is going to have trouble bringing in enough fodder for them. Two fields are still so flooded that they cannot be used and the other two are sodden. Neil said he keeps hoping he can last out, but there is little grazing left in these two fields and if there is more rain it will be some time before he can move them back into the fields currently under water.

He is going to go off on another run to find ewe nuts rather than hay and wants Martin to go with him for safety. I can't object, even though I feel uneasy about any of us travelling any distance in these difficult times. They will set off tomorrow, but hope to go no further than Dorking at most.

In the meantime, Neil decided he should slaughter a couple of last year's lambs, hoggets as they are now. So we hung the carcasses in the garage and collected the blood for black pudding again. Some of the joints we'll take to the pub for the Saturday barter market, but for tomorrow, when Neil and Martin successfully return with feed for the sheep, I'll slow cook lamb shanks on the fire.

I collected three brown eggs today but two of the Legbars were sitting when I went in the henhouse this afternoon. I'm hoping that means they're laying again.

Friday, February 14

Valentine's Day is dark and wet and my husband is absent. He left this morning with Neil at 8am. It is 3.30 and they have not yet returned. I am trying not to worry, but cannot help feeling anxious, knowing that there are malicious marauders out on the roads. The wind has picked up again today and it has been raining for at least six hours, so their journey will be hazardous even if they don't encounter any suspicious characters.

I am trying to keep my mind occupied cleaning the house and preparing our supper. I marinated the lamb shanks with herbs, oil, seasoning and a little red wine vinegar. Wine alone is too precious these days to use in cooking, though in the past I would always use a good couple of glasses in this dish. Then I dried and browned the shanks before placing them in a deep copper pan with onions, carrots and stock to simmer by the fire.

I've added a couple of spoonfuls of redcurrant jelly as well, to make the gravy richer and more flavoursome. I usually like to add flageolet beans about half an hour or so before the end, but I don't have any here so I shall add pearl barley in about an hour. That bulks up the dish and makes it very satisfying. I think mashed potatoes and kale will go well with the lamb.

As it's Valentine's Day, Anna has made hearts of twisted willow twigs for everyone, even Neil and Linda, who will be joining us for supper tonight after the search for sheep feed. I have warmed a pair of dry socks for Martin when he returns and I have picked the flower heads of some of the darkest, deep purple hellebores and floated them in a glass bowl for the table. Let no one say that in these powerless times there is no electricity.

Saturday, February 15

It was dusk before the men returned yesterday. We were beginning to get quite worried as the wind had picked up considerably since the morning. When I fed the hens it sounded just like a London Tube train roaring through the tunnel.

But they were back, laden with feed sacks from Dorking and full of tales of their time on the road. We heard all about their adventures while we ate last night. They had set out on the route we were used to taking, but soon found that one country road after another was blocked with fallen trees or flooded. So they turned back onto the main roads and after Guildford came across an army truck parked by a set of dead traffic lights.

Martin and Neil thought they would ask the soldiers what the roads were like ahead, but suddenly found themselves under suspicion. The men jumped out, fully armed and started interrogating them, wanting to know where they were headed and why. The soldiers were very suspicious of Neil's gun, but they could see from other items in the Land Rover that he worked with animals, so eventually accepted his explanation and let them both go on their way.

At the corn merchants outside Dorking, where Neil still has an account, they didn't have to pay for the feed. Neil had taken some cuts of lamb, but his offering was dismissed with a wave of the hand as they'd had their fill of mutton and lamb from grateful customers. So we had more lamb to take to the pub today in exchange for vegetables, which we need just as much as meat. There were fewer regulars there today because of the terrible weather. The wind howled all last night and although we've had a couple of bright spells today, we've mostly been lashed with rain. I expect the hens will be sulking again when I go out to feed them shortly.

Sunday, February 16

When I shut up the hens last night, just after dusk, the full moon was rising behind stark black trees. And this morning we woke to a frost and bright sunshine. I rushed to get some washing done and was tempted to stay here and put more laundry out as it was so sunny, but the girls told me they'd take care of it so I could go to church.

We walked in such bright light that Martin and I were quite cheerful after yesterday's downpour and wind. He even held my hand as we waded through the pool at the end of the lane. Maybe he is turning into a romantic after all these years. He surprised me on Friday with a gift of a red balloon which he found in a village shop when he and Neil were coming back from Dorking. There was little else there for Valentine's Day but the enterprising proprietor was offering balloons to any customer in exchange for goods or money, so Neil and Martin agreed to give him two lamb chops as they hadn't had to hand them over at the corn merchants.

I was very glad we went out today, not just because it was so lovely and warm, but also because everyone in church was talking about the posters. We didn't see them until we walked back, but pinned to the oak tree with the circular seat on the green and also above the seat outside the church, there were notices advising the public to 'boil water before drinking'. Honestly, everyone is laughing at this, as if we didn't have an ounce of common sense and haven't been doing just this since the mains water went off in October. No one knows who put the posters up, but we all think the army sneaked through in the night, wanting to avoid confrontation. This information might be necessary in towns, where sewers could be contaminating fresh water supplies, but out here, where most of us have cess pits and wells, we don't need to be told how to look after ourselves.

Monday, February 17

Another dry day, which gave the boys a chance to collect kindling around the grounds after the recent storms. And I was able to hang out washing which has dried quickly in this breezy sunshine. I would love to be able to iron clothes and linen too and think I must make more of an effort to see if we can find a flat iron from somewhere, though it will still be much less efficient than my favourite steam iron.

After the wind had dropped to a steady breeze, Martin could take a closer look at the damaged trees. As well as the little cherry, we've also lost a mature rhododendron, both of them savagely uprooted.

When we had our lunch of soup, he said the split pine will surely come down very soon. It's a week since I last looked so I went down there this afternoon to see it for myself. The vertical splits have opened up completely so the trunk looks almost hollow and it's starting to break on its south facing side. I hope Martin and Stephen will be very careful when they are working nearby, as when it falls it is likely to take some big branches down with it or even another pine.

We're bound to have some more trees down before this winter is over and today we found out that another one has fallen over the road just past the house of our neighbours Robin and Deidre. It hasn't blocked the lane as much as the one that fell before Christmas and with the upper branches removed it forms an arch that a car could pass under quite easily.

The hens seemed to be in better shape after two dry and sunny days. I collected two brown and two blue eggs today.

Tuesday, February 18

We're still laughing about the official advice posters on boiling water, which we saw on Sunday. When Martin came down this morning while I was heating water and coaxing fires, he joked that I'd better make sure the water was boiling before I used it. And everyone who came into the dining room during the morning made the same joke, till I was quite bored with it.

If we're drinking the water we use rainwater wherever possible, so we know it's as pure as it can be. We still boil it, but if the water is for washing then we heat it only as much as we need. It's such hard work fetching water, logs and kindling, building fires and keeping them stoked, that we can't be boiling large quantities of water constantly. However, I do always keep a kettle hot by the side of the fire once it has boiled, ready to make drinks whenever they're wanted. I've been using a catering size blue and white enamel kettle, which previously idly decorated the kitchen and has now been called into active service. And an old copper kettle which was left behind after a church jumble sale has also proved useful.

Obtaining water is not a huge problem for us at present, as we have two rainwater butts as well as the well and, of course, have had an endless supply of rain for the last couple of months, which we have collected in buckets. As the rain has been so heavy in recent weeks, the water table will stay high for a long time, so the well should keep us supplied even if we have a dry spring.

Wednesday, February 19

Martin is my hero and he is triumphant. He has caught the mole at last. After weeks of molehills wrecking the lawn and invading my precious flower beds, he has finally caught the beast. I say caught, but he made me pull up the trap to check.

The mole must have been in the middle of tunnelling, for Martin had set one trap and was just setting a second a short distance away, when he heard the first one snap. He came rushing indoors to find me, as he hates dealing with rodents, although he is not at all fussed about shooting birds and other animals. I must admit I huffed and moaned, as he rarely snares moles with these sprung traps and I was in the middle of making lamb meatballs. But I wiped my hands and followed him outside to where he pointed and pulled out the trap. And there it was, neatly garrotted, its head limp, its spade-like paws dangling. Martin backed away. He really can be such a wimpish girl at times. But I stroked the fur and admired the pink nose and the way its front paws have evolved into such efficient digging machines. Then it was up to me to take it over to the wood and dispose of the body. The foxes will soon take it, of course, though it will be no more than a snack for a fox used to the carcasses of pigs, sheep and deer.

Despite his sensitive disposition, I thanked Martin for his perseverance as I was becoming quite distressed by the hills and tunnels being dug under and around my much-loved hellebores. There was even a mound disturbing the stones in the courtyard which borders the bed and I've heard that moles can lift paving with their tunnelling. Hopefully, there was just one mole in this area and not a community. We shall have to watch carefully.

I then went back to making the meatballs. They're meant to include breadcrumbs but as we can't get regular bread, I crumbled some flatbread. I also added a pinch of five-spice, which is unusual in an Italian recipe. Instead of crushed pistachios I've substituted chopped chestnuts, the last of the autumn harvest.

Thursday, February 20

First it was moles and now it's mice. We had an infestation of mice in the house about a year ago and so I know the signs well. You'd think droppings would be the first clue, but no, it's nibbled packets, shreds of paper in unexpected places and emptied nutshells.

This morning I was sure I saw something dart under the heating pipe in the kitchen. I wasn't sure what it was at first, but I decided to look in the back of the larder and my suspicions were confirmed. I found a nest in an old insulated cool bag. The lining had been chewed to shreds to make a cosy winter home. I suppose the recent wet weather has washed away their food and now the mice are moving into better accommodation, just as they did last year when it was very cold.

In the past, we relied on our expert mouser Maisie, who disappeared on her last great mouse hunt last summer. Or I would have rung our pest control man, Tom, who deals in all manner of vermin. But in these powerless times we can't call on his help as he lives too far away. I remember him saying once that the acid test for determining whether or not there is a mouse in residence is a chocolate biscuit. Of course, we don't have that luxury any more. I can't think when we last saw a biscuit, let alone a chocolate one. I don't even have any long forgotten chocolates hiding in the back of the larder. We don't have any traps either, as we've always relied on our clever cat before. I told Martin we shall definitely have to get a cat again if this becomes a serious problem. And then I remembered that last year, when the mice were being a nuisance, I had put a humane trap inside the breakfast room window seat. So I've retrieved it and baited it with a fragment of one of the gilded and sugared almonds, which decorated our table at Christmas over a year ago. They're never eaten, so I'd saved them as decorations and now they're being put to good use.

Friday, February 21

Today is cold but it's sunny and dry, so maybe the mice will soon move out. The humane trap has done nothing but sit there looking like a black praying mantis. It has been ignored by the mice and I expect they are sitting in their hole, replete and fat, waiting for more crumbs to fall from our table.

When we first moved to this old house and mice were running through all the kitchen cupboards, we had to use the old fashioned spring loaded traps as there were more mice than our cats could catch. The traps were effective, but we hated dealing with the results. Eventually, after removing a dead mouse with its eyes forced out of their sockets, I said that was enough. I'd never use them again and we've relied on cats ever since. So we are really missing Maisie, our champion mouser and I'm determined to ask in the village tomorrow if anyone knows of a cat in need of a home.

But although there are no bodies in the house, there is one in the field. I'd just fed the hens this morning when I noticed tufts of white on the grass and then I realised one of the old white ewes had keeled over. Neil said he heard a disturbance last night, but couldn't see anything. He thinks she's died of old age but the weather and poor grazing hasn't helped. As she has already been partly eaten we won't use her ourselves, but Neil may give some bits to his dogs.

The hens look happier with the drier weather and have laid four eggs today.

Saturday, February 22

Last night Martin asked me what I planned to do if I caught a mouse in the humane trap. Was I going to let it out in the field so it could run back to the house? Throw it in the pond and watch it drown? And I realised that I'd only ever considered using the trap with the help of a cat. A clever cat like Maisie would sit and wait while I opened the trap and let the mouse out to run as fast as it could before she pounced.

So today, when we went to the pub, I asked everyone if they had heard of a cat in need of a good home. And we're in luck. One of the elderly ladies who died last month had two cats, which are being fed by a neighbour at present, but in these difficult times she would be happy not to have the responsibility of feeding them. They are a brother and sister, both neutered, and are about five years old.

Martin and I went to see them before we walked home. The boy is sleek and black and the girl is a brindled tortoiseshell. Their names are Tom and Tickles. We couldn't take them home with us straight away as we hadn't brought our old cat boxes, so we shall use some precious petrol tomorrow to drive to the village to collect them both, then hope they will soon settle in and earn their keep.

I feel much happier now, knowing we will fight the mice together. As long as we don't get rats in the henhouse again, we shall cope.

Sunday, February 23

We collected the cats today after church. They yowled on the way home and we've realised that as their mother was half-Burmese they are going to be somewhat more vocal than our previous cats. We have settled them in the spare bedroom for now, with the cushioned bed they had slept in, until they are used to their new home.

I had some trouble working out what to put in a

litter tray for them to use while they are shut away upstairs. There is no cat litter to be had in the village shop and the garden is still too wet for the garden soil to be any use. I eventually used a combination of wood ash, soil and gravel and dried it off by the fire first. It won't form convenient clumps like normal cat litter, but it will do for now until they are allowed out.

We also can't buy commercial cat food in tins or as biscuit, so these cats will be spoilt with natural home-cooked food and may turn into the most pampered animals we have ever had. As we were having pheasants again today, I cooked up the giblets for stock and them chopped them up finely for the cats.

Tom is extremely friendly, rubbing around our legs when we enter the room and allowing us to stroke behind his ears and under his chin. Tickles is a little more aloof. She stares at us with knowing eyes and makes little sharp purry yaps. I'm glad we have found two cats though, especially as they are related. I think they will settle in well and keep each other company. And they'll keep each other warm while they are shut in the unheated bedroom. I was a bit worried they'd be cold, but Martin told me not to be so stupid as they have fur coats, after all. But I have given them an old fleecy dressing gown to curl up on.

Monday, February 24

Neil has lost another ewe. She too was old, so could have gone at any time, but the poor grazing these past weeks won't have helped. The foxes and crows got to her overnight and early this morning, so she won't be much good for us to eat, but as we now have the cats I've asked for some of the offal to cook up for them. Linda said she thought she might be able to use the fleece, but when she examined it more closely it was ripped and bloody.

When I looked in on the cats this morning, with a fresh litter tray, they were eager for food. So far they are not desperate to escape their room, but I'll give them another couple of days to settle in. After that I'll leave the bedroom door open so they can explore the house and gradually discover the outside world in their own good time. I think once they become used to having regular meals here they'll feel very much at home here and won't stray. There are no more signs of mice for the moment, but I'm sure the cats will still find enough prey to keep them interested.

It really does feel as if spring is coming at last and we might feel warm once more. All the daffodils and narcissus are up and ready to burst open. There are more primroses by the day and delicate pale mauve crocus are scattered under the trees. Our seed potatoes have sprouted, so we hope we shall be able to plant out early potatoes in about another week. I've also sown cabbage, turnips and parsnips in trays in the greenhouse and washed down the glass to clear away the green winter algae.

And the hens are behaving well and gave us five eggs today. I rewarded them with some fatty scraps and a good dig of their run to help them find the worms.

Tuesday, February 25

When I went outside to feed the hens this morning I

could hear barking and then I noticed all the sheep running as one across the field. I thought at first that Neil was rounding them up for some reason, but then I realised that they were being chased by a small off-white dog, which was yapping as it ran. So I ran too, over to the caravan, wondering all the while where Neil and Linda were. But it was shut up and there was no one there.

I then realised that the dog had cornered one of the old white ewes, who was stubbornly butting it while the dog bounced up and down, still barking. I had some baler twine in my jacket pocket, so I climbed over the fence and started walking towards it, thinking I could tie it up or drag it away. I called to it and it turned and looked at me, but as I got closer and was maybe a couple of hundred yards away it suddenly raced off and over the stile onto the road towards the village.

I took a close look at the ewe, which had suffered nothing worse than a bloodied nose, then went indoors to write a note to leave at the caravan. Neil came across at lunchtime to thank me and said if the dog turned up again he'd take a gun to it. Any landowner or stockholder has the right to shoot if a dog is worrying sheep. We don't know whose dog it is and it could well be a stray from a nearby town, but that doesn't mean he can risk his livestock, particularly as a number of ewes will lamb in a few more weeks. He said he'd checked the flock after seeing my note and that none of them had come to any harm, but we both know what damage even a small dog can do. When I used to keep sheep I once had an over excited Jack Russel attack my small flock. Its owner had let it off its lead and in a frenzy it bit at the neck of a lamb and nearly ripped the ear off its mother. I tore a strip off that dog owner and made her pay the vet's bill for stitching up the ear and would have no hesitation in shooting a dog attacking sheep.

Wednesday, February 26

Everyone was very cross with me for going into the field after the dog. I didn't think about it at the time. I was just concerned to get it away from the sheep before they were harmed or miscarried. But when I told the family about it later yesterday, Martin, Jane, Anna and Stephen all said I'd been very reckless and could have been bitten myself, even though it was only a small dog.

On reflection I know they are right and if any of us is injured in these difficult times we don't know how easily we can be treated. We have heard that the hospital is attempting to stay open for emergencies, but minor injuries and births are all being treated at home or in local doctors surgeries. So if any of us sees the dog again we have all promised to involve Neil and not try to tackle it ourselves.

After that ticking off, I tried to lighten the mood by getting everyone to talk about what we miss and don't miss during this endless power cut. I said I miss my oven, washing machine and iron, as well as running hot water, TV, friends and relatives further afield, fresh bread and wine. But I don't miss newspapers, rolling news reports, noisy traffic and airplanes. Martin said he missed his regular work, the internet and being able to watch boxed sets of *Deadwood* and *The Sopranos*. He doesn't miss the train journey to London, unproductive meetings or phone calls.

And then Anna said she missed her family and for a moment she was near to tears and we all began to think this maybe wasn't such a good game to play after all. But she pulled herself together and said although she missed her parents and her brother and sister, she didn't miss her aunts interfering and telling her what she should and shouldn't eat or do in her condition, or trying to suggest names for the baby. So then we were all laughing and she seemed fine. Stephen then said he missed football matches so Jane threw a nutshell at him and we all agreed that was the last thing we miss.

Thursday, February 27

The stupid dog came back again today. Linda came over and said Neil had heard it barking first thing this morning, but before he could get outside with his gun, his two sheepdogs had it cornered. Apparently it was very friendly once he got hold of it and he found its name and address was on the collar. Linda says it's one of those strange cross-breeds which were all the rage, a cocker doodle doo or something. That means it would have been expensive and would also have been much loved, we assume.

So Neil has decided, as the sheep have not been harmed, not to shoot it, but to see if he can find the owners. They aren't from the village, but the address is only three miles away.

We've been having spells of sunshine and showers today, making it difficult to decide when to hang out washing. I gave up in the end and have left everything on the racks near the hall fire. They'll smell of smoke, but we have to get them dry.

Anna has been feeling more movement from the baby. Still flutters rather than kicks, but it's a good sign and is making her feel optimistic and less inclined to worry. I suggested we might want to think about preparing for the baby soon, since we can't head off to Mothercare as we would have done before the power cut. The mothers at the school have been doing a regular children's clothing exchange at the beginning of each month, so we might go to the next one on Monday. There's no guarantee we'll find everything Anna might need, but if we start looking now we should be able to have enough laid by for when the baby arrives in the summer. I told Anna I'm happy to help with sewing but she can't expect me to try knitting as that was never one of my skills. She laughed and said if her aunts knew about her pregnancy they'd be producing hideous knitted garments by the dozen, so she's glad to be saved from that delight.

Friday, February 28

The weather has been rough today, so I thought it would be safe to let the cats explore the house. They're not likely to want to go outside in windy rain and hail. I left the bedroom door open when I took their food and clean litter tray upstairs this morning and didn't see a sign of them for an hour or so. Then, about mid-morning I saw a little dark face peering round the door into the dining room, where I was preparing lunch on the table by the fire.

Tom was bold and friendly and he was soon

followed by Tickles. They had a good look around the room and under the table, then rushed out again when Martin came thumping inside, kicking his boots off in the kitchen . Once he had sat down by the fire to warm up I soon saw them peeping round the door frame again, at the bottom of the stairs.

By mid-afternoon I think they had explored half of downstairs, hiding every time anyone opened a door or walked through. I'm going to give them their evening meal in the kitchen and start feeding them in there regularly from now on. If they want to retreat to their room upstairs tonight to sleep that's fine, but I want to encourage them to feel comfortable down here as soon as possible so they can detect mousey smells and start working for their living.

The wind had died down a bit by the time I fed the hens, but they clearly weren't impressed with the change in the weather and only gave us one egg today.

Saturday, March 1

The wind has dropped today and at least there hasn't been more rain. We hung out some washing for a while but I told the girls to keep an eye on the weather while Martin and I walked to the pub for the market. We took the wheelbarrow again as we badly need potatoes and other vegetables. It will be a long time before we can start cropping our own.

There was a lot of talk at the pub of thefts from the allotments. Some of the older villagers were blaming the refugees from the town, but they have no proof. Those poor people have come here with nothing and need pity not prejudice.

Reverend James said that the team from the church who normally organise the Lent Lunches every year, are turning their attention to helping the community living in the village hall. They usually make soup every Friday in the period leading up to Easter, with the proceeds going to charity. This year they will be making soup for anyone in need. They'll each make a large portion of soup at home, then bring it down to the hall to heat on a makeshift barbecue outside. That way, both the residents of the hall and anyone passing can have a bowlful. Next week they're making potato and onion, so I've said I'll join them with my contribution. A bowl of soup once a week is not much, but if you've nothing in the world it must help a little.

When we came back from the village, the cats both scooted across the hall and up the stairs. They then sat there at the top, staring at us while we packed away our vegetables. But they soon ventured down when I showed them a dish of giblets.

Sunday, March 2

The enormity of the current situation was brought home to all of us today, when Linda called in to tell us that Neil had been to find the stray dog's owners. Their house isn't that far away, but it's very isolated, buried deep in woodland. Maybe their nearest neighbours hadn't thought to check on them, maybe they didn't even know them.

She said Neil, who as we know is a steady, unshockable type, used to country ways and country life, was quite shaken by what he found. He thinks the couple were only in their late sixties or early seventies, but they were both dead. How they died, he couldn't tell. But the back door was splintered and open and the place had been ransacked.

So that's how the dog escaped. It must have got hungry and come looking for food. Neil had taken it there with him, hoping he could return it to its rightful owners, but he's brought it back home with him and is now wondering what to do next.

I said the first thing to do was deal with the bodies. Martin cycled off to speak to Reverend James and make arrangements. The couple aren't from our village, they're between villages, but they can't be left where they are, so the matter has to be dealt with immediately. With no means of contacting the authorities who would normally be responsible for such tragedies, we have to make decent, responsible decisions as a community.

When Stephen and Anna heard the awful news they said maybe we could keep the dog. Linda said Neil won't want to keep it, as he only has working dogs. And I said we'd have to think about it as we've only just taken on the two cats. It's hard enough feeding humans let alone animals in these times. Even the hens are on strict rations and can only produce an egg or two now and then.

Monday, March 3

We were all in a sombre mood this morning after yesterday's dreadful news. Reverend James is organising a funeral with the help of the local carpenter, who now makes coffins, and a former roadworker who now digs graves. The doctor will give his opinion on the cause of death and issue a certificate.

A notice signed by Reverend James and David Henderson, Chairman of the Parish Council, will be posted at the deceased couple's house, notifying any relatives who may call there at some point in the future, of the actions that had to be taken. Two other members of the Parish Council, who both happen to be lawyers, are checking through their personal papers to identify next of kin if possible, but it appears they did not have any family in the immediate area. If this information can be found, along with any other important financial papers, they will be stored safely in the hope that the appropriate steps can be taken in the future.

I spoke to Neil today and said how sorry I was that he had to be the one to make this distressing discovery. He simply said he was glad he hadn't gone there in the height of summer. He thought the wife might have been dead for some time. She was upstairs in bed but her husband appeared to have collapsed in the kitchen on the floor. Maybe it was the flu from a few weeks ago, or perhaps it was just malnourishment.

This afternoon was a little more cheerful, as Anna and I walked to the school to see if we could find any useful clothes or equipment for the baby. We were only able to get a smock top for Anna herself, but the mothers helping there know now what we'll need and will pass the word on to others.

The sunshine over the weekend has promoted the hens' productivity. They all laid well today and I collected six eggs, three brown and three blue.

Tuesday, March 4

I thought Anna seemed a little downcast after our visit to the school yesterday and our failure to find anything for the baby, so I suggested we could start making our own preparations. We went up to the attic and found the old Moses basket which I had used for both Stephen and Jane. I had originally lined it with sprigged cotton from Laura Ashley and made a little coverlet to match. But I know Anna will want to trim it herself for her baby, so we looked through the store of fabric scraps and found a remnant of blue striped from the same shop.

The basket itself only needs a good brush and the mattress needs airing then recovering. I no longer have the tiny sheets and blankets I once used. I think they went to Jane's doll's pram long ago, so we found an old flannelette sheet to cut down and Anna will knit or crochet her own blanket.

It was such a pleasure retrieving the basket and remembering the excitement of my own first baby. I'm sure we can help to make this time just as happy for Anna, even though she can't go shopping in Mothercare. Jane wants to help as well and I left the girls talking about sewing little nightgowns and making nappies from old towels if they can't find enough baby clothes at the school.

This was a much more cheerful subject than the other matters we have been dealing with, including another dead sheep in the field. It was an old ewe, who had lived out her days, but it is always sad to see an animal stiff and still, being pecked at by crows.

Despite the sunshine, the egg count was meagre. Only two today.

Wednesday, March 5

Just as we were about to have supper yesterday, Jane suddenly said she thought it was Pancake Day. I wasn't sure and none of us was certain because we lose track of dates so easily these days. Without the constant reminders from newspapers, TV and radio telling us when and what to buy, we are surprised by dates. So I searched for last year's diary on my desk and found she was right.

But it wasn't too late to celebrate Shrove Tuesday and although we didn't have milk for the batter, we made pancakes of a kind from some of the white flour ration that was left in the village, our own eggs and plain water. They weren't as good as they would normally be, but spread with honey and jam they were still delicious. And we had the fun of taking it in turns to each toss our own pancake. Martin was impatient and tried to toss before his was cooked through, so his stuck and broke. Anna and Jane both managed fairly well but Stephen did one of the best, tossing it as high as the low ceiling would allow and catching it so it lay flat and finished cooking evenly.

Today we've had warm spring sunshine all day, which meant we could hang washing on the line. It was even sunny when I first woke, although there was a hard frost and the ponds were thinly iced. The temperature must have dropped considerably last night and when I shut up the hens before suppertime it was already very cold and there was a sliver of new moon high in the sky. The hens enjoyed the sun as well, digging in the drier areas of their run and trying to take their baths. Four eggs today.

Thursday, March 6

It has really felt like spring today, with warm sunshine and birds singing, but I had to spend much of the morning indoors making soup for the village hall soup kitchen tomorrow. Martin wasn't too happy that I was cooking food to give away, so I've had to make extra to keep him quiet.

It's only potato and onion, because that's what the organisers agreed to make this week, but it will be hot and filling. I wish it could be leek and potato, with extra cream, but these days we have to cook with whatever is available. If these were normal times and I could make whatever soup I liked, I would do either minestrone, with a wide selection of fresh vegetables, including green beans and courgettes, or cauliflower and fennel, which sounds like an odd combination but is surprisingly successful. It will be wonderful if our own vegetables grow well this year and we have a choice again.

Neil has been making enquiries about the stray dog, whose owners' funeral will take place soon. It seems that nobody wants to take it on. I suppose that in these difficult times when it is hard enough to feed a family, it is understandable that people would not want an extra mouth to feed, not even one belonging to a very attractive, cuddly, friendly dog. And Neil doesn't want to keep it either, because he already has two working dogs to feed and he says it is not a good idea to keep a pet dog with sheepdogs, as the untrained one is inclined to get the wrong idea. Also, as this dog has already chased the sheep a couple of times already, it cannot be trusted. I asked Linda what Neil plans to do with it now and she said if no one wants to give it a home he will have to shoot it.

I thought as I fed the hens how hard it is to put down an ailing animal, let alone a healthy one. It is a soppy dog with a stupid name. Buggles, it said on its tag. The hens agreed with me and gave me four eggs.

Friday, March 7

I knew as soon as I told everyone last night that the dog might have to go, that the girls and Stephen would start pestering to keep it. Martin objected, quite rightly, but Jane in particular, said it really did seem very unfair on the dog, which has already lost its owners and its home. I said I had never wanted a dog and as we have just acquired the two cats we already have enough animals to look after.

But I might have known that wouldn't be the end of it and halfway through the morning, just after we'd hung out the washing in the sunshine, Neil turned up at the back door with the stupid dog. It sat there looking very pleased with itself, wagging its tail. And Neil said he'd brought the dog, as agreed. I didn't know what he was talking about then Jane leapt forward, picked up the dog and said she'd been across first thing this morning and told Neil we would keep it. She said she couldn't bear to think of it being shot, just for being homeless and unwanted.

I've put my foot down. I'm not feeding it or walking it. But Jane says she will look after it and train it to behave and I have to say it does seem to be taking to her. Which is more than I can say for the cats. Tom and Tickles, already established in their new home, are being very wary. They decided to keep an eye on the dog (Buggles, I ask you!) from a high vantage point on top of the redundant fridge and freezer in the kitchen. I may have to put out their food when Jane takes her new pet upstairs to bed tonight.

I don't normally approve of pets sleeping in bedrooms, but the dog might whine if it is left alone. I've told Jane she will have make sure it doesn't misbehave and if it causes any problems, I'll be sending it straight back to Neil for him to deal with. And I said she has to train it not to bark at the hens either, now they are laying well again. There were six eggs today.

Saturday, March 8

Yesterday I wheeled my soup to the village hall in the wheelbarrow. It was such a lovely day I didn't want to use the car and we try not to use the little petrol we have left. I didn't have a suitable storage container to transport the soup, so I had to use an old nappy bucket. It was well washed and was last used for the kit I had to have close by for lambing. But I rinsed it out with bleach and boiling water just to be safe and to satisfy the housewife brigade I knew would be startled by my choice of container.

As the weather was so warm it was really quite pleasant walking down the lane to the village and the makeshift barbecue outside the hall was glowing hot by the time I arrived. All the soups were poured into one huge preserving pan to heat through and we soon had plenty of hungry mouths to feed. We'd all made flatbread to eat with the soup, so it was quite filling.

I chatted to a young couple who'd left Guildford the day before the terrible storm nearly a month ago. They said the countryside felt so much safer than the town with its overflowing sewage, rats, stray dogs and stray people. Even though they are living in temporary accommodation, they are well fed and clean here and are enjoying working on the allotments which should produce a good crop in a few months.

Today the wheelbarrow was put to good use again when Martin and I walked to the pub for the barter and market. We collected potatoes, cabbage, carrots and kale, then left promptly as the weather was so sunny and we wanted to get back to our own garden. I know I should be concentrating on growing our own produce, but I found some seeds left over from last year, so I couldn't resist sowing some trays of cosmos and sunflowers. Knowing there will be flowers gives me hope.

The Rhode Island Reds didn't do so well today and there were no brown eggs, but the Legbars had laid four beautiful pale blue eggs.

Sunday, March 9

I'm very scratched and very dirty, but I'm also very happy. Today is the first day for months that I have felt thoroughly warm, in fact I'm actually hot. I've been sweeping the garden clear of all the debris that the winter storms threw at us and the sun has been shining all day.

It has put us all in such a good mood. Martin has

lit big bonfires to burn the twiggy bits that won't make good kindling. I've been brushing off the benches and chairs on the terrace outside the kitchen so we have somewhere clean to sit in the sun. And the girls have made lamb kebabs and a salad of grated carrot mixed with early ground elder and bitter cress, tossed in a mint dressing. They've made flatbread to wrap around the meat and baked potatoes in the fire indoors. Stephen has lit the barbecue and although we don't have charcoal, he has managed to make it very hot with our own wood.

We feel almost civilised again for the first time since the power cut began. The sun shines, we have good food, there is washing blowing on the line and we are really warm. The cats have ventured outside and are sunbathing when they tire from chasing leaves and birds. The dog has explored the garden and has now befriended Martin. Our hens are enjoying dust baths in dry soil at last and they've made a new nest where I found four eggs today. What more could we want for? Tomorrow there is a funeral, but today the sun is shining and we can eat an early meal outside and be glad we are all alive.

Monday, March 10

Although the sun has still shone and bright green buds are emerging on all the trees, our mood has felt much greyer. Today the husband and wife Neil found last week were buried in the village graveyard following a short service in the church.

The funeral was quite well attended, considering none of their family were present. Reverend James made an announcement in church yesterday, asking for us to support these people in their onward journey, even though they were not known to us. Letters had been dropped off at houses that neighboured the woodland cottage and two people came from nearby, although they said they had never become acquainted with this reclusive couple.

We sang the hymns for two strangers, including 'When I needed a Neighbour', which was a poignant choice. And although none of us present had known these people, I think we all reflected on how sad it would be if no one noticed our passing. But by the time the service finished we all felt we had come to know them a little. We knew their names – John and Barbara Ruggles – and we knew, from the vicar's address, how old they were, when they were married and that they had cared for each other very much. He couldn't add much information as he hadn't been able to speak to their friends and family the way he normally would in preparation for a funeral, but he and the parish councillors had obviously gleaned some information from documents they had found in the house.

And as we left the church, Martin made a joke which cheered me up. He said, "So that's how the dog got its stupid name." I didn't understand at first, then he said, "Barbara Ruggles. Buggles." And we both started laughing and held hands all the way home.

Tuesday, March 11

While we ate our supper last night, we were all talking about the funeral and the loneliness of the couple in the woods. Martin has never been a great one for making friends, but even he agreed that we should check on our neighbours more often. I said we must make a point of seeing them at least once a week, so today I've called on Robin and Deirdre as well as looking in on Tony and Gail and their family.

Jane seemed the most concerned and said she was worried that if the rest of us became very ill, she wouldn't be able to cope. We've all been wondering why the Ruggles died alone. I suggested that it was because they were elderly, they'd run out of petrol and perhaps, when Barbara became seriously ill, her husband didn't like to leave her. Anna thought the husband should have walked into the village to find a doctor, but maybe he wasn't fit enough to walk such a distance or was afraid he wouldn't return to her in time.

I told Jane that our situation is vastly different to the Ruggles couple and if any of us falls ill and needs a doctor, we will let our neighbours know, just in case. She seemed reassured by this and said if we all went, she wouldn't stay in the house but would ask Mick if she could move into the pub with Buggles. She said she'd leave the cats here and let Gail have the hens.

I think the cats would cope quite well. I found the remains of some wild thing in the kitchen this morning. I assume it was a mouse they'd eaten, but they still rubbed around my legs purring and asking for food. And the hens would cope too. They left four more eggs in their new nest today.

Wednesday, March 12

Breezy sunshine has meant washing out on the line and I've hardly missed my tumble dryer and steam iron. The clothes smell fresh and after a good blow on the line they are hardly creased. Although the actual washing is still a laborious chore, fetching water, slowly heating it on the fire, then the endless rinsing and wringing, it is much easier in good weather. Martin has suggested we could heat water on the barbecue and do the laundry outside when it's fine, which is also easier with all the splashing and sploshing that it entails. We still have to fetch the water of course, and as the well is the other side of the house, that's still hard work.

Anna and Jane have been scouring the flower beds for the first shoots of ground elder. They are popping up everywhere, but they are easier to spot on bare earth. We'll eat them like spinach and this constant picking will weaken this annoyingly vigorous weed which continues to invade all the beds.

The strangest occurrence today was the discovery of a large number of plucked hellebore flowers arranged in a circle the size of a dinner plate in the border. Jane found it and called me to see. I've grown hellebores for more than fifteen years and I've never known this to happen before. Although I assume it was done by a cheeky pigeon or a pheasant, it gave me an eerie feeling looking at the display, for all the world like a sacrificial offering. Each flower had been nipped off at the very top of its stem and laid on the soil so the speckled petals were open to the sun.

No such mischief from the hens. There were two eggs in the new nest and two under the old work bench in their stable, so I had to get down on my hands and knees to reach them.

Thursday, March 13

Today Martin planted out the potatoes we prepared a few weeks ago. It is still early, but because the weather has been mild we think they should do well. I've noticed that the seeds from the other week have sprouted already, so I'm hoping we can give these an early start as well.

There are other signs of spring too. When I was clearing leaves from the kitchen terrace, I found a toad nestled in a corner, so I tucked him up again to keep warm. The days are much milder but the temperature really drops at night. I also came across a large frog on the lawn, which should have only just emerged from its winter sleep. I think it may have been dropped by the heron I've seen flying in and out of the garden recently. I picked up the frog and took it to the edge of the big pond so it could slip back into the mud.

And this morning, as I sat at my dressing table, trying not to look in the mirror or think about my greying hair, my lines and eye bags, there was a tap on the window. A little coal tit was clinging to the leaded window and flitting from one pane to another. Then it was joined by a blue tit which also pecked at the frame. They must have been looking for insects or searching for moss to make nests. I was happily enjoying the sight when Tom suddenly jumped up on the windowsill and scared them both off. I do hope these cats don't become bird killers. I hate finding feathers in the house. I only want them to catch mice.

After throwing leaves and weeds into the hen run, the hens have done well and there were four more eggs today.

Friday, March 14

In the thick mist that hung over the fields this morning, Martin thought he had seen an eight-legged sheep. It wasn't of course, it was two sheep, or rather it was a ewe and her lamb. The first lamb of the season, wobbling on thin legs, its mother licking it dry as it steamed in the early chill of morning. A couple of hours later there was another one and by the end of the afternoon three had been born, all snuggled up against their mothers.

These black Welsh mountain sheep are hardy and rarely need help with lambing. Neil is keeping a close eye on them and has already banded their tails. He's only had tails to deal with so far as they are all ewe lambs, but if they are male they get an extra band. Martin doesn't like hearing about that one, but I don't mind helping to hold the lambs while Neil performs the operation.

The mist was burnt away with the sun by mid-morning, so we could hang out washing, which was almost dry by the end of the afternoon. It smells so fresh, liked toasted bread, when it dries outside. Much better than the slightly smoked smell it acquires when we have to dry everything indoors near the open fire. Even in the days when we had electricity and could use a tumble dryer I still preferred to hang the laundry outdoors for the sake of that lovely clean smell.

This run of good weather is keeping the hens very happy too. They laid another six eggs in their new nest, so we have plenty and will have some for breakfast tomorrow.

Saturday, March 15

I held a day old lamb today and felt its heart beating fast against my fingers. Its black fleece was like rough towelling and it smelt clean, like fresh grass. It was quiet at first then gave a pleading bleat, so once Neil had slipped the band over its tail I had to let it run to its mother, who was watching anxiously and giving that snickering cry which is peculiar to new mothers, then sniffed it all over to check it hadn't been harmed as it butted her udder to suckle.

Days like these help us to forget what difficult times we are experiencing in this endless power cut. Life goes on when ewes give birth untroubled and the sun shines all day. Then Martin and I walked to the pub with our wheelbarrow to pick up potatoes and hear the latest news. There was talk of aid reaching Aldershot, but that may just be to sustain the army and there is still no sign of anything reaching us here. We will run out of flour very soon and candles and rice would be useful too.

But we are coping and the village isn't starving. And there was good news today too. Neil thinks he may be able to get me a mangle! I never thought I would be so thrilled at the thought of such an old fashioned contraption, but if I can get it I will be delighted. To be able to wring out the washing more than we can do with our bare hands would be wonderful.

We had eggs again for breakfast as the hens are laying so well. They gave us four eggs today.

Sunday, March 16

I am really upset today. I went out first thing this morning to feed the hens and found they had all gone. It was my own fault as I had forgotten to shut the henhouse door last night, but the gate to the run was still closed and nothing had dug under the high wire fence.

When I saw the run was empty, I looked all around inside the henhouse, thinking at first that they could all be laying, although they are usually eagerly pecking to get out and have breakfast. But there was not a feather to be found.

It seems very strange, but I have heard stories of mink climbing into runs and killing the hens then taking them out one by one. It certainly isn't the work of a fox as they would kill the whole flock and only eat or take what they needed immediately. The last time a fox broke into the run I discovered six hens dead and two dying. I loaded the bodies into the wheelbarrow and threw them into the field, where the foxes probably ate them all later at their leisure. If that happened now, in these difficult times, I wouldn't let the foxes have the dead hens, I'd keep them for ourselves.

But I'm most annoyed about the loss of the eggs. The hens had been laying so well recently and the eggs were most welcome, even though we can find extra supplies in the village once a week. I will have to make enquiries about getting more hens and also be less careless in shutting them up at night.

And then, after this disastrous discovery, we went to church to contemplate Lent, which is particularly difficult this year as we have already lost so much. There is not much more we can deny ourselves during this challenging time. The theme of the sermon was 'counting our blessings', which I am trying to do but am finding very hard now the hens have gone.

Monday, March 17

Martin and Stephen have both been really annoying about the disappearance of the hens. They don't seem to appreciate how devastating this loss is and why I am so upset. Martin just said, at least there weren't any bodies to collect this time and now you won't have to remember to shut them up at night. Then yesterday evening, around 6.30, Stephen noticed there was a full yellow moon rising behind the trees. He pointed it out to me and I thought I was simply meant to comment on how beautiful a sight it was, as the pale yellow traced with bare black branches was quite striking. And in the absence of electric light and aircraft our night skies are stunning. It was a clear night and the stars were already emerging, but he startled me when he then said, it could be a sacrifice. I didn't immediately understand what he meant, then he laughed and said, maybe the hens were taken as a sacrifice for the full moon.

I was so cross with him. I told him he wasn't to talk like that, even if he was joking, and he certainly shouldn't say any such thing to Anna, in her condition. She doesn't need to be unsettled by such fanciful nonsense.

And then this morning Martin came out with his own theory. He said he's been thinking that the hens were stolen, not by an animal, but by a human thief. I asked him what on earth made him think that and he said he thinks the idea they were taken by a mink is rubbish and that in these difficult times, with such a shortage of food, it could well be a chicken rustler. So I had to tell him off as well. I told him to shut up as the very thought of a robber prowling around here in the dead of night was enough to terrify me, let alone a young expectant mother.

He went quiet for a bit, then said he was going to have a good look around the garden and grounds and see what he could find. So I told him that whatever he found he was not to tell either of the girls. We all need to stay calm and have steady nerves. The jitters are the last thing we need.

Tuesday, March 18

I am really missing the hens. I always loved the way they were so eager to escape from their house every morning and scratch in the dirt of their run for worms and whatever I had taken them to eat. And although sometimes it was tedious waiting for them to go inside to roost in the evenings, I enjoyed shutting them up too. Walking out there in the dark, hearing the sounds of the night, then as I closed the henhouse door I could hear them making soothing sounds to each other as they slept.

Recently, since the power cut began, that evening

chore has actually been even more enjoyable as the nights are quieter and darker. With no cars, no aircraft and not even the distant rumble of the London trains, I've become more aware of the sounds of the country at night. I'd hear a deer leaping through the brambles, an owl calling for a mate and if it was just past dusk, the hooting of swans and geese flying home.

And the skies have never been blacker and clearer. Now the surrounding towns are blacked out, we are astonished at how many stars have been hidden from sight all these years. Before this crisis I've only ever been able to see the Milky Way on empty moorland. I don't know my constellations, but Martin has been out many times recently with binoculars marvelling at the sky.

Last night I went outside anyway, just to hear the night settling in and walk in the moonlight.

Wednesday, March 19

Men can be so childish. Last night I went outside, just to enjoy the moon shining on the grass through the trees and Stephen nearly gave me a heart attack. He crept up behind me, making a strange cry as I stood looking at the sky. I was so cross with him, then even crosser when he said he still thought the hens had been sacrificed.

I really gave him a telling off then. But he said there was the circle of flowers the other day and now the hens, so what are we to make of it? And then he said didn't I think there was something strange about the fact that it was all to do with things beginning with 'H'? You know, he said, first hellebores, then hens... it will be hedgehogs next. So I gave him a sharp clip round the ear, which was quite difficult to do as he's been six foot tall since he was seventeen.

And today Martin said there are footprints on the bottom lawn and he thinks someone has been wandering around the grounds overnight. He also said he's found fag ends near the garage, which makes him think someone has been spying on the house. I told him to show me exactly where he'd found them and when he did so I realised it was precisely where Joe and his occasional assistant gardener used to park before the power cut started. They both smoked so I think the stubs date back to then. They look very old, so I don't think anyone has been snooping around recently.

However Martin says he will continue to be vigilant as he is convinced the hens all ended up on someone's plate and not in a fox's den.

Thursday, March 20

Martin has gone up in my estimation. Not only did he find the mangle, following Neil's directions, but he has been to collect it. Neil was the one who first heard the mangle was available, but he is busy with the sheep, so Martin cycled off to double-check that it really was in working order. He found it in the garden shed of an elderly lady who no longer has the strength to turn the heavy handle and was glad to think it would be put to good use. It is a little rusty, but some oil will soon put that right.

Then Martin returned with Stephen in the car, as it needed two of them to lift the heavy contraption. And now it has been assembled and is standing on the kitchen terrace. No longer is this area an elegant patio for pre-dinner drinks and nibbles, it is fast turning into a working laundry. There's the barbecue where we are heating water on dry days, an old metal bath and an old baby bath for washing and now the mangle nearby. It's all very convenient, almost like a quaint retro chic utility room, with the washing line in easy reach.

I haven't used the mangle yet as there was such a cold wind today I didn't fancy getting frozen, but will do so tomorrow if the weather is fine. Jane and Anna are intrigued and want to take turns with the handle and pushing the laundry through the heavy wooden rollers. We shall collect the waste water in a large basin and use it for topping up the cistern in the cloakroom.

It's so funny to be so excited by such an old fashioned piece of machinery. But in these powerless times, without spin cycles on washing machines and the aid of a tumble dryer, laundry is a real chore and this mangle is going to be an enormous help.

And the cats are helping in their own little way too. They left two mice in the kitchen this morning. I must be feeding them too much as they didn't even try eating them.

Friday, March 21

I held another lamb today. This one is rather unusual as it isn't black, it's dirty beige with dark brown legs and black patches on its face. Neil says it is 'badger faced' which meant I immediately had to start calling it Badger. It was very calm and quiet in my arms and if we still had power I would have liked a photo.

None of us have old-fashioned cameras with real film, just phones and other gadgets which no longer work without power. As it is, I shall just have to commit the experience to memory.

Badger was light to hold, but he didn't smell as sweet as the first lamb I held this year. I think Badger is four days old and has lost his newborn freshness. He now smells like a urine-soaked tramp from butting his mother's nether regions when he feeds, but he was still lovely to hold.

Still, the cats smell sweet. They are increasingly friendly and now starting to seek strokes and laps. They smell of dry leaves and grass when they have been sunning themselves outside and smoky fires when they have been warming their fur inside. Tom has decided he likes to sit on a large upturned log, which provides a steady seat right by the fire. Tickles prefers a softer bed and after being shooed out of the basket of dried and folded bed linen has opted for a firm cushion by the hearth.

Tomorrow we go to the pub for the market and I will ask if there are any hens available. I don't have high hopes as everyone must need to keep as many chickens as possible in these troubled times, for the eggs and for the meat. I am going to take some of our black pudding sausages, dried mushrooms and potted meat in the hope that these can be bartered for hens in lay.

Saturday, March 22
I suddenly realised today that we are in real trouble. I don't mean the inconvenience of this prolonged power cut, the burden of household chores or the

shortage of staple foods, I'm talking about toilet paper! Martin was able to find a large supply on an abandoned pallet at the big supermarket just before Christmas, but we are down to the last two rolls now and there are five people living here. I hadn't noticed until this morning, when I went to pick up another roll. I asked Martin where the rest of the packs were and he just said, that's it. That's all we've got.

I'm staggered, because we had tons. Martin accused me and the girls of being profligate with the paper, but I said I've been very careful right from the start and have always used it sparingly. So we went off to the Saturday morning barter market at the pub in a very bad mood and the conversation there put me in an even worse mood, when I explained our problem. Rob, who used to run the village shop said it wasn't a problem, just use newspaper. Well as we haven't seen a paper since this darned crisis started I don't know how we're supposed to lay our hands on some.

I remember visiting an old aunt on her unmodernised farm in the 1950s, when I was a child and she had squares of newspaper hung on a string in what she called the 'privy'. It was a seat height, smooth plank with two large circular holes over buckets. I was horrified, but now I'd be very glad of some handy newspaper.

Martin said he won't bother, but I've told him not to be so disgusting. Stephen said couldn't we be like the Romans and use a basin of water? It may come to that if we can't think of anything else. We've managed to remain quite civilised so far, retaining our flushing toilet, but now we are being reduced to basic needs.

The pub didn't produce any leads on hens either, so today was altogether a bad day.

Sunday, March 23

I woke very early to sun streaming through the windows, highlighting all the dust and candle wax that has dripped on windowsills and floors during this crisis. There was a hard frost which may have caught the magnolia flowers, just as they are emerging.

And then, as I gazed at the beautiful light softly illuminating the grounds, I remembered. There is an immediate problem to solve and if I don't address it we shall all be in terrible trouble. Stephen's Roman solution won't work, I'm sure. I can't rely on the men to rinse and clean the basin every time and anyway, what would we use, in place of a sponge on a stick? I don't think Stephen and Martin realise how important hygiene is to women and girls, especially an expectant mother. No, I must solve this problem quickly, before we run out of paper altogether.

As we walked to church in the bright sun, Martin asked me if I was in a mood. I said I certainly wasn't, I was just thinking. He asked me what I was thinking about and I said, what else is there to think about? Aren't you aware of how serious this is? He looked blank. I honestly think he'd forgotten overnight about our dilemma. When I reminded him, he just said not to blame him – that at least he'd brought back loads of toilet paper in the first place. I said that was true and we were very grateful, but now we have to stop blaming each other and think how we can solve the problem.

He nudged me as we were sitting in the pew in church, just before the service began and flicked the pages in his hymn book. Paper, he hissed at me, lots of paper here. I glared at him and turned my attention to singing 'Love Divine, All Loves Excelling'.

Monday, March 24

Although I was very annoyed with Martin's irreverence in church yesterday, he set me thinking. We have loads of books in the house, many of them destined for the charity shop anyway. But when I told Martin, he rushed to my bookcase and picked up my much loved copy of *Pride and Prejudice*. No, I shouted, not books we want to keep!

He shrugged and put it back, but I don't trust him or Stephen, so I've said I'll decide which books can end their days as toilet paper. I think unwanted paperbacks can work quite well. By keeping them intact and ripping out pages as they are needed, the paper will be neatly contained, like a pack of old-fashioned Izal paper, which came as individual sheets in a cardboard box.

Of course, I also realised that paperbacks, while printed on thin paper, are not made of soft toilet tissue, which can be flushed. So I think we may have to resort to the method we had to get used to in Corfu, of disposing of the used paper in a bin. It always seemed unpleasant, but we soon got used to it and we don't want to have a blocked toilet.

Quite how long this will provide us with an adequate supply, I'm not sure, but I've already started sorting out books that we'll never read again.

Stephen's said we can have all his Dan Browns and I
found a couple of Jeffrey Archers too. And Jane
shocked me by coming downstairs with a copy of
Fifty Shades of Grey and when I said I was very
surprised at her, she said all her friends had been
talking about it and she wanted to see what all the
fuss was about. She says she never finished it.

Tuesday, March 25

The weather has been so much colder, almost the
coldest we've had all winter, so it hardly feels like
spring, although the daffodils are all out and the
bluebells are already in bud. I've run out of chilblain
ointment and my toes are hurting, so I've not been
happy today.

But Neil is happy because the lambing is going
well and there have been no still births. Two sets of
twins have been born so far and all are thriving.
Twins are the greatest worry as sometimes the fox,
which is ever watchful, will steal the first lamb while
the mother is still in labour. These Welsh Mountain
sheep have mostly single lambs and twins only
occasionally, but Neil says if any are abandoned or if
there is a triplet struggling to feed, I may have a lamb
to care for.

Yes, I know I have my hands full with washing,
cooking and general chores, we still have no power
and there is the toilet paper crisis to worry about and
I also have a pregnant daughter-in-law, but it is
immensely satisfying to bottle feed a lamb. I have
only ever done it once and that lamb is still alive,
although he is now an eleven-year-old brute with a
patchy fleece that leaves his hind-quarters naked. But

he came to us as an abandoned triplet who took his bottle eagerly, once I had bought the formula he was used to, and he fell asleep on my lap every evening like a big baby in a fleecy baby-gro after drinking his milk. And a bottle-fed lamb becomes very tame and friendly and my grown lamb still comes to the fence to greet me even though he now has the company of fifty ewes. I don't know what formulation could be concocted if we can't get the right kind of powdered milk, but I'm sure Neil will advise.

Wednesday, March 26

I was outside early this morning and I saw a ewe give birth to twins. She was still licking her first-born dry when the sac started to emerge with the second, glistening and steaming in the morning sun. Half an hour later, both lambs were standing and one gave a little jump, trying out its new legs, as the mother nudged and snickered at them in her special sheepy baby talk.

This event quite put me in a good mood and I was in an even better mood when Martin cycled back from the village with the last remaining tube of chilblain ointment from the chemist. If my toes don't throb I might be more cheerful, he said. But he had also heard that some hens might be available soon. There is a chap down near the church who has a garden full of hens and not enough food for them, now that supplies are so hard to come by. We have come to rely on our own eggs, so I shall be very glad to stock the run with new hens.

Martin and Stephen then got on with splitting the pine tree that fell in the high winds last week. I'm relieved it has finally come down as it was the one with the splintered trunk, which had been threatening to fall since Christmas. Luckily it didn't bring any neighbouring trees down with it, only odd branches. And I couldn't help noticing, as they were working over by the copse, that Buggles has abandoned Jane and seems to be following Martin everywhere he goes.

Thursday, March 27

Blasted dog, Martin keeps saying. Follows me all the darn time. I think it's really funny. Martin has never liked dogs and never wanted us to have one, but Buggles seems very attached to him. And I suspect that Martin is secretly enjoying the attention, as I swear I saw him pat Buggles on the head when they were outside this morning. He definitely didn't shoo him away.

We used the last of the toilet paper this morning and now there is a pile of books in the cloakroom, next to a plastic bin which was originally the electric paper shredder we bought but never used. It's hard to break the habit of tossing used paper into the loo, but I've stressed we must do this if we want to be sure of having a flushing toilet. We'll burn the paper outside when the weather is dry. I wondered about putting it on the fires indoors, but I'm not sure it will add to the ambience the way a scented candle could!

Stephen cycled over to the other side of the village today to speak to the man with the surplus hens. He is prepared to let us have five, providing we also take on a young cockerel. I wasn't too keen on this, seeing how aggressive the last one became. But if this one gets too feisty he can end up in the pot too. The hens will cost us a delivery of logs, which is fair exchange and as we would need to take the car to collect them anyway, it will be worth using the petrol.

I'm really looking forward to collecting them and helping them settle into their new home. Stephen shovelled up all the old sawdust and straw from the henhouse today and added it to the compost heap. Poultry manure is very potent and is an excellent ingredient in the compost mix. We were a bit stumped at first as to what we could spread in the empty henhouse, but then we realised that our old pig's shelter still contained dry straw, so Stephen recycled that with a helping of dry leaves. It now looks fresh and clean and awaits its new occupants.

Friday, March 28

We have chickens again! They are mostly Rhode Island Reds, which are dark reddish brown, but there are two light brown mottled Legbars as well, which I am glad of as they are the ones that lay such pretty coloured eggs. We brought them home in a selection of containers; a large cardboard box with holes, two cat baskets and a picnic hamper. Mr Christopher, who bred them, had rounded them up ready for us and helped us by grabbing them and stuffing them into the various carriers.

Once we were back we took them inside the henhouse, which was ready with food and water, then shut the outer door before releasing them. They squawked at first, then started investigating. We shall leave them shut up in the house for at least twenty-four hours before allowing them out into the run, so they become used to their new home. As we have lost our old flock, we don't have to worry about the hens fighting or bullying each other. If we were introducing new chickens to an established group we would have to separate them for a longer period, so they became accustomed to each other.

So all seems well in the animal part of the household for now. The hens are settling, the lambs are feeding, the cats are killing and the dog is loving Martin. I think the feeling might be mutual. Martin came back to the house after we'd unloaded the hens and, as he kicked off his muddy boots, he said, "Bubbles was very interested in the new chickens". "Bubbles," I said, "who's Bubbles?" He looked sheepish then said, "Oh, you know who I mean. Anyway, I always thought Buggles was a stupid name." I tried not to laugh too much. It's rather sweet.

Saturday, March 29

After several days of very cold weather and frosts, we have sunshine again. Working outside we feel quite warm and have even thrown off our winter sweaters at last. But the house is still very cold at night and we huddle round the fire for warmth. If there was power we'd be having the central heating on until late into the evening and maybe even some of the day as well. Martin keeps saying that the only good thing about the long power cut is saving money. But I can't help thinking that while there is no way of spending money or accounting for it, how can it be important?

We went to the pub today as usual and returned

with supplies of beef, carrots and potatoes. I'll make a large stew which will last for at least a couple of days, eking it out with dumplings. The gossip there was all about raids on the allotments again and Martin didn't help by telling everyone about the strange disappearance of the hens and the significance of the hellebore circle. I don't see the point in fuelling suspicion and superstition, especially in these difficult times. It can only create uncertainty and fear and I've told Martin he's to stop doing it. I think men are worse gossips than women.

When we returned home, Jane said the dog had been desperate to go with us and she'd had to tie him up to stop him following us down the road. Martin said she should have let him come and then untied Buggles, I mean Bubbles, and they walked off together to collect more wood for the fire.

Sunday, March 30

I always wake early and since this crisis began my body clock has been governed more by daylight than by the ticking of a mechanical clock. But today we realised that in normal circumstances the clocks would have gone forward overnight, so Martin spent some time adjusting all the clocks in the house, which he still winds up every couple of days. I don't really see the point, but I suppose if everyone else is on Summer Time then I may as well conform. At least it meant I got to church on time and I didn't know until I got there that today was Mothering Sunday. But Jane and Stephen somehow knew and they gave me a little bunch of primroses when I came back.

Martin wasn't tempted to filch any pages from the hymn books this week, but when we returned home I noticed that our little pile of paperbacks in the cloakroom has diminished. I thought at first that we were maybe being liberal with the paper, after strictly rationing the last of the toilet rolls. I looked through the stack of books, trying to remember which titles I'd selected for our use. I know I was being selective and don't want to rip up my favourite books unless we get desperate.

I told Jane and Anna that we seemed to be using up the books very quickly, but they didn't know what I was talking about. Anna was excited by the offer of the loan of a cot from Gail, as Alfie will be two in the summer and can move into a bed a few months after the baby is born. But they don't have any newborn clothes to pass on as everything was left behind when they had to escape from London.

Tom and Tickles must have been hard at work again today. They left a gory little pile of guts on the kitchen doormat which seems to be their favourite place for eating their prey.

Monday, March 31

I've finally solved the mystery of the paperbacks in the loo. I knew I had put out twelve books originally and as I seem to be the only one who removes the covers from the cloakroom when the book is finished, I was sure I hadn't miscounted and now I know that I was right.

I stripped our bed this morning to wash the sheets as the weather looks bright enough to wash them and I noticed a book sticking out from under the divan base on Martin's side. I pulled it out and there it was. *Fifty Shades of Grey*. He hasn't said a word, so I'm not going to either. I'm just going to wait and see if he dares take it out to read.

I opened up the henhouse for the new chickens yesterday. They peered out of the door at first and only emerged slowly, but they obediently went in to roost at dusk, just as they are meant to. This morning they were more confident and when I went to feed them this afternoon I found the first egg, which I hope will be the first of many. Once they have all begun to lay we could have as many as five eggs a day, which will be plenty. I may even think of letting a few hatch once the cockerel gets into his stride if the hens get broody.

It is a real pleasure to have chickens here again and hear them clucking at each other and see them wriggling in their outdoor dust baths. The cockerel is still young, but he is strutting and puffing, pausing now and then to crow. His cry hasn't yet fully matured and still has treble croaks in amongst a richer tenor. But soon his cry will be my most efficient alarm clock.

Tuesday, April 1

Today should have been happy and joyful. The sun has shone all day long, Stephen remembered it was April Fool's Day and played jokes on us all, the weather has been warm and my iris are in bud. But when there is death, even though it is a death that might be expected, there is sadness, despite the flowers and sunshine.

Neil told us a couple of days ago that he had

noticed two lambs had disappeared. He suspects the foxes and, as a seasoned shepherd, always knows that there will be some losses during lambing. When he first told us he had lost them, I immediately said, no, not Badger, as I have become fond of him with his two black eye patches and little black stripe under his chin, which makes him look like a smiling clown. Luckily it wasn't him, he is growing fast and running with the other lambs, so the two missing lambs weren't ones I felt I knew.

But yesterday I saw another ewe give birth to twins in the morning and by early evening, when Martin and I were strolling in the garden, they had both rested enough to play hide and seek around a tree trunk. Little black Lowryesque lambs playing as dusk fell.

So this morning I couldn't resist going out to look for them. I know they are not my sheep, but they graze, breed and give birth on our land, so I feel responsible for them and get to know them. I looked through the mist and could not see the entire flock clearly, but the ewe which I was sure had lambed on Monday morning was sitting next to the fence and had only one little one by her side. I walked up and down the fence, I looked in the ditch which runs close by, I looked at the back of the wood and I searched the edge of the field. And then I went to tell Neil that I thought another one has gone.

Martin thinks it might be a human thief, not a fox. But Neil is sure the fox is responsible. He has put a paraffin lamp in the field to warn it off. I'm glad the fox is not taking an interest in the chickens, but sad that it has taken a lamb that only lived for a day.

Wednesday, April 2

This power cut has lasted six months now and we are all surviving. At first it seemed disastrous and I know it has been terrible for people in the cities and larger towns, but out here, surrounded by green fields and trees bursting into leaf, it is quite bearable. Now that the winter is over, with all the frosts and floods we endured, we feel sure we can survive.

I have settled into an efficient routine with the laundry, which is so much easier with the warmer weather and the recent acquisition of the old mangle. Our clothes and bed linen smell of fresh air and sunshine instead of damp floors and smoke. The girls are happier too as they can wash their hair outside and let it dry in the warm breeze. Stephen is keeping the barbecue supplied with kindling so we can heat water, which we are still recycling for the downstairs toilet cistern.

Fetching water, feeding the fires and foraging for wild food seems normal after such a long time. I am sure there are people somewhere who have generators or secret supplies of Calor gas, who have managed to devise petrol driven systems or even invented ovens, but I have not heard of anyone in this village who has succeeded in doing so. But despite us managing very well, I am concerned about what lies ahead. We had a very wet winter and the water table must still be high, but we shall struggle for water if we have a hot summer and there is drought. I worry about Anna and hope the birth will be easy and I fret every time Stephen and Martin are felling trees and cutting logs. One slip of the axe and a man could be disabled for life and with no emergency services on call one mistake could cost a life.

But in the meantime, there is supper to cook, water to boil and hens to feed. I've collected four eggs today and shall worry tomorrow about what may happen next.

Thursday, April 3

I woke to mist with the sun just starting to melt through and heard the cockerel's fractured cry. His call is louder when he is boasting out in the run, but muffled when he is shut in the henhouse overnight. I let them all out before breakfast as they are so keen to enjoy the open air and scratch in the earth of the run for worms.

Jane and Anna are busy every day searching for the new leaves of ground elder and bitter cress for us to have as salads and to serve wilted with warm food. Anna is still able to bend down to pick, but soon, as her baby bump grows bigger, she will have to use a hoe and let Jane do all the bending.

I used to throw all these weeds to the hens, but we need them for ourselves now. However, there are plenty of other weeds growing vigorously this spring and as I cannot bear for my herbaceous borders to deteriorate completely, we are gathering dandelions, milk thistle and groundsel for the hens. They would like to come and find food in my flower beds for themselves, but from past experience I know that they would eventually start scratching at the plants they're not allowed to eat and then create great dust baths in amongst my precious plants. Having given over half the garden to vegetables, I am reluctant to lose the last of my flowers.

Several pairs of ducks have been investigating our ponds this week. I am sure one pair has already made a nest in the ivy above Anna and Stephen's bedroom window, as I saw a cluster of speckled feathers below yesterday. But the other ducks seems to be courting and making up their minds about where to settle. Martin suggested getting some for the pot, but the pheasants are easier targets and we shall have one for supper in a casserole with onions and herbs.

The new hens have settled and there were eggs from everyone today. Five in all.

Friday, April 4

Today I took soup along to the village hall in my large preserving pan. We are running low on vegetables this week, so I wasn't sure if I'd be able to produce anything, but then I noticed yesterday that the nettles had started growing, so I picked a stack of young shoots and made a nettle soup. It would be all the better for the addition of butter and cream, but those ingredients have not been available since this wretched power cut started.

There was talk at the village hall of more aid coming to this area soon, but no one had any definite information. One woman said she had seen an army truck on the A3, which is only a couple of miles away, but there has been no sign of the army in the village since the last delivery of supplies of bottled water and flour over two months ago. People were muttering about how they felt abandoned and how shocking it was that no more help has come this way.

But I don't see the point in moaning. No one has starved. No one has died in the village because we don't have electricity. People may have died here because they have been careless with paraffin or because they could not call for help, like the elderly couple in the woods, but the majority of residents are in reasonably good health. I think we must continue to be resourceful, work hard and help each other. Our lives are no longer those of the 21st century, they are like those of our great great grandfathers. We have to think how they survived and lived to tell the tale.

My great grandfather went to work as a shepherd boy on the South Downs, at the age of thirteen, then ran away to sea after two years. I feel that resilience in my blood and feel sure we can endure this crisis. So I came home and weeded the garden and threw a pile of green stuff to the new hens, who are working hard and had laid four eggs. Three brown and one blue.

Saturday, April 5

We all walked to the pub this morning as the weather was dry though cloudy, but I rather wished we hadn't as the place seemed to be full of grumblers today. A group of men had gathered round David Henderson, Chairman of the Parish Council, saying they wanted action. Martin and I stood on the edge of the group to hear what they were saying and it seemed someone had heard that the cities now have generators and some towns have received plenty of aid.

The men were saying our village should send off a

delegation. They thought petrol reserves should be pooled and two parties should drive to London to make a stand and find out what is happening. There are foreign radio reports saying aid is reaching the country, but there is not enough specific information. David Henderson said he could not stop them going if they wanted to do so, but that he felt his role was to stay here with local people and help as best he could on the ground.

This didn't go down too well with the group which started insisting they should requisition petrol from anyone who still has supplies, as they would come back with useful information and maybe rations as well. At that point I pulled Martin away, as I didn't want him saying he'd join them. I saw Gail do the same with Tony and we exchanged a look. I know what she was thinking. After their narrow escape in London she would never want to risk returning until they know for certain that all is safe.

We then collected vegetables and some stewing steak and left. Hopefully the girls didn't hear too much of the unrest. I don't want Anna fretting and I want everyone to feel secure where we are now. It is a shrunken world we have at present, but it is a safe one. Whereas we once thought nothing of daily commutes to London and journeys to the far ends of the country, now I am content to stay in this village, where the highlight of the week is the Saturday market at the pub and my hens lay eggs every day.

Sunday, April 6

Grown men don't cry, but even a hardened old shepherd can look a little misty. Before this wretched power cut, back in the days when there was television, if we were following a reality TV programme in which a male contestant became tearful, Martin and I would both yell "Stop blubbing!".

But now, although his eyes did not fill with tears and his chin didn't quiver, I think I have seen a grown man's heart sink, for today another lamb died. And this time it was not the fox, it was not a sheep rustler, it was just nature.

I saw it first. A white lamb lay beside its black mother, its legs outstretched, so still that I knew straight away that it was lifeless. I went back again after ten minutes and felt sure that it had gone and that I had to tell Neil. He was mending fences with Martin on the furthest field and hadn't noticed. And when he walked across, slowly, so the mother would not be startled, I could see his face fall. He glanced at the little body, then picked it up by its legs. "I hate it when this happens," he said as he looked the lamb over.

I left him then but we talked later and he said the lamb was only born yesterday. A healthy lamb, a good weight, but not able to survive. Luckily most of the ewes and lambs are doing well and only one other ewe has lost a newborn and she was able to adopt a triplet, so she is not bereft. But the dead lamb's mother is still searching and calling for her child and must feel her milk bursting.

Monday, April 7

Anna and Jane went to the school today, hoping to find second-hand baby clothes and maternity wear. Although Anna has been coping well with large sweaters and old shirts, combined with leggings, she says she would like dresses in case the weather gets very warm.

They came back rather disappointed, with only a couple of babygros and some terry nappies. I think they were lucky to get the nappies as that worries me the most. I know terry cloth and muslin are meant to be environmentally friendly, but they are hard work and I was very glad that disposables improved in fit and absorption in my time as a young mother. But now, unless the power and supplies are restored by the summer, there will be no choice and Anna will have to make do with the old-fashioned ways.

However, once they were both home we talked about alternatives and, yet again, I suggested they look through the wardrobes upstairs for old clothes and pieces of fabric which can be cut up or adapted. They soon came down with two Empire line maxi dresses which will do very well for Anna, plus some soft cotton from which they can sew little nightgowns. Whether it's a girl or a boy, the style of garment won't matter for the first couple of months. I've also sorted through my linen cupboard again and found some old towels to cut up for nappies. And I'm sure I have large safety pins somewhere.

The hens seem very happy in their new home. The cockerel is in full cry, but isn't attacking me when I enter and I collected five eggs today.

Tuesday, April 8

Martin has gone and done it again. He must think
this power cut crisis is some schoolboy adventure,
not a case of life or death. He has agreed to go with
other villagers on a recce into London. I am simply
furious with him. I know we are managing fairly
well here, but who knows what might happen once
they reach the city? I can't dissuade him, he says he
has given them his word. He said he tried to
persuade Tony to go as well, but Linda put her foot
down and Tony said he didn't fancy facing the
horrors of London again, after their lucky escape
months ago.

We've had a huge row because of this. I'm afraid
for Martin's safety and also for ours. We need him
here to manage the heavy jobs of fetching water,
cutting logs and bringing them inside. I know
Stephen is very capable, but he has a young pregnant
wife and has to think of her welfare and he mustn't
take risks.

Martin says I'm making an awful fuss and that
he'll only be gone for a day at the most. I'm not going
to talk about it any more. I can't speak to him
without losing my temper. He's upstairs now,
sorting out his 'gear' as he put it. I suppose he means
a torch, his gun and ammunition. I threw some socks
at him and told him to put a sock in it. At least I've
managed to make him promise not to take our car,
although he is donating some of our fuel to the
expedition.

He's leaving in the morning. I shall give him some
of the bottled water that was left in the village and
also some greens and beef wrapped in flatbread, as

there is no way of knowing what food there will be on their journey. And I shall try not to fret about these foolhardy men thinking they are helping us by abandoning their families and setting out into the unknown. I shall concentrate on what needs to be done here to keep us fit and healthy, gathering spring greens, making nettle soup and feeding the hens which laid four eggs today, two brown and two blue.

Wednesday, April 9

Martin left early this morning. He wanted to cycle into the village to meet up with the other men who are going on this ridiculous expedition, but I put my foot down. Not only was he prepared to risk leaving the bike outside the pub, where anyone could have taken it, but we desperately need it here. What if Martin doesn't come back and we run out of petrol for the car and Anna suddenly needs medical attention? He really isn't thinking about the welfare of the whole family, he is just so caught up in the excitement of this stupid venture.

I'm afraid he left with my cross words ringing in his ears. He stormed off because I wouldn't let him take the bike, saying he was glad to be away from me for a while. So I told him we could manage perfectly well without his mad schemes. I hope I don't come to regret my words.

And then I concentrated on making sure all was calm and orderly here. I know the country is in crisis, but by being resourceful and resilient I feel sure we can come through this. It has been a bright sunny day, although there was frost first thing, so the girls helped me heat water outside for washing and we managed to get a good load of laundry on the line by mid-morning. Then Jane and Anna continued picking young nettles and ground elder for soups and salads, while I watered my seedlings.

The cats are very active in the garden as so many birds are flitting about making nests. I found a robin has built its nest in the ivy in the courtyard beside a window, within easy reach of sharp claws. I have protected it with a piece of chicken wire, leaving a gap at the side. The robin flew out when I first approached, but I checked later it had returned to its nest behind the protective barrier and I could just see its defiant beak and beady eye. So all is well here, with the chickens laying four eggs and I hope all is well on the road to London.

Thursday, April 10

Today started well with the birth of twin lambs. At first, when I saw the ewe with one lamb on its feet and noticed the second supine, I was afraid it was another death, but in minutes I realised she had only just given birth and in no time at all both lambs held their heads up high and suckled.

But there is no news of Martin and the other men. We have no way of contacting them in these powerless times, so we can only wait and wonder. Late yesterday I suddenly realised that Bubbles was missing. I had assumed he was following Jane around, as he normally stays close to Martin, but when I asked her where he was she said she hadn't seen him all day. She went outside calling for him but there is still no sign, so now we are wondering if he went with Martin. He is not a guard dog and loves everyone, so he won't be much help.

At least they have good weather for their expedition. Here we have washed and dried sheets and pillowcases, aired blankets and swept floors. We have watered seedlings, hoed beds and gathered greens. I don't like to imagine what will greet the men in London. In the country we have fresh air, green buds and vegetables bursting through the soil. Today we have seen nesting birds, butterflies and a mother duck trailing her ten ducklings towards the big pond for their first swim. In the city there will be vermin, trash and destruction.

The chickens laid five eggs today and enjoyed the groundsel and milk thistles the girls found for them. But I can't stop thinking about a man and his dog.

Friday, April 11

I woke early today, forgetting that Martin had gone. No alarm to wake me, not even the cockerel or a snoring husband, just the sun of a new day. And then I remembered and began to worry again.

So I have tried to keep busy all day. I have no idea how long he will be away or if he will ever come back and I won't let my worries affect the others, especially Anna, who is blooming and healthy and deserves to enjoy this happy time of waiting for her baby. As the day was so fine I began boiling water even before breakfast, so more laundry could be dried in the sun.

By the time Anna and Stephen were down, I had clothes soaking and had fed the chickens and been to look at the lambs. Yesterday's twins were tucked up against their mother's woolly flank and all looked calm across the field. Neil was doing his rounds and came over to say how well the sheep looked on the grass, which is growing fast after the winter floods. Twenty lambs so far, despite some losses and another half dozen ewes still to produce.

He has decided not to keep one of his young rams from last year, so it was slaughtered today and we shall have hogget in a couple of days' time. It would normally be hung for at least four days, but we don't have the luxury of a chiller in these powerless age, so we shall have to eat it sooner. However, with Linda's help we have made black pudding today and shall have some of the liver for supper tonight, which will help all of us, but especially Anna, stay healthy and strong. I doubt if Martin and the other foolhardy men will be eating so heartily tonight.

Our new chickens continue to lay well, with four eggs today.

Saturday, April 12
I didn't go to the pub for the market today. I sent Stephen along with Anna and Jane, as I couldn't face the gossip and the morbid speculation about what may have happened to the reconnaissance party. My own imagination is hard enough to control, without other people putting on a show of concern and thinking the worst.

So I sent them off with some black pudding to barter and told them to come back with vegetables, particularly potatoes, as that is what we are most in need of. They did well and returned cheerful and said they hadn't stayed to chat to the old fogies.

And I stayed here, to hoe the borders and the veg patch. Then I made a pot roast with a piece of the hogget Neil prepared yesterday. I've cooked it slowly over the fire with some onions, swede and turnip which were brought back from the pub market. For flavour I've added thyme and rosemary from the garden and some wild garlic, which is growing in the shade by the pond near the hens. The garlic has been spreading so I've also lifted some seedlings and potted them up in the hope of having a good bed of garlic in future.

Neil and Linda will join us tonight and I've invited Tony and Gail as well. They are bound to ask about Martin's absence, but they are all good friends so I know they will be supportive. And now I've just remembered that there is an old jar of red currant jelly in the pantry which I can stir in with the pot roast juices before serving. If Martin returns in time there may be some supper for him too.

The hens were eager for the weeds hoed from the beds and laid five eggs today.

Sunday, April 13

I went to church today with Gail and Linda and we enjoyed singing 'All Glory Laud and Honour' loudly at the top of our voices, as it is Palm Sunday. It helped me to forget about Martin and what he might be doing, as we walked in procession around the church. There were no palm crosses distributed this year, but some people had come with ones they'd kept from previous years.

As we walked home, I felt reassured by the good people around me. If Martin doesn't return soon, I still have the support of friends and family and will feel able to put my energy into helping the younger ones learn how to manage the house and garden.

This afternoon I worked in the garden, pulling weeds in the courtyard for the hens and was feeling quite cheerful until I noticed crows hovering around the duck pond. I'd counted twelve ducklings there yesterday afternoon, but when I went across to check, there were only seven. Every year the delight of seeing ducklings is tainted by the knowledge that their numbers will decrease hour by hour, as these predatory crows and magpies pick off the fluffy babies. Jane says she doesn't even want to know there are ducklings as she finds the slaughter so upsetting. And I get annoyed with the mother ducks who are so careless after all their laying and nesting, leading their young directly across the lawns in full view of the marauding birds.

I checked on the ducklings again when I went to feed the hens at five. The mother was sitting on the bank with some of her brood tucked under her wings, but one solitary duckling was swimming frantically round and round in the pond, unable to climb the bank to safety and warmth.

Monday, April 14

Jane is missing Bubbles. She has grown quite attached to him since he came to live with us. But I am trying not to admit to missing Martin, since I am still cross at him for being so inconsiderate, going off on this silly escapade without a thought for me and his family.

Today there has been a chilly breeze but the day

has given us warm sun for washing and airing clothes. We sat outside with our lunchtime soup to feel the heat of the sun then spent the afternoon gathering kindling as we still need fires for cooking and to keep the house warm at night. Stephen is working twice as hard in Martin's absence and now realises just how much his father normally does in a day.

Anna decided today that she needs to rest in the afternoon. I think she must be near the start of her third trimester as she is due in early July. Without the usual antenatal classes and checks, it is hard to be absolutely sure of dates and the welfare of mother and baby, but Anna certainly looks as if she is glowing with health and we can only hope that her baby is too. I worry about vitamins and iron, but we are gathering all the greens that we can and she has eaten lambs liver and black pudding recently, so she should be getting a good balance of nutrients.

Tonight we are having a hotpot of hogget with wilted ground elder. The mint has been growing vigorously for about a week now, so we can have some on that on the side too. Martin will be sorry to miss the first fresh mint sauce of the year and I wonder what he is eating in London, if anything.

The hens laid well again today, producing four eggs, but the duck has lost more of her brood and is down to five ducklings.

Tuesday, April 15

I woke several times last night, thinking I could hear thumps and bumps in the house, so I was very tired this morning. Maybe it's because Martin is still absent and I'm worrying. This old house does ease its joints with creaks and groans at night, though less so now as we can't run the central heating without electricity.

Then when I came downstairs I realised the noises had probably been made by the cats, which had disrupted my study, rucking up the rug and knocking over a pile of books, in their night time mouse hunt. The guts were on the carpet, but no tails or heads this time.

With this mystery solved, I should have felt calmer, but I didn't. There is no way Martin can contact us, nor can we reach him. With mobile phones, computers and telephone lines out of action we have no way of knowing if he is safe and he cannot check on our welfare either. But I can't help thinking he won't be concerned about us. He will assume that I will manage, as always.

Jane came down for breakfast of eggs and black pudding and said she was worried. But she asked more questions about the dog's welfare than her father's. She really has become very fond of Bubbles in the short time he has been part of our household.

But we have tried to be positive today. I found some embroidery silks and showed Anna how to do smocking on the little nightgowns she is making. She chose yellow, pale blue and white and the stitches remind me of the forget-me-nots which have just come into flower in the garden. Jane is unpicking an old cream sweater for its wool and wants to make a little blanket for the Moses basket.

I collected five eggs today, but didn't see any ducklings. That may or may not be a good sign. She has either lost the lot or has taken them to a safer place.

Wednesday, April 16

Today I noticed that the thermal socks I have been wearing ever since the power cut started, have finally begun to wear through. I have five pairs of thick knee-length socks with I have washed and worn in turn for more than six months during the cold, wet winter and all are developing holes, which I shall have to darn as there is no hope of buying more pairs.

I haven't had to darn a sock for years. In fact I don't think I've ever darned a sock. I don't even have the right yarn or a darning egg to help me do the job properly, so I've had to use a china egg that's meant to fool broody hens and unpicked an old sweater. My socks are light and dark grey and the sweater is red, so I have conspicuous patches on my feet.

And when I looked at them, my worn socks, on my purple, chilblain blistered feet, which wear wellington boots half the day, I felt unkempt, dejected and ugly. Then I thought, maybe this is why Martin hasn't come back. Why would he want to come back to a woman with unwashed hair, rough hands and drab clothes? Perhaps London is filled with scented women who bathe regularly and have clean dresses to wear.

I nearly cried then, all because of my socks. But tears won't do the washing, nor the cooking, so I sniffed a lot and went outside in the garden for a while. There was an early frost but the sun shone in a clear blue sky all day and a second duck visited the front pond with thirteen ducklings, all much larger than the ones I saw a couple of days ago, so they stand a good chance of surviving. Then I collected five eggs from the hens and felt that all will be well and we shall all survive too.

Thursday, April 17

Another difficult day, despite the sunshine and warmer weather. I am really beginning to think that Martin won't come back. Stephen cycled into the village to see if there was any news of the other men who had made up the expedition and came back saying none of them have yet returned.

My anger at his departure has now changed to deep anxiety. How and when will we know what has happened? If the power doesn't return, we may never know. Will we mourn or will we keep hoping? I'm praying for the safety of them all, praying that the most that can have happened is the loss of their vehicles or a shortage of petrol.

But I daren't speculate about the worst scenario. I won't think about disaster movies, post-apocalyptic films and programmes about the depravity that can engulf men. I started reading *The Road* once and had to stop half-way through. I can't stop hoping.

So today I've taken advantage of the weather again and washed all the bedclothes and aired the blankets, fusty from the winter of smoke and damp. I've thrown weeds to the hens, which had laid four eggs and watered the seedlings. I've scrubbed the tiles on the kitchen floor and left the doors and windows open so it dried quickly. Jane picked greens for our dinner and Anna embroidered her baby's clothes.

And I felt calmer and more hopeful and all seemed well until Neil told me someone had obviously tried to force the field gate open last night. The field is full of lambs and ewes, with some yet to lamb. He is going to keep watch.

Friday, April 18

I slept well last night, despite Neil's concerns over the field and when I woke I felt full of optimism that Martin will soon be back, full of stories about his adventures. So I was humming while I boiled water first thing and scrambled eggs to eat with flatbread made with almost the last of our acorn flour. Then Neil knocked on the door and I could see straight away that his face was grim. They didn't get them, he said. The lambs run like whippets, but one of the ewes miscarried because they used a dog. I told him to sit down and have some breakfast, but he wouldn't. He said he had to get back out and count the lambs again, just to be sure.

So when Stephen and the girls came down, I wasn't quite as cheerful as I'd hoped I would be. Then Jane said she'd been looking at her college diary and realised that it was Easter and I felt even worse, as today is Good Friday and I would have liked to go to church. At that point I went out in the garden for quiet reflection. I'll go to church on Sunday, which will make me feel better. This is so different to the kind of Easter we used to have. There would be a turkey some years and sugar coated speckled eggs in chocolate nests, Easter egg hunts when the children were small and one year a little grey rabbit joined our menagerie of pets. I have made no preparations at all this year and have no chance of making any either.

Then I made myself weed the beds and tried to cheer myself up by noting the changes in the flower beds. But at that point I saw a strange disturbance in the bed where the tree peony grows. At first I thought it was a molehill, left over from when the moles had wrecked my borders several weeks ago. There were tufts of black fluff and I wondered if a cat had found a mole and eaten it. But when I touched it, the black was woolly, not the velvet of a mole's coat. And one tuft was hard with horn. It was the tiniest lamb's hoof and I realised with horror that this was where a fox had devoured a newborn lamb. I don't believe in omens, but this has really disturbed me. I am trying to concentrate on the good things about today, the five eggs from the hens, the fine weather, Anna's health, but it is very hard.

Saturday, April 19

I so wish I had not gone into the village today. Last week I avoided the gossip-mongers at the pub, but today I thought I could cope and I felt I needed to escape the confines of this house and garden. So I walked with Stephen, Jane and Anna along the lane in the warm sunshine, with the new green leaves of the trees overhead, the white blossom of the blackthorn on the roadside and birds singing and flitting overhead. But as soon as we got there I regretted my decision. David Henderson immediately came up to me and asked if I'd had any news. I shook my head and then he said that half the party had returned, in one of the cars, having had a terrible time. I was so shocked and felt even worse when Rob Harvey, who used to sit on the Parish Council, came sidling up and said he knew it had been a foolish idea to go off to London.

Eventually I asked what had happened and David shook his head and said the men still wouldn't talk about it, but they were dirty and bruised when they returned. Then Rob said there were gangs everywhere and the men were lucky to get back in one piece. I couldn't take any more after this and made my excuses. I told Stephen to look after the girls then started walking home on my own. I can cope as long as I can have hope, but when I only hear bad news I begin to despair.

So I came back and found Neil had brought us some cuts after culling the ewe which miscarried yesterday, so we can have a mutton stew tonight, which is simmering now with rosemary. I calmed down once I was home and fed the hens some rendered mutton fat along with greens in return for five eggs. Then I made another mistake. I decided to inspect the garden and went to have a close look at the ferns I grow in a corner of the courtyard. There is maidenhair and dryopteris and also two Japanese painted ferns, their pale fronds outlined in dark purple. Then, to my horror, I saw the most revolting sight in the corner by the old wall, where a hart's tongue fern grows in deep shade. A snake had a toad in its jaws, its fangs piercing the head and drawing blood. Why am I finding death all around me every day?

Sunday, April 20

'Jesus Christ is Risen Today' – we sang heartily in church and finished with 'Thine Be the Glory'. I insisted everyone came with me as it is Easter Day and a time to celebrate. The church was in darkness as it is all the time now, but candles were lit after the first prayer and everyone lit a small but precious candle which we were allowed to take home.

As we walked back, we remembered previous Easters with chocolate eggs and simnel cake. And although we are missing the usual treats, we recalled the Easter egg hunts and the surfeit of sweet things with pleasure and laughed as we walked.

So we arrived home in a good mood, even though it started raining heavily. I had planned to cook over the barbecue but had to rethink our meal and managed to make a mutton stew which was close to being a tagine with its spices and a few raisins. And when we sat down, Jane produced painted eggs in egg cups to decorate the table. She had blown an egg for each of us and decorated the shells with intricate patterns, so we all had an Easter egg of sorts. The broken egg can be scrambled for breakfast, so there is no waste.

It was a cheerful meal and I managed to feel hopeful. My husband may be missing, but Jesus Christ is Risen and my family are here. But the hens didn't like the heavy rain and only gave us two eggs today.

Monday, April 21

He's back. Martin came back in the middle of the night. I woke in the early hours of the morning, thinking at first that I was dreaming, then I realised someone was knocking and calling my name. I opened the bedroom window and looked down and there was Martin, standing by the front door. I rushed downstairs and unbolted the door. You took your time, he grumbled.

I don't know where he's been or how he got back. All I do know is that he was hungry and wolfed down the eggs and black pudding I quickly cooked for him last night on the fire. He mumbled about being too tired to talk. He was filthy but washed himself before falling into bed. I couldn't go back to sleep. I just lay there wondering what had happened to him and the others and whether we would ever hear the full story.

And now he's still fast asleep and we still don't know any more. The girls and Stephen know he's back, but they are more worried about the dog. There is no sign of Bubbles and we had assumed he had gone with Martin on this foolish escapade. Jane keeps asking if her father is alright and I've reassured her that he's fine, just tired and hungry. But to be honest, I don't know if he is alright and I have no idea whether he or any of the other men achieved anything as a result of their enterprise.

But I cannot spend the day fretting while Martin sleeps off his exhaustion. There is gardening to do, hens to feed and meals to cook. The weather is cold but dry, so Stephen has lit the barbecue and we are cooking mutton kebabs with onions. I'm worried that the meat might not be tender enough to cook this way, but we long for different flavours, so I've marinated it in oil from an old jar of sun-dried tomatoes lurking at the back of the larder, rosemary and a sprinkling of that fragrant Moroccan spice ras-el-hanout. Potatoes are baking in the fire indoors and we have a salad of bitter cress, ground elder and dandelion gathered from the gardens. When Martin wakes and smells the food perhaps he will feel able to give us a full account of his adventure.

Tuesday, April 22

I'm rather worried about Martin. Not only did he sleep all yesterday, only getting up to eat early in the evening, but he then went straight back to bed and slept late this morning too. And on top of that, he's hardly said a word about where he's been and what he's been doing. It's not like him at all. He always likes to talk about himself.

So I'm beginning to wonder if he might have experienced some terrible trauma. He doesn't appear to have any injuries as far as I can see. He was dirty, tired and hungry, but other than that there is little to show for this risky eleven day escapade.

Stephen is as mystified as I am. He said that his dad always likes to show off about his exploits. It's not like him to be so quiet. The girls aren't so concerned, they are just glad he's back home and I'm no longer worried about his safety. Jane is more bothered about the absence of Bubbles and keeps saying she can't believe her father lost him.

When he finally emerged this morning, Martin gulped his nettle tea, ate some scrambled eggs and then went off to the fields without a further word. I think I'm just going to leave him alone until he is ready to talk. If he is suffering from post-traumatic stress, he will need time to recover but talking will help him to come to terms with his experience in the end.

In the meantime, Stephen and Jane worked hard today bringing in more dry kindling and logs. There was heavy rain all last night and the weather still looks unsettled. If we are in for a protracted spell of cold and rain we shall need plenty of wood for the fires. I'm glad of the rain for the vegetable beds, but hope it doesn't pour day after day and stops me staying on top of the washing.

The rain benefited the hens too, bringing up more worms to boost their protein intake. They laid five eggs today, three brown and two blue.

Wednesday, April 23

Martin has been keeping out of my way. Last night he wolfed his supper then went straight to bed. This morning he was up before me. He made himself some breakfast then went outside and by the time I was ready to go out and feed the hens he had already gone off into the village on the bike.

He came back at lunchtime and came inside for some soup and when I said we really would all like to know what happened during his time away, he just grunted and said there was really nothing to tell. We just drove around, he said. And where's the dog, I asked. He shrugged and went outside again.

I was so exasperated I vented my frustration on Stephen and the girls when they came into the dining room for lunch. Jane said she didn't understand because she thought her dad really loved Bubbles. Then Stephen said it wasn't fair to keep us in suspense and he would try talking to his father. He went off to find Martin and came back after only twenty minutes saying he couldn't get anything out of him. He sat down for a while, deep in thought and then said he'd had an idea. He didn't tell us what it was, but he cycled off to the village moments later and was gone for a couple of hours.

It's all very well having these angst ridden men mooching about, but I could really do with them pulling their weight and bringing in the fire wood. The sooner they stop being so introspective the better. If Martin doesn't get his act together soon I'll just have to give him a piece of my mind. We've got to cook, heat water and stay warm. Even though the days are milder it is always cold in the house and the nights are quite chilly.

At least some men are still sane. Tony popped round to say their rhubarb was growing faster than they could eat it and brought us some early pink stems. It will be quite sharp without sugar, so I think I'll use it on the side with meats. It goes rather well with duck. And Neil called in with sad news about the twin lambs born yesterday. The white one was taken overnight but there is still a black ewe lamb for the mother to suckle. And the cockerel is looking after his wives who have laid four eggs.

Thursday, April 24

So now we know. The truth is out. Martin and most of his fellow travellers didn't even make it into the centre of London. They were held on the outskirts, questioned for a time, then told to go back home. No wonder he didn't want to tell us. He must have felt a total fool, worrying us all over nothing.

Stephen came back from the village with a smile on his face. He'd had the bright idea of finding David Henderson, the Parish Council chairman, and telling him we really needed answers because I was so concerned that Martin and the others might have post-traumatic stress syndrome. Apparently David laughed when Stephen said that, but he was sympathetic and took him to see Simon Carter, a tree surgeon who was one of the other intrepid adventurers. And he told Stephen the full story.

Simon said that when the two vehicles reached the London end of the A3, on the roundabout just before it meets Putney, Martin's car had to stop because the dog had been sick. They all got out and Martin took Bubbles out onto the grass on the edge of the common. Simon's car was slightly ahead and they were waiting for the others when suddenly they saw an army patrol with guns apprehend Martin's group. Simon said they would have waited, but the guns made them nervous so they drove off, down Putney High Street, over the bridge and on into London, where they were finally halted by an army blockade outside the Tate on the Embankment. They were taken into the bowels of the gallery for questioning and released after a week.

He said they were all well treated and fed basic rations. They learnt that the army was concentrating on restoring order to the cities and conurbations, with the help of overseas aid and imported generators. Tankers are bringing in fresh water and the army has pulled in volunteers wherever they can to clear debris and bodies. Simon said London looked messy, but not much worse than it has during dustmen's strikes in the past. I told Stephen to invite

Simon over tomorrow. I can't wait to see Martin's face.

Friday, April 25

I don't think Martin thought it was very funny, but I did and so did Stephen. Simon came round mid-morning and I didn't tell Martin he was coming, I just called him in and said there was someone to see him. Martin's face fell when he saw Simon, who laughed and said he'd been wondering how Martin had got on since they'd last seen him at the top of Putney Hill.

Then Jane came in to listen to the story and asked what had happened to Bubbles after they'd got out of the car. It turns out he has a new career. He is now a squadron mascot. Jane looked very cross, but Martin said they fell in love with him. All these young homesick soldiers adored Bubbles and he loved these big tough men right back, so Martin said he could stay. They aren't going to call him Bubbles though, that's far too twee for army chaps. They've settled on Bombardier, Bomber for short.

But what I wanted to know, I said, is what did you do all that time? And where were you? Martin said his group were kept in what used to be Putney High School, just down the hill. The school is closed because of the power cut and the army has commandeered the building for the time being.

So you spent over a week in a girls' school, I laughed at Martin, and everyone else did too, particularly Simon and Stephen. Did they give you homework, I asked. Martin said, oh you think you're so funny. You try standing up to an army squadron who are demanding to see ID and pointing their guns at you. I had to agree that probably wasn't very pleasant and then Martin said if we'd all had our fun he'd like to get on with chopping some more wood, as someone had to keep the fires burning. Then he turned his back on us and stomped out.

Simon told me Martin's group were quite lucky as his crowd met some trouble on the way back when they stopped to change a tyre and that was why they were all bruised and dirty when they returned. But otherwise both groups had survived unscathed. But you all went off to demand help for the village, I said. I know, he said, but when you see what the city is having to cope with, you realise how lucky we are out here. We're all healthy and well fed, aren't we?

That's very true. We are and we'll continue to be if we can all work together and look after each other and not indulge in silly boys' own adventures. But I still laughed to myself when I went about my chores.

Saturday, April 26

We've had more than our fair share of April showers. We'd all hoped that the rainy season had finished for good in March, but the last couple of days of rain have swelled the river and the nearest field is flooded again, with water spilling over into the grazing containing most of the ewes and lambs.

I noticed the silver water glinting in the first glimmer of sunlight today when I looked out of the hall windows. I knew Neil would be on top of the situation, but I couldn't resist going to check whether he was thinking of moving the flock into the next field. He said he thinks the water has peaked and they will be safe, but it worries me to see the smallest lambs venturing near the bursting ditches.

However, there is a plus side to the flooded field. It attracts Canadian geese, ducks and the occasional swan. And Martin is in my good books again as he managed to bag a goose today. It's hanging in the garage and we'll have it tomorrow. We've had a lot of mutton lately, so it will make a great change. Some of that sharp rhubarb will be good on the side and I'll be sure to save the fat for roasting potatoes in a pan on the fire. We've agreed not to talk about the London episode, as I call it, any more. Jane is disappointed that Bubbles didn't come back with her father, but she too is amused that a dog that was once lost now has a whole squadron of devoted owners and is the bearer of three names. He never did answer to his old names, she said, he just runs up to whoever looks friendly, and pants. Names mean nothing to him.

Sunday, April 27

I knew I was right to worry about the water. This morning I saw a very small black lamb on a spit of grass while its careless mother was on the other side of a full ditch. I couldn't see Neil anywhere nearby and I was ready to leap the fence and jump to the rescue, when the ewe moved away and the lamb scrambled through the deep water, wet up to its chin, to reach her. And she didn't care, but just kept slowly moving across the grass to find another mouthful while her baby bleated pitifully and tried to shake itself dry.

I told Neil later what I had seen, but he just

laughed and said tough little chaps, aren't they. I know he is right and that they can survive almost anything, bar foxes, but I do feel anxious when I see them coping with these difficult conditions.

And the bad weather has put a stop to our regular outdoor laundry. I've decided not to try to wash much other than underwear and socks until we have a dry spell. We've caught up with sheets and large items recently, so we can have a washing day once we get a good sunny breezy day. It's such hard work trying to wash and wring out in the rain, then dry indoors. And I much prefer the fresh scent of sunshine on my clothes and sheets to the smell of damp smoking firewood.

The hens aren't happy about the weather either. They gave me one egg yesterday and only two today. There's not much I can do about it, other than hope the sun shines at length soon.

Still, the goose is cooking over the fire as I write and the fat is dripping into a pan as it cooks. It's making the fire smoke, but we are all looking forward to some succulent meat.

Monday, April 28

I don't think I dare tell Neil what I did today. I'm not even sure I should tell Martin, he's such a terrible one for tittle tattle he'd be sure to tell Neil or Tony at some point. But I told Jane, who then told Anna and Stephen and they all said I should have kept it. They wanted to raise the baby fox as a pet and name it Ferdy.

I have such mixed feelings about the foxes now. I used to think they were nature's dustmen, clearing away the bodies of dead deer and other animals. Then I was annoyed and somewhat distressed when they killed all the hens and left the dead and dying littering the hen run. And lately I have come to see it from Neil's point of view, when a newborn lamb is taken so soon, when it has just found the springs in its legs. So Neil won't be pleased to know that I have rescued a fox cub from drowning.

It happened this morning, soon after I'd fed the hens. I was walking round the garden to see how wet it all was after yesterday's downpour. I had to empty some pots in the courtyard of their pools of surplus water and then I walked across the lawn to admire the new silver leaves of the whitebeam, when I noticed a strange screeching cry. I thought at first it was an angry squirrel quarrelling with one of the cats, or maybe a young magpie calling hungrily for its parent. But it was an odd noise so I crossed the ditch towards the wood where so much had fallen in the winter. And I was just about to turn back when I saw it. A little bundle of dark fur crawling on the edge of another ditch. I went over to look and realised it was a very small cub, still with its charcoal baby coat, crying crossly for its mother.

I thought I should leave it for its parent to rescue, but then I thought how close it was to deep water, how near it was to drowning. It was much, much smaller than the little lamb that sprang out of a watery ditch the other day and I was so afraid that it would drown before its mother returned that I had to pick it up. As I held it in my hands I thought it looked more like a very small bear cub than a fox. Its front paws were square and spade-like, its nose was snub and not yet elongated and its fur was soft and dusky, with not yet a hint of red. I couldn't put it back down on the grass with swollen ditches close by, so I carried it into the wood where I knew a fox had dug its earth in previous years. Sure enough, there were signs that the burrow was back in use, so I placed the cub by the entrance and watched as it sniffed, then waddled down the slope and into its home. I hope its mother will return soon and that it will survive, though I'm not sure Neil would agree with me.

And when I went back out late this afternoon to feed the hens, who delivered five eggs today, I couldn't resist creeping across to the wood again. But all was quiet and there was no sign of the little fox or its parent.

Tuesday, April 29

Such good news today! Stephen had cycled to the chemist to pick up iron tablets for Anna and came back to tell us supplies have reached the village. I doubt if it has anything to do with the efforts made by Martin and his fellow adventurers the other week, but it is quite a coincidence that one minute we are being ignored and the next we have rations delivered by the army. So maybe they did achieve something after all.

There is flour, rice, sugar, tea, cooking oil and salt being distributed at the church. The stocks are being guarded and handed out by members of the Parish Council, to ensure there is enough for every local household. As soon as Stephen told us, we decided to go straight over there with the car. We could have walked with the wheelbarrow, but the weather is

unreliable today and we would not have wanted
these precious supplies spoiling in the rain.

And when we got there, amidst the excitement of
actually having tea again, we found there was also
powdered milk, coffee, soap and toilet paper! These
feel like the greatest luxuries after so long without.
So as soon as we were home with our supplies we
made a pot of tea and I set about making drop
scones. We still have jam as I made so much at the
end of the summer, so we could actually have
afternoon tea and feel almost civilised. And the soap
is very welcome as we are almost at the end of our
supply of tablets given to me in previous
Christmases and the bars in the cloakroom and
bathroom both have blackened cracks, but I was
determined to use them down to the last sliver.

Martin said he'd never known a cup of tea to taste
so good, so we treated ourselves to another pot
immediately and can now look forward to real tea
first thing in the morning. If they had been able to
deliver fresh bread as well, that would make our
breakfasts complete. But we shall content ourselves
with fried egg, black pudding, drop scones and a
good strong cup of tea.

Wednesday, April 30

Last night I made a pilaff with the last of the goose
and some of the rice from the newly arrived supplies.
It certainly isn't a classic dish and it may not be one
I'll make again, but it was wonderful to have
different textures and flavours after all these months
of unvaried, albeit still nutritious, meals.

We all talked about foods we are missing again

and, as always, fresh crusty bread was top of the list. Second was cheese. Not special continental cheeses, but plain old English Cheddar which we could have on toast, or eat in a sandwich or sprinkle on top of a baked potato. But we are grateful for the supplies that have been delivered and talked about how to make the most of them.

Jane pleaded for pasta, which she can easily make now we have flour. So we plan to have a carbonara tonight as we don't have tomatoes, butter or cheese, but we do have eggs and bacon. Anna says she craves cucumbers and avocados, which we can't possibly obtain, but she says she will enjoy the pasta too. Stephen longs for burgers, which we can manage to make if we bring back mince from the pub barter market on Saturday. Martin says he misses cauliflower cheese, which we also can't make, but I said that when we can find a cauliflower we could serve it with a white sauce, now that we have powdered milk and flour, so he was fairly happy with that.

And I miss sweet things. I know I shouldn't but I've always had a sweet tooth and liked having a biscuit or a cake with my morning coffee and afternoon tea. I'm struggling to think what I can make apart from drop scones and soda bread and then I suddenly remembered that I still have dried yeast in the pantry and so I am going to make little doughnuts. I will try to make some filled with jam, but even plain ones, sweetened and rolled in sugar after they are fried will be a sweet treat. If they are disastrous the hens will gobble them up and maybe lay more eggs. They gave us four today.

Thursday, May 1

My doughnuts were a triumph! I managed to make them in time for tea late yesterday afternoon and dusted them with sugar. The jam leaked out of one or two and made a bit of a mess of the oil, but if I strain it I can still use it. Everyone had one of the little cakes and we all agreed that they were the best things we'd ever tasted.

Then Stephen pointed out that now we had oil we could make chips and everyone started rhapsodizing about how wonderful that would be and asking when we could have them. I don't really care for chips but I said if Stephen was so keen he could make them, as long as he was prepared to peel and cut the potatoes. He's going to make them for supper tonight and we'll have them with fried eggs if the hens have laid enough for us.

There is a cold wind despite the sun today and so warm food is still very important for us, particularly as we are all working hard at various chores every day. Jane helped me with a wash outside as we wanted to take advantage of the sun and the breeze. Anna is getting tired easily now as she only has two months or so to go, but she still helped to turn the mangle and peg washing on the line. Stephen was out chopping wood and Martin hoed the vegetable beds. The hens were hard at work too, scratching in their run, having cleansing dust baths in a dry corner and laying five eggs, so we have enough for supper tonight.

Friday, May 2

I now wish I'd never made the doughnuts. I should

never have let Stephen try deep frying. It was disastrous and he is going to take a long time to recover.

I feel it was all my fault. I didn't emphasise enough how important it is to keep the pan steady on the trivet. But of course he hasn't been cooking regularly on the open fire, like I have for the past seven months since the power cut began. He knows how to cook on a modern oven and knows not to leave a chip pan unattended, but he hadn't thought about what could happen with the fire. I suppose we are lucky the fire wasn't worse. But I am very worried about his foot.

And we were all so excited and feeling so jolly about the simple prospect of having egg and chips for supper. Such an innocent request that ended so terribly.

He had peeled the potatoes and chipped them, then he waited for the oil to get hot enough and I reminded him to test the heat with a sliver of a chip. I'd normally use a cube of bread, but we don't have any, so he dropped a test chip in the pan, then poked it with a knife and then, before he could say whether it was ready or not, he'd spilt the pan over the fire and over himself.

The screams, the shouting and the swearing were terrible. Flames leapt up the chimney and rapidly licked across the oil spilt over the brick floor towards the table and the logs stacked either side of the inglenook. Jane and Anna jumped out of the way and Jane said she was running outside for water, while I was shouting that we couldn't throw water on an oil fire and Martin was grabbing my decent Turkish rug to throw over the flames flickering across the floor.

Stephen was hopping around repeatedly shouting 'bugger' at the top of his voice and once we'd killed the fire and prevented it spreading further, my main concern was for him. Luckily he was wearing thick socks and heavy boots, so the upper part of his foot and ankle bore the brunt of the hot oil. We plunged his foot in cold water and he tried to sleep with it draped in wet muslin all night. But he is still in dreadful pain and Martin has now driven him to see the doctor.

And all for the sake of a plate of chips. We never managed to eat last night and now the hens have laid more eggs we have plenty to spare. But we shan't try cooking chips again.

Saturday, May 3

Stephen is still in terrible pain. The doctor couldn't do much for him, other than a small amount of morphine and the promise of antibiotics if he can get hold of them. He has to rest as much as possible and try not to put any weight on his foot.

He doesn't want to stay in bed, so he has spent most of the day sitting in an armchair in the dining room where we cook and eat. His foot is resting on a low cushioned stool and he keeps complaining his leg is getting stiff and how much it hurts.

I'm trying to distract him and have persuaded him to roll up the wool Anna has unravelled from old jumpers to make some clothes and a blanket for the baby. So far he has managed to make only a couple of balls before moaning that he is bored. Jane is threatening to teach him to knit and Anna keeps checking on him and asking whether he'd like a drink or any food. I think he is just so annoyed with himself about the accident. I've been blaming myself, but he is an adult and he should have been more careful.

I didn't feel like going to the pub today because of Stephen's accident, but Martin went with Jane as we needed potatoes, carrots and minced beef. I thought I could at least make Stephen his favourite beef burgers, even though we don't have rolls or chips to go with them. I thought I could bind the meat with some of the coarse acorn flour and egg, and add chopped onion.

Martin said there was lots of advice in the pub about the best way to treat burns. I know they mean well, but really the suggestions that came back are more likely to make things worse in my opinion. One remedy involved minced onion, which I think would aggravate the wound and cause tremendous pain. Another involved a poultice of oatmeal, which is probably quite soothing, but if anyone round here has any oatmeal left after the difficult winter we've had I'd be very surprised. I think the best course of action is keeping the burn, which in total is about the size of my hand, really clean. It has blistered and I know we mustn't burst the blisters. The doctor applied a sterile dressing and said this should be changed every couple of days until the area has healed. The doctor called it a minor burn and Stephen said he might think it's minor, but it feels pretty major. He says he won't try cooking again. We had plenty of eggs as we didn't eat many the other day and the hens laid four more today. So I gave Stephen a fried egg with his burger.

Sunday, May 4

We didn't go to church today. I would have liked to go, but I felt I was needed here. With Stephen out of action and Anna's energy needed by the baby, we all have to work harder. Martin is on firewood duty full time, Jane is fetching clean water for cooking and washing, then recycling dirty water for the toilet and I'm stoking the fire for cooking and doing numerous jobs.

Stephen keeps saying he wants to help, but if his foot and ankle are to heal quickly, he must rest. I suspect the blisters have already burst and his dressing must be changed later on today. He will find that immensely painful, I know, but it must be done if we are to keep infection at bay.

So my prayers will be private ones for today and I took advantage of the bright breezy weather to wash clothes and hang them out to dry. Anna turned the mangle for a short while but I won't let her do very much work. We don't want another casualty in the household. But she was able to water the seedlings and feed the hens without finding that too tiring.

Being laid up is very boring during this power cut. There is no TV for distraction and no daily papers. Stephen is not a great reader, so I let him have the radio for a bit. We have to conserve the batteries so we can listen to news bulletins from time to time, but he found a music station and that took his mind off the pain for a while. Anna persuaded him to come outside and sit in the sun, then they both sat together discussing names for the baby and the cats decided that a pair of idle laps were just what they needed.

Then hens have enjoyed the sun too as their run is completely dry and they have had the best dust baths they have had for a long time. As a result they felt happy enough to give us five eggs today.

Monday, May 5

The optimism of youth brought a much needed spark of joy into our lives today. Jane suddenly announced at breakfast this morning that it was a bank holiday and therefore we should all have a day off from our chores. Stephen joined in from his armchair, where he'd been eating scrambled egg, and agreed with her and said, yes, we usually go to the seaside on a bank holiday.

Martin disagreed at first, saying he never wanted to go anywhere on a bank holiday, because of the crowds, but he wouldn't mind having a break from work today. Then Anna and Jane said we should leave it to them and we all had to be ready to leave at 12 o'clock. I said that would give me time to get ready, so I immediately swept up, rinsed out some washing, hung it out, then stoked up the fires. Martin brought in more dry wood and stacked some freshly cut logs outside. We can never afford to be behind with our firewood.

By 12 we were all ready, the sun was shining and the day was warming up. Stephen was lying on a blanket with cushions in the trailer that is pulled by the garden tractor, when we have petrol. Jane carried a picnic basket and Anna had prepared hats for all of us. She gave Stephen and Martin white knotted handkerchiefs and the girls and I wore straw sunhats decorated with daisies. Alongside Stephen were long forgotten buckets and spades she had found in the shed. Then we set off, pulling the trailer around the garden, till we reached the bench by the big pond, where the girls had spread blankets and cushions so we could recline and have our food.

Jane and Anna had made a feast. We had hard boiled eggs and they had found an old bottle of salad cream as well. They lit a little old barbecue and we had black pudding sausage with fried onions in flatbread, as that was the nearest they could get to hot dogs. We had tea made with water boiled outdoors, served in old tin mugs and we talked about rides on piers, sand in sandwiches and melting ice creams. I nearly mentioned chips with vinegar, but that's a sore subject at present, so I kept quiet. But when the girls said how they longed for a cornet I suddenly knew what I could do. I told everyone to stay where they were and wait for me. Then I ran indoors, glad I had stoked the fire before leaving, and quickly caramelised sugar in a pan and came back with toffee apples.

We crunched on our apples with our feet splashing in the pond and were so happy, laughing about our own bank holiday.

Tuesday, May 6

Our neighbours called in today and asked why we hadn't gone to the village May Day celebrations yesterday. I hadn't realised there was anything special happening, as I've been so wrapped up with Martin's adventures and Stephen's accident. Tony said there was maypole dancing and a May queen, both organised by the school.

I'm glad that local people had a good time, but I'm not sorry we didn't go. We all had such a lot of fun with our own bank holiday outing. I told Tony and Gail what we'd done and they agreed it had been a good idea. They said some of the locals had got very drunk on some kind of homebrew of their own devising and there were a couple of unpleasant scenes on the green yesterday evening, luckily after the younger children had been taken home.

Tony said it was the tug of war which really got the lads going. There was a lot of rivalry between the men from the cricket club and the British Legion, with accusations of cheating. Martin said he wished he'd been there to see it all kick off and Tony said it was quite exciting, as they slithered on the grass and took swings at each other. But I could see from Gail's raised eyebrows that she didn't think it was something she'd like to witness again. There's another bank holiday at the end of May, so we agreed we'd find out if anything special would be happening in the village and if not we'd organise our own entertainment again. We could have a tug of war here Martin said. I think we'll see about that. With Stephen's injury and Anna's pregnancy I'm not sure who will be fit enough to take part.

We ate a lot of eggs yesterday, so I gave the five laid today to Gail as they don't keep hens. There were four brown eggs and one blue.

Wednesday, May 7
I tired of taking the washing in and out today, so eventually I left it outside all day and ignored the showers. The afternoon was breezy though not very

sunny, so the laundry almost dried and we brought it all in by 5pm as the sky was growing dark. It looks as if we may be in for some heavy rain tonight.

Stephen has been keeping himself occupied by learning a couple of new songs on his ukulele and says he will treat us to a recital this evening. Home-grown entertainment has been one of the good things about this power cut, since the absence of television means we have to find other ways to fill our evenings. Martin's guitar playing has improved and Jane has taken up the piano again, saying she really missed playing while she was away at university. Anna doesn't play an instrument but sings well, so we often have sing-songs we all enjoy.

The music helped to take Stephen's mind off his painful injury, but he still winced and groaned when his dressing was changed by Anna today. It looks very raw but there is no sign of infection at the moment, so hopefully the burn is starting to heal. He is getting very fed up sitting all the time, but I don't think he should try walking much for a couple more days.

Despite today's showers my garden is giving me a great deal of pleasure. The warm weather at the weekend has encouraged the iris to fully open into scented silky flowers. The light purple Jane Phillips, which smells of Parma violets, and the rich maroon and yellow of one I think is called Maharajah are particularly striking. So I allowed myself a little time weeding in the courtyard so I could enjoy the scent and then threw the weeds to the hens and collected four eggs.

Thursday, May 8

Linda called in this morning to see how we are doing for meat. We have used all the beef mince from the other weekend and could do with more soon. She was asking because Neil thinks he should spray the sheep soon and that will mean none can be butchered for more than a week after treatment. He was worried that he won't be able to shear this year, as he can't contact his usual help, so he wants to spray now as a precaution.

The weather today has been cooler with a fine misty rain, but it could quickly change and hot sun on damp fleece would soon encourage fly strike. Linda said she thought it would be a good idea if Neil slaughtered one of the older ewes today to tide us over and then he can go ahead with spraying. I wondered whether he had been able to obtain the chemical spray normally used, but Linda said he had just enough for the flock right now. If they aren't sheared this summer and he needs to spray again and can't get any more Crovect, he will have to use diluted paraffin.

I said I'd like to help this afternoon when he penned them up, as it's a chance to observe their characters first hand. So I've ended up with a very busy day as Linda and I made more black pudding with the blood from the butchered sheep this morning, then this afternoon I was out in the field with the flock. Linda said she'd finish cleaning the intestines for sausage skins, so I had the job of marking each sheep or lamb in turn as it was sprayed.

Badger has grown tremendously since I first held

him and he and some of the other ram lambs already have horns a couple of inches in length. They and their mothers all made an immense noise and fuss about being treated, even though it is entirely for their own good. But my original bottle-fed lamb, who is now an old brute of eleven years, refused to enter the pen and said it was not for the likes of him. Then he stood still, feeding from a bucket, while Neil sprayed him.

Friday, May 9

I shouldn't be cross, but I do feel somewhat in despair. It was bad enough losing Stephen's help, but now I've lost Martin's as well. Two men are laid up and three women, one of them very pregnant, have to run the house and tend the garden.

I suppose we should be thankful that Martin isn't more seriously injured, but as it is, he will be out of action for a couple of weeks at least. If it had happened during the depths of winter it would have been worse, but it is still bad enough now in spring, as we need so much wood chopped and fetched, as well as water drawn and carried.

It happened when he was splitting logs. He is very experienced and has never had an accident before, but maybe he was tired. He says the axe was blunt. Just as well, otherwise the injury would have been much worse. It slipped and he caught the side of his foot. If the blade had been really sharp it would have taken his little toe. As it is, he has ruined his boot and badly cut his foot. I had to drive him down to the surgery and he's had stitches, tetanus and antibiotics.

So now we have both Stephen and Martin hobbling around and complaining. Jane and I thought we would have to start splitting logs, but Tony has come to our rescue. We have such a pile of wood here from trees that fell last winter as well as this, that he says if he can have some logs he'll be happy, with the help of Brad and Flynn, to split and stack them. That means Jane and I will only have to worry about replenishing the kindling. If it was winter, we would still be keeping two big fires going all day, but now it's milder we are only using the one inglenook, where we cook and boil our water. But the need for firewood is still crucial and on fine days we also heat water for laundering on the barbecue.

While Martin is recuperating we shall also be short of game birds. So maybe I'll have to find out if our neighbours are good shots and lend them the gun. At least the hens are reliable and laid four more eggs today.

Saturday, May 10

The men are hungry and bored but we women are exhausted. Jane and I have fetched water and boiled it, scrubbed clothes and hung them out, weeded the vegetable beds and fed the hens, brought in dried kindling and stacked damp wood to dry, piled logs and stoked fires, as well as sweeping floors and dusting. Anna cannot undertake heavy work, but has folded laundry, watched the fires, boiled kettles and prepared our supper. And the men have moaned.

I know they both have injuries which could have been serious, but they are of their own making and my patience is wearing thin already. Martin keeps asking for tea, which Anna can make for him and Stephen, as we received supplies a week or so ago, but at this rate they will soon consume our stocks and leave nothing for the rest of us hard workers. Stephen was proving to be fairly resilient before Martin's accident, but now he too is indulging in the moan fest.

I told Anna to ignore them when she is busy. It is more important to keep the fire hot and prepare a good meal than make constant pots of tea, which only result in frequent trips to the loo that produce enormous groans and hobbles from the two of them. Anna is a good cook and has made a tasty mutton tagine-style stew for us, which we'll have with some of the rice ration. However, bending over a hot fire is not the easiest task for her with her baby bulge and she must take care.

Jane and I picked lots more ground elder, which is still flourishing because of the sun and showers. We'll have this as our green vegetable with our meal. Other weeds from our hoeing have gone to the hens, which laid overtime today, producing six eggs. With the longer daylight hours I think one of the Rhode Island Reds must have laid one yesterday evening and then another today.

Sunday, May 11
I thought it would do me good to get away from the patients today, so I walked to church with Gail and Jane, where we sang a lovely version of the 'The Lord is My Shepherd'. We also sang 'Brother Let Me Be Your Servant', which was ironic in the circumstances and I could not stop myself muttering under my

breath that I would not be making that request once I was home again.

Today was cold and windy until about 3pm when the sun really shone, so I decided that once I had finished the main chores and could see that supper was simmering nicely, I could allow myself some time on my flower beds. The bearded iris are a joy at present and a very pale one, almost white tinged with a subtle hint of lavender, has just opened amongst the Purple Sensation alliums.

An hour or so amongst my favourite plants, despite bending and weeding, always puts me in a good mood and I was much more cheerful and amenable when I came back inside. Anna had made a pot of tea and drop scones, which were most welcome. Martin ate more than anyone else and I can see that if he doesn't get back on his feet again soon, he will have extra weight to worry about. But he managed to hobble outside this afternoon to sit in the sunshine and said he'd heard the cuckoo again. We first heard it about three weeks ago and it seemed to be very close then.

At the end of the day I threw all the weeds I'd collected into the hen run and found four eggs.

Monday, May 12

Although today has been mostly sunny and bright, there have been some dark clouds too and not just the ones overhead. Yesterday evening I'd walked across to see the sheep and noticed that yet another ewe had just lambed. She had two tiny black twins nestling beside her.

But by this morning she had only one. The fox

must have been out hunting again. Neil is furious and says he will stay up all night until he's shot it. Martin says as soon as he is able to patrol the grounds he'll be looking out for it with his shotgun too. And I feel guilty for saving the fox cub and still haven't told Neil what I did. This year I think the fox has fed well on five lambs and every time it has been a twin.

Neil has blamed himself for not leaving a light out in the field last night. He'd noticed the new arrivals but was tired, so for once he didn't hang his storm lantern nearby. Strange lights can help deter the foxes but they still aren't a cast iron guarantee.

On the bright side, Jane and I managed to get a good wash completed and hung out this morning. It was almost dry when the sky darkened this afternoon, so we brought it in with Anna's help. And the girls went to the school to see what baby goods were available and came back with another smock for Anna and some terry nappies, which will be vital in the absence of disposable ones these days. Anna was tired by the walk into the village and although she is still keen to take some exercise I think she will soon find it is better for her to stay here and rest.

The hens have done well on their regular feeds of lush green weeds and produced five eggs for us today.

Tuesday, May 12
When I woke early this morning, I thought how loud the birdsong was and then I began to think how much more aware of the natural sounds we have become, since the power cut started. Without the

distractions of morning radio or TV we hear all the voices of birds and animals more clearly around us. There is no buzzing of aircraft, no clattering overhead of helicopters, nor the drone of traffic or the occasional distant rattle of trains.

Last night as I shut up the hens in their run, long after they had finally decided it was dark enough to retire to bed, I heard the sharp cry of an owl. Today I've heard the screech of a heron flying past and the irritated quacking of a female duck being pursued by three drakes. One of the cats chased a squirrel and it chattered angrily from a pine tree, and I also heard swans fly overhead, their wings whooshing through the air.

But I've heard sad sounds too. Neil and Linda had to go away for the day to visit Neil's elderly mother near Alton, so I said I would keep an eye on the sheep, despite my many chores. Mid-morning I saw the sheep which had had her lamb taken by the fox, nudging her remaining baby as it lay on the ground. It was floppy, trying to lift its head now and then and I could see it wasn't well. The mother kept licking it, urging it to stand, muttering in her baby language. And by the end of the afternoon it was lifeless. It had lived for two days, longer than its sibling, but still not long enough and its mother is still lying beside it talking to her little one.

However, the hens are cheerfully clucking and the cockerel is crowing boastfully. They have given us five eggs again today.

Wednesday, May 13

Well, I was wrong. It wasn't dead. There was still a

flicker of life.

I kept watch until early evening, by which time the mother had abandoned her lamb and wandered off to the far side of the field to rejoin the flock. I know that Neil doesn't leave the dead out as it encourages foxes, so I climbed under the barbed wire and over the stile, carrying an old compost bag to collect the body. As I approached, a crow flew off and I knew that the carrion eaters had already spotted the lamb.

I was dreading what I would find, but to my surprise as I bent down to pick up the body, I found it was warm and breathing. The crow had pecked at the top of its head and there was a little blood, but at least the bird hadn't gone for its eyes. I held the little black lamb and stroked its tightly curled fleece, knowing that if I left it in the field it wouldn't last the night. I thought it stood little chance of surviving, but I couldn't bear to leave it there to be pecked at by crows and torn to shreds by foxes.

So I brought it back here. I was sure it was going to die soon, so I wrapped it in a fleecy blanket then shut it in a little hut we once used for geese. I thought that would be kinder than leaving it outside in the dark for predators.

And early this morning, even before I'd dressed, I went outside in dressing gown and wellies, expecting to find it stiff and cold. But it was still alive. Its breathing was fast, but it tried to lift its head and kick its legs. I carried it indoors and dripped some warm milk into its mouth, then rocked it in my arms and wondered what to do. I haven't the stomach for putting it down and it has fought to stay alive this long, so I decided to bottle feed it. I wasn't sure where I'd find bottles, teats and formula, but when I told Gail about the frail lamb she said she still had all of those in the house from when Alfie was a baby. The milk is not as rich as a ewe's, but it will have to do.

The lamb sucked weakly at first, but has suckled well on the hour since mid-morning, consuming almost half a bottle. It still can't lift its head and it may still die, but we have done our best today.

Thursday, May 15

Martin complained today that he was not being looked after half as well as the wretched lamb. And I'm afraid I said that as he wasn't likely to die after dropping the axe on his foot, he and Stephen were not a priority. He then went into a sulk and said I'd be sorry if his injury became infected and stopped him working for another week, so I felt obliged to help him by changing his dressing and bathing the wound.

It is healing quickly and I really don't think there is any cause for concern, nor do I have any worries about Stephen, who is hobbling about nimbly and able to keep an eye on the fire and boil water.

Neil turned up this morning, just as Jane was giving the lamb its third feed of the day. He was amused by our attempts to save it, but had to admit the little ewe is a fighter and we may save her yet. However, he said he isn't interested in bottle feeding her and we can if we want to. If she survives she may be reintroduced to the flock when she's weaned, but he doesn't want to care for her until then.

So Jane and I are enjoying looking after our new

patient. She is quieter and more amenable than our human ones and her short black fleece has the texture of a good quality Axminster carpet. Her ears are velvet and her little hooves are carved ebony. She sucks hard on the bottle and has already dirtied both our laps when we've been feeding, so I've suggested we cover ourselves with a heavy duty gardening apron when we are holding her. Anna isn't allowed to help as pregnant women are vulnerable to infections from sheep.

And of course the girls want to give the lamb a name. I was reluctant as she may yet die, but they insisted, so she is now called Sooty. Martin offered to name her Jessica, but Anna and Jane ignored him, so Sooty she is for as long as she lives.

Friday, May 16

Martin and Stephen have been listening to the radio more often recently, because they are both still somewhat indisposed. They mostly want to hear if there is any sign of solving the UK power cut, so they tune into regular news bulletins, but of course these also contain news about other parts of the world. And it struck me today, as I half listened while I made them breakfast of scrambled eggs and drop scones, that although the power cut has been devastating for many areas in this country, there are more terrible events happening elsewhere.

My dear husband shook his head and yelled at the radio, when it was announced that the problem here has still not been solved and after a few expletives, I felt I had to point out that in this house, in this village, we are not that badly off. We have been able

to eat well, we have stayed relatively healthy
(apart from self-inflicted injuries, I remarked) and we
still have each other. Elsewhere in the world, since
the power cut began, there have been major natural
disasters. Recently there has been an awful mining
accident, the sinking of a ferry with huge loss of life
and the kidnapping of a large number of Nigerian
schoolgirls. Compared to these calamities, our
problems in this household are insignificant. I know
we are lucky to be here in the countryside and not in
a city and I know that our life is inconvenient and
difficult while the power cut continues, but it is not
going to kill us and we should be thankful.

Once I'd made breakfast I left them to grumble to
themselves while I fed the hens, which gave us five
eggs today. And then I watched Jane feed Sooty, who
managed to lift her head a little and waggle her tail
as she took her bottle.

Saturday, May 17

By the end of yesterday we were all in a much better
mood as the day was glorious. Summer has suddenly
arrived with such a burst of warmth and sunshine
that we all feel that winter is finally over. Even
Martin has cheered up and is managing to do more
for himself now.

Today looks set to be another beautiful day. I've
woken even earlier than usual to find the sun shining
at 5.30am and it looks so fine that I can't go back to
sleep. We cooked on the barbecue last night and will
be able to do so again today. However we shall still
keep one fire going indoors for heating water and as
the weather is so good I will want to use the

barbecue to heat water for the laundry first and I can't have it smoking while the washing is drying on the line nearby.

While the family were still sleeping I've swept floors and fetched water to boil. I've given Sooty her first bottle of the day and she attempted to butt my hand, just as she would nudge her mother's udder to make the milk flow, so that is a very good sign. She is still very weak, but she is holding her head higher and sucks vigorously. I cleaned up her tail end with warm water, then tucked her back in the straw in the old goose house. Yesterday we left the door open so she didn't overheat in the sunshine. Jane wanted to take her upstairs with her last night, but sheep are creatures of the open fields and need a good flow of air to avoid respiratory infections.

The hens were ready to start their day early too, so I opened their house at 6am and threw them some scraps then dug over the soil so they could find the worms. With these long hours of daylight they will be laying well again today.

Sunday, May 18

Such glorious weather, my day began very early with boiling water for the washing and for breakfast. We should be able to eat outside again this evening, so I'm keen to dry the laundry before we start barbecuing tonight. Tony and Gail brought us hamburgers they'd picked up at the pub yesterday and we all sat outside until nearly 10 o'clock, then Jane gave Sooty the last bottle feed of the day.

We were in a celebratory mood last night and rather wished we'd had something stronger than tea to toast Martin's success as a crack shot. He'd been sitting at the back of the house enjoying the early evening sun, when he spotted a fox with its nose to the ground in the field. He sent Jane to fetch the rifle then went back to quietly watching and got it in one shot as it followed a trail on our big lawn.

I know I've praised the foxes for their efficiency in removing dead and rotting corpses, but I have come to like them less since the lambs have been born this year. Around five twins have been taken by the fox and it is heartbreaking to see the mother with a sole remaining twin less than twenty-four hours after the birth.

So Martin was toasted for his heroic actions in tea. Less heroic was his reluctance to deal with the body. Not only could he not hobble across the lawn to satisfy himself that it was well and truly dead, because of his wound, which is not yet healed, but he would not be keen to do so even if he was fleet of foot. Martin is squeamish about small furry creatures and all dead ones, so I had to check for him. It was quite dead and it was a female, which means there may be young ones which will also die, so Neil will be pleased to hear about the kill. I threw the vixen into the wheelbarrow and took it to the far side of the wood as it won't be eaten by its own kind and only crows and magpies and eventually insects will dispose of the body.

I'm sorry for any cubs that may now starve, but I am not sorry that our little black lamb and our hens will be safer. The hens laid well today, giving us four eggs, but one had broken in the nest and I may have to determine whether they are eating their eggs or the shell was soft and broke as it was laid.

Monday, May 19

Barely any time to write in this diary. Weeding, watering, washing, fetching water, collecting logs, preparing meals, sweeping floors, feeding hens, cats, men and Sooty the lamb, take up all our time. Anna needs to rest in the afternoon and Jane does as much as me and is in charge of the bottle feeds.

There are no shortcuts and no household appliances to help us do all the work quickly. And the fine hot weather, though welcome, means young plants need to be watered, adding to our list of chores. So no time to write.

Tuesday, May 20

I'm not sure if the lads are feeling better or just bored, but both Stephen and Martin are back on their feet. They are hobbling, especially Martin, when he sees anyone looking, but they are helping. It is such a relief, even though they aren't quite up to full speed yet and can't do all the heavy work they normally undertake, but it is a great help having them load the wheelbarrow with logs and bring them up to the house, then stack them in the inglenooks. They are also able to fetch heavy pails of water from the well, which is still our main source for the present.

And there were a couple of heavy showers of rain this afternoon which were also welcome as I was starting to think we would have to water all the vegetable beds ourselves. Under normal circumstances, with power operating the water treatment plants and pumping out fresh water day and night, we've never questioned the wonders of having clean supplies on tap and through the garden hose. Of course we've moaned about the hosepipe bans that were imposed most summers, but we've never before had to think about where our water has come from. We've just used it and now we are aware of every drop.

The water butts and various buckets collect rainwater, which we boil for drinking and laundry. The well gives us murky water for cooking vegetables and washing. Then all the waste water from washing-up and doing the laundry is recycled to flush our toilet. Water has become a precious commodity.

And I gave the hens well water to drink to help them keep up their egg production. They need plenty of water to help them make good eggs and they gave us five today, which I found in another new nest in their henhouse.

Wednesday, May 21
Tony came triumphantly down the drive this afternoon, bearing supplies of flour, butter, cheese, oil and dried milk. Another delivery of rations reached the village today and as we can't manage to get there, while Martin and Stephen are still recovering, Tony collected our share for us.

We haven't tasted cheese for months, so we are all very excited about the big block of very ordinary pale yellow Cheddar that's arrived. Martin said he'd like cheese on toast, but there isn't any bread. Jane wanted to grate cheese over a jacket potato and Stephen said he'd just like cheese and biscuits, but we don't have any crackers.

In the end we agreed to make homemade pasta,

cooked with the young leaves of ground elder and nettles, which taste very like spinach. Anna is rolling the dough through the pasta machine and cutting it into strips, like tagliatelle. Then we'll cook the pasta, wilt the leaves in the cooking water and toss with butter and grated cheese. I still had some pine nuts in the larder so we'll add those as well for extra flavour and texture.

We all long for different foods, even though we have, on the whole, eaten well ever since the power cut started. There has been lamb, mutton, beef, pheasant, duck and goose. We've had potatoes and cabbage, onions and carrots. Soon we shall cut our own lettuce and pull radishes too. But it's variety that we miss and we long for the simplest of foods too. Freshly baked bread would be more welcome than any gourmet dish right now.

If we could have bread, I'd boil one of our fresh eggs and dip a crust of thickly buttered bread into the deep yellow yolk. That would be such a delight. And we have eggs, four more laid today, but no bread, only the meagre flatbread we can make on the fire. It really isn't the same as the crunch of a crust over soft doughy crumb.

Thursday, May 22

I have been despairing about the grass. Not the grass in the fields, for they are providing lush grazing for the sheep, but our lawns, which are growing thick and fast. Early in the season Martin agreed to cut them with the petrol mover a couple of times, but now he is reluctant to use any of our precious fuel. But today I begged him to cut the garden lawns some more and he relented. I think he is bored of not being able to be as active as normal, while his wound continues to heal, so he sat on the tractor and cut a winding path through the big lawn, then cut strips around the edges of all the formal lawns. He cut the kitchen lawn completely, as that is the one where we mostly sit if there is sun during the day.

So now I am happier. I can kneel and reach into the borders to weed and the garden looks neater. I know it is not the most essential job at present in these difficult times, but it breaks my heart to see my lovely garden becoming bedraggled and overgrown. And I keep thinking this power cut surely cannot go on forever, and we have the kerosene stored, so it wouldn't hurt to use a little of it for the grass.

Then Stephen said he could resurrect the old cylinder mower, that requires man power, not petrol power. Now that Martin has employed the tractor to do most of the work, Stephen says he will sharpen and oil the blades of the rusting mower and he will push it around the paths and edges as his foot is much better and he would like the exercise after these inactive weeks since his accident.

The hens loved the grass cuttings. I left them scratching through a pile we'd thrown into the run after I'd collected four eggs today. The cockerel was feeling very proud of himself, puffing his chest and shuffling his feet before he pounced on one of the hens. She put up with his advances, then, once he had finished shuddering over her, she shook her feathers as if she was rearranging her hair and powdering her nose after a lusty embrace.

Friday, May 23

As Martin and Stephen are much improved, I decided that I would be able to help at the soup kitchen in the village hall today. I made a mutton broth and Jane and I took it down in two large containers in the wheelbarrow. We added more water once we were there, so the soup wasn't too heavy for us to transport. I've missed coming into the village while the men were both indisposed with their injuries, so it was good to feel part of the community again.

Of course much of the gossip was about how little news there still is on progress with resolving the power cut. There were grumbles about the limited supplies brought into the village this week and moans about our restricted diet and the lack of alcohol in the pub. This last gripe brought sniffs of contempt from some of the older ladies, stalwarts of the WI, who said that was a good thing.

And then one of these formidable elderly ladies said we weren't half as badly off as they were during the war on rations. I said I thought we were managing very well and the latest supplies were most useful and welcome, though I miss baking and sometimes long for a cake with afternoon tea. Then she said I should try using a biscuit tin. She told me how to punch holes in the lid, surround the tin with embers and use it as an improvised oven. She said she had learnt to do it in the Girl Guides, many years ago.

So this afternoon I gave it a go. I can't say it was the best cake I've ever eaten, but it was tasty and it has been devoured by the whole family. I used some of the flour and butter that was delivered this week, with baking powder, bicarbonate of soda, sugar, spice, dates and nuts from my larder, all mixed with two fresh eggs. I wondered whether to put the mixture straight into the biscuit tin, but decided to use a small roasting tin, lined with greaseproof. I settled the tin in the glowing embers of the fire, gave strict instructions that no logs were to be added, as I wanted it to bake, not burn, then watched as it steamed and cooked. I tested it with a skewer after half an hour, which is the time it would normally take to cook in my oven and decided it needed another ten minutes. It smelt of nutmeg and cinnamon and although the crust was not as firm as it would be in a conventional oven, it was delicious. Thank goodness for our hens and for the army who delivered our supplies. And thank goodness for the old Girl Guide.

Saturday, May 25

The cats are in my bad books. I know that felines are natural killers and I welcome the killing instinct where house mice and rats are concerned, but I have to draw the line at birds, especially small ones. And I don't know which of them caught it, but I had to rescue a very frightened robin today.

Tom and Tickles were being particularly attentive, calling for my attention and I thought they wanted food or a drink. I checked their bowls and told them not to fuss, but still they miaowed at me continually. I stroked them both and talked to them, thinking they were feeling unloved as the weather has suddenly switched off summer and reverted to cold and damp spring, but still they seemed unsettled.

Finally, when I went to put my raincoat on a peg in the hall porch, they both followed me. As I hung up my coat I thought I heard a footstep outside the front door. I opened the door and nothing was there, but both the cats became excited. I shut the door and then heard another sound. A flapping. I looked up and a robin was fluttering around the porch lantern, indoors.

The cats were trying to jump up, but the robin was fortunately out of their reach. As it panicked, it left droppings on the wall and on my raincoat. Eventually it perched where the old wall juts out from the oak beam, high above where Tom and Tickles were trying to work out how they could scramble up the walls and coats to reach it.

I had to act fast. I grabbed both cats in one armful. I pushed open the hall door and threw them inside, then I opened the front door wide, so the bird could see the daylight outside. It stayed where it was for a minute, then perched above the pegs, dripping some more onto the cream trench coat. After a second it flew down, sat on the iron latch of the heavy door, twisted its head to look outside, then flew away over the lawns and ponds. It was safe and I hope it didn't die later from shock, but it looked more or less in one piece.

Back inside the house, I found two bemused cats, wondering where their friend had flown to, plus several tail feathers in my study. I think the robin had a very lucky escape, unlike my coat which I shall attempt to wash.

Sunday, May 25

I suddenly realised today that this last week has traditionally been the time of the Chelsea Flower Show, an event I've attended and enjoyed many times. Not only the big showpiece gardens, sponsored by major financial institutions, but the small courtyard gardens celebrating original creativity have caught my imagination and encouraged me to try new planting schemes at home.

And then I began to think about the many activities we used to take for granted before this extended power cut, which are now an impossibility. We can't order books and groceries online or research and reserve holidays. We can't catch a train to London for visits to theatres and galleries or for shopping in the famous department stores. And the times when we fretted about catching planes on time, or queued in irritation for a major exhibition or complained because the newspaper delivery was late, now seem totally unimportant and I really don't miss them.

Of course, if I think about our pre-power cut life too much I miss having my hair cut and coloured every six weeks, I would love a chilled glass of Pinot Grigio and I long for an avocado or a banana, but I don't find myself thinking about these things all the time. I told Martin what I had been thinking and he said he didn't half miss cold lager and watching a box set. But we both agreed that our life here, during this difficult time, when so many people have truly suffered, has been bearable and we are grateful to have remained well fed and healthy. Apart from his injured foot, Martin pointed out. Well, at least it's almost healed now, I said.

And I think my garden looks glorious with a profusion of purple alliums and this year it doesn't feel inferior to the gardens of Chelsea, for there are none. So I felt happier, as I tossed more weeds to the hens, who laid five eggs today and had vigorous dust baths in the sunshine.

Monday, May 26

This morning Martin asked me if I realised today was a bank holiday. I wasn't aware of the fact, as I lose track without regular newspapers and news bulletins on the radio. Then he said, well, we're stuck here with nowhere to go. And I said, but you never like going anywhere on a bank holiday. You don't like crowds and you never want to drive when there's likely to be heavy traffic. True, he said. But a change of scene would be nice. A day out, a bit of sea air, that's all I'm saying.

I left him to grumble that it was typical bank holiday weather too, grey and drizzly, as he hobbled off to fetch wood. Then Jane came down for breakfast and I noticed she was looking very red-eyed. I asked what was the matter and she just shrugged, but next minute she was crying in my arms and I held her like she was still a child.

Once her tears had subsided, she said she'd dreamt about being with her friends, about being able to go out and have fun. I hate it, she said, I hate being stuck here all the time.

Then she sniffed and I hugged her some more, made her tea and gave her scrambled eggs and she apologised and said it must be worse for other people and she worried about her friends. And I tried hard to help her see how fortunate we are and how there are still many things to look forward to. I reminded her how well she is doing with feeding Sooty and she smiled at last.

The little lamb is much stronger and can now stand and even tries to hop. She no longer needs feeding all night, just a late feed and then a bottle as early as possible, which I usually give her. And yesterday Jane took Sooty out for a little walk on the grass and she sniffed it then tasted a few blades of grass. Jane adores Sooty and the lamb is very attached to her, bleating when she sees her and waggling her tail furiously at the sight of the bottle.

Then I told Jane about Martin's moans and we hatched a plan to make today a bit special. I said we'd do it to put Martin in a good mood, but really it's for Jane. I'll do anything to keep her cheerful and give her hope. Then I sent her off to feed Sooty and I fed the hens and collected the first egg of the day.

Tuesday, May 27

A day of good news and bad news. It started with us all in a happy mood because we had enjoyed the special evening that I had prepared with the help of the girls. We commandeered the dining room where we cook all our food on the fire and said Stephen and Martin couldn't come in until supper time. Martin was a bit miffed at this until I took tea outside to him and he kept coming up to the door to the kitchen asking if he could come in yet. I think he was feeling the cold as there was a chilly breeze blowing.

And when we did finally open the door they were

astonished at how we had draped the room with remnants of brocade from the attic and rearranged most of the cushions in the house, so it looked like a kasbah. Anna had made the men Arab headdresses, but she drew the line at draping the women in black, so we wore long dresses and had old necklaces draped around our heads. Jane looked particularly fetching in a chain belt which she had retrieved from the dressing up box, which I think I last wore in about 1970. Then we sat down to eat mutton pilaff and carrots with caraway seeds, flatbread with nigella seeds and a beetroot dip. We had mint tea as the mint is growing well now and then told stories like the ones in *One Thousand and One Arabian Nights* until it was dark outside.

But later today our mood changed when Tony came up to the house to say that large numbers of refugees had arrived in the village and had set up their tents wherever there was open space. They are camping on the village green, outside the pub, in the churchyard and on the common. And there's more coming this way, he said, they're all fleeing the big towns and cities now the weather has improved and the days are longer. We could soon be inundated.

So I shall make sure I shut up the hens as soon as they go in to roost. We need their eggs and they laid five today.

Wednesday, May 28

Martin and Stephen have more or less recovered from their foot injuries, but they aren't up to walking into the village yet, so we're relying on Tony and his son and son-in-law for news. I don't want Jane going into the village alone, until we are sure that the incomers are behaving decently. The few stragglers who reached us during the winter and were accommodated in the village hall, were all grateful for whatever help we could give them and their numbers could easily be absorbed into the community, but now we are hearing that a couple of hundred or more have arrived so far.

Tony, Brad and Flyn went to see the encampments this morning and came back saying the farm butcher has donated two hog roasts already, but that won't go far with these numbers. The Parish Council are in a panic and have met in the church with Reverend James, to decide how to distribute rations. They are asking every village family to donate a portion of the supplies that came the other week.

The travellers arriving say there are ration centres in places like Aldershot and Guildford, but the queues are vast and the rations so meagre, people finally lost patience and that's why many are escaping into the countryside to fend for themselves. Tony said the new arrivals seem thin and ill, for the most part, and are astonished at how well-fed the villagers look.

Part of me wants to help, of course, but I'm worried about our little family here too, particularly with Anna's baby only a few weeks away. We must stay strong if we are to protect new life.

I've been thinking about this problem all day and when I went to collect the eggs late this afternoon I discovered that one of the Legbar hens has gone broody. I slid my hand underneath her and found she was sitting on five eggs. I've left her one, which I marked so I shall know which are fresh if she lays

more. But I am in a quandary. What is the greater
need? Eggs today or new hens tomorrow?

Thursday, May 29
Last night we all talked at length about the new
arrivals and whether there will be a problem, then
we decided that I should go into the village today
with Tony and Neil to see for myself. Martin and
Stephen really wanted to come, but they aren't up to
walking that far yet, so I left them to fetch logs and
water and keep the fire going. It's been chilly and
drizzly today, so I can't do any laundry outside and
we've needed both fires for cooking, boiling water
and keeping warm.

Martin thought we should go in the car or Neil's
Land Rover, but I said that would draw too much
attention, so we walked across the fields and I wore
even drabber, scruffier clothes than usual. We all
carried heavy walking sticks, just in case, and as we
approached the village green we could hear
shouting.

Then we rounded the corner and there was the
green crowded with tents, looking like the end of the
Reading Festival. The two young oak trees planted to
mark the Jubilee and the Millennium had been
snapped off and a crowd of men were cheering two
others fighting near a smoking heap, on which they
had presumably tried to burn the young trees.

David Henderson and Reverend James were both
standing to one side and when we joined them they
said the fight had broken out over the distribution of
rations, even though the refugees had been well fed
with the hog roasts and were receiving equal shares

of supplies. I noticed that there were very few women in the crowd and no children to be seen. Reverend James said that families with children had either been squeezed into the village hall or were camped in the church and churchyard, as it was thought this would be safer for them. David said he believed some kind of alcohol had been circulating amongst the men and that it would be best to wait for the furore to die down. We left soon after that and returned home feeling troubled and gloomy. I shut up the hens as soon as I could and Neil said he would leave his dogs to guard the fields at night from now on.

Friday, May 30

Martin said he wanted to go into the village today. He insisted his foot wasn't troubling him, but I know it is and said he might manage to walk there but he wouldn't be able to run back, if he had to, so he shouldn't go. I thought he'd listened to me, but late this morning I realised I couldn't hear him chopping wood and he wasn't trundling logs up to the house in the wheelbarrow either. So I went up the drive to see Tony and Gail and found that he'd ignored me completely and had gone off with Tony and Brad.

Gail was pretty annoyed too. We've had enough of the men thinking this is all one great game. So we both spent an anxious hour or so waiting for them to come back. When they did, we were both waiting with grim faces, which made them laugh and they told us there was no danger on the green this morning as nearly all the travellers were still out for the count. The booze they'd managed to find, illicit or legal we don't know, had knocked them out and the few who were awake were in no fit state to fight.

But that doesn't mean to say we shouldn't be wary, I said. And you shouldn't go taking risks either. All three of them laughed again and I can see that Gail and I will have to keep a close eye on them. They are bound to want to check on the situation again soon. So I tried to put my dark thoughts behind me for the rest of the day.

Although the weather hasn't been good, Jane has been encouraging Sooty to exercise. This dear little lamb is getting stronger by the day and Neil says he believes she definitely has a chance now. Another week and he thinks Jane should try feeding her lamb nuts to gradually wean her. She is tasting the grass already and trying to do little hops and skips. Jane carries her some of the time, but when she puts her down on the grass Sooty walks at heel, just like a little black poodle.

And my hens are comforting with their soft clucking and the broody hen puffs herself up over her clutch of eggs, which are all marked so I can still take the freshly laid ones indoors.

Saturday, May 31

I wouldn't let Martin go into the village again today, even though we could do with some vegetables from the barter market at the pub. But Gail said Tony was going anyway with Brad and Flyn, so they could fetch our supplies, in return for some duck, rabbit or venison the next time Martin is able to go out with his gun. They didn't come back till early afternoon and when Tony came up to see us he was empty

266

handed and apologetic. He hadn't been able to get supplies for us or for his own family. The new arrivals have taken it all.

I couldn't believe what I was hearing, but he said it was chaotic. They may have been comatose yesterday, but they were fully awake today and as the local growers and the farm butcher started setting up at the pub, they just launched themselves at the goods and took it all. Tony thinks the farmers won't dare to come back while the encampment continues and the arrivals have also taken over the pub and Mick has moved into the vicarage. That will be a culture shock for him, I said, but it was the only moment of amusement in Tony's account of the situation.

We're all shocked at the change in circumstances these badly behaved people have brought on our village. Up to now, through all these months, we have been civil and decent, sharing what we have and ensuring that no one really suffered. But now, without any sense of fairness, we will all be worse off. No one will dare to go into the village to exchange surplus produce.

Tony said that there are other signs too of how inconsiderate they are being. Any wooden fence fronting the road is theirs for the taking, back gardens are being raided for vegetables and eggs and most villagers are learning not to answer a knock at the door. Thank goodness we're tucked away here, I said. But Tony said we shouldn't count on it. They'll start searching further afield soon, he said. The only good piece of news he brought us was the rumour that rations are being increased and there should be a delivery early next week. Let's hope they bring some potatoes, I said.

Sunday, June 1

I badly wanted to go to church this morning, but I
wasn't sure about going without Martin and
Stephen. It sounds utterly stupid to be afraid of
walking through my own village, where I have safely
walked at all times of day and night for years, but
now I am truly nervous. I used to be scared of the
traffic, not the people, but now I just don't feel safe
and I'm beginning to think that, for once, I want the
men to be foolhardy and rally themselves. It's
ridiculous letting a rabble of only a couple of
hundred rowdies take over a village of two
thousand.

I talked to Martin about it after breakfast. He
nearly choked on his tea and said he didn't think I'd
want him anywhere near the troublemakers. But if
we don't do something, I said, they will squander the
supplies when they arrive, as well as the produce
they filched at the weekend. Don't tell me they can
eat all that meat and vegetables. It will be going to
waste, as they won't be able to cook it all before it
goes off. We can't have that happening from now
until things get back to normal. If they ever do,
Martin added. But he promised to talk to Tony and
Neil and our other near neighbours.

So I went about my usual jobs feeling a little
relieved that we might be able to address the
situation. Jane and I managed a big wash yesterday
and it finished drying today as it is sunny with a
little breeze. Then Jane took Sooty off for some
exercise and when Neil saw her he said if she

continues to grow like this she'll be able to join the flock in two or three weeks. Jane is still shutting her up in the goose house at night and barricading the bolted door with a wheelbarrow, but on fine days like today Sooty plays on the grass and then falls asleep in the sunshine.

The broody hen is continuing to sit, but I make her leave the nest once a day so I can check for newly laid eggs. There were four today so she is sitting on five, which I feel is enough to spare.

Monday, June 2

I slept badly last night, waking at every little creak of this old house, then worrying about what might be happening in the village. So this morning Martin spoke to Neil and Tony and I think they might have an idea. Neil asked how much petrol we still had and then asked the others to walk the fields today and keep watch tonight if he doesn't make it back. I don't know what he's up to, but I think he's got a plan.

I've tried to distract myself with normal chores and gardening, but even that doesn't stop me feeling we are living in difficult times. I went to check on my delphiniums and found a dead snake on the lawn. I expect it had been plucked from one of the ponds by a heron, then dropped when it was disturbed. But it was about a yard long and was partially eaten by a crow, which flapped away on its huge black wings when I approached. I lifted the snake with a garden fork and threw it into the ditch.

Seeing the crow reminded me of the one that had pecked the poor little abandoned lamb's head, so I went round to see how she was today. The injury on her head has completely healed and she is always eager for another bottle, butting our hands when we approach with her feed and waggling her tail furiously. Jane found her following at heel into the house today, just like an obedient puppy.

And then I found a crow trapped in the hen run with the hens and cockerel squawking at it madly. I shooed it out with the spade I use to dig the run for worms and it found its way out. I hope it doesn't make a habit of diving in when the chicks hatch or they won't have a chance. There were four fresh eggs today laid in another nest, well away from the bad-tempered broody.

Tuesday, June 3

I don't know what time Neil got back or what he got up to yesterday, but there was no sign of him last night and Martin and Stephen, Tony and his two boys organised the overnight watch between them. Then this morning I noticed them all gathered in the field, huddled with Neil, all nodding and waving in the direction of the village. I know they are up to something, but I'm guessing they don't want to worry me, as all Martin will say is that Neil says everything will be alright.

I'm trying not to think too much about it and there certainly is enough here to keep me occupied. But I'm worried about the next delivery of rations if the situation in the village isn't brought under control. There will be enough for everyone if it is properly distributed, but if these ruffians commandeer the lot it could be wasted.

Talking of supplies, I made a happy chance

discovery today when I decided to clear out the cupboard in my study. Sandwiched between some files was a whole box of Maltesers! I'd always thought I'd mislaid a box the year I asked for only Maltesers and bath foam for Christmas. And there it was, unopened. It says best before May 2012, but I've tried a couple and although the chocolate is less shiny than usual and the centre is not as crisp, they are delicious and I'll set up my own rationing system so everyone has a few to enjoy. We haven't tasted chocolate for months. Martin asked if I was sure they were safe to eat, but he soon took a second one after his first sample.

And the other delight has been seeing Sooty have her final bottle of the day. I watched Jane feeding her and the dear little lamb fell asleep in her lap. It's going to be hard sending her off to join the flock when she is bigger and stronger.

Wednesday, June 4

Hurrah for Neil and 'the boys'! The rabble has been routed and we have rations. I don't yet know all the details, but we shall have a full account tonight with a celebratory dinner here by the fire. We have potatoes, onions, flour, rice, tea, butter, long-life milk and bacon! Oh how we bless bacon for its mouth-watering smell and lingering flavour. I could kiss all the boys for bacon!

All I know is that Neil drove out of the village the other day on the back roads and visited all his cronies round and about, on farmland and smallholdings and gathered together a band of fearless men, who all own and use shotguns,

prepared to give the troublemakers a shock. They
came across fields and farm tracks, over the common
and through the woods. On a network of bridle paths
and footpaths they came, avoiding the obvious roads
into the village and they approached the village
green from the south, the east and the west. Driving
tractors, harvesters and Land Rovers, mounted on
giant shire horses and hunters with satin coats, they
circled the green at dawn, before the idle ruffians
were awake and then they waited.

And that's all I know for now. Neil has promised
to tell all tonight. Martin is desperate for the inside
story as his job was to stay here and keep watch, in
case there was an attempt to hide in the fields. So I
am preparing a feast of an onion and bacon pudding,
with mashed potatoes and gravy. And I'm
concocting a sweet rice pudding which I'll top with
melted Maltesers, which is probably the best way to
eat stale chocolate.

So tonight we shall be happy, until the next
obstacle rears its head. We have no electricity, but we
have food, a baby is coming and we have saved a
lamb from being pecked to death. And the hens are
laying and the broody one is sitting.

Thursday, June 5

Such laughter there was last night, as Neil related his
story of derring-do. All the boys were up for it, he
said. He didn't have any trouble rousing his
homemade army. They know how to fight fair, he
said and in the end they didn't even have to fight,
they just said boo. I imagine the sight of these burly
farmers, armed with their shotguns, coming from all

sides in their machines and on their mounts, must have terrified the troublemakers.

We thought we'd wake them up, Neil said, so at the agreed hour of five o'clock, just as the sun was coming through the river mist, we all sounded our horns. That woke them up, alright. There were girly screams and squawks from all their makeshift tents and hovels they'd draped over benders and garden chairs, then the first few started to crawl out, bleary eyed and shaking. And one of them screamed when old Bob's shire horse Rosie shook her head and stamped her foot by his tent. Get that thing away from me, he shouted, get it off me!

How we laughed and then he told how the farmers force demanded to see a leader, a representative of this shabby crew and eventually, after much muttering, an enormous, bald-headed man with a gallery of tattoos was pushed forwards. By then, Neil had fetched David Henderson, our Parish Council Chairman, and Reverend James, and the tattooed man was told he had to deal with these two stalwarts of the village if they wished to stay, but first he must tell all his men to bring out the supplies they had filched from the pub market on Saturday. And out it came, Neil said. The meat was no good, what was left of it, but they gathered together the vegetables, preserves and eggs and told them how we run things round here. They didn't take much persuading, the wimps. And after that, the real army turned up. Neil's boys entertained them with the tale of their recruitment and manoeuvres and the soldiers unloaded the hard rations allocated to the village. They have promised to return early next week with more, now that the local population has increased. I guess we shall see how it goes when the market returns to the pub this weekend, but for now, order has been restored, thanks to the old boy network.

Friday, June 6

Sometimes the reality of our situation hits home with the tiniest thing and I am reminded just how much our lives have changed, since the power cut started. It sounds trivial, I know, but today I noticed the date and realised that exactly a year ago I had a very grand afternoon tea with three old school friends. Two of them I had known since junior school and we had all been a close gang throughout our time at secondary school. Despite personal tragedies over the years, we were still the same girls who had shared jokes at the back of the class and mocked the boys, chased the boys and married them.

We met in a country house hotel on a sunny June day and promised to meet again a year on. That day, twelve months ago, we were served finger sandwiches, dainty pastries and scones with two kinds of jam and clotted cream, all presented on tiered cake stands. The menu devoted two whole pages to varieties of tea, some of which we had never heard of before. Two of us wanted strong 'builder's tea' while the others sipped Darjeeling and a Ceylon tea called Lovers Leap. It was another world, that seems so long ago. Now, we are lucky to have any tea at all, let alone pastries and cream.

I have no way of knowing how my friends have fared during this challenging time or if they have even survived. Without phones, mobiles, computers or even a basic postal service, we cannot know how anyone beyond our immediate locality is faring. But I like to think, because we are all from the same post-war era, that they too have tackled this crisis with determination and resilience. They might not have inglenook fireplaces in which to cook, but they would be resourceful, meeting the difficulties of everyday survival with stoicism and cheerfulness. That happy afternoon, reminiscing about our school days, seems so long ago now.

And I must confess, as I wondered how the girls (for we shall always be girls to each other) have fared, I did feel a tear welling up, which I brushed away in annoyance, as I cannot weaken after so long with so much more still to strive for. I will pray for my friends of over fifty years, but in the meantime I will make a cup of 'builder's tea' and think of them.

Saturday, June 7

We were woken by a crash of thunder at 4am and the rain poured down. It poured again right after breakfast and then turned into hot sun, masked by the occasional cloud from midday for the rest of the day. We quickly put out buckets to catch the rainwater this morning and are glad the water butts filled too, in case we get a prolonged spell of hot weather. Martin remarked that the heavy rain should quell any rebellious spirits on the village green today, as he prepared to go to the market with Tony and the boys. I didn't want to go, in case there was any more trouble, so I kept busy hoeing the vegetable beds and sowing more salads. I've picked our first lettuce and spinach and need to sow more to keep them coming. I've also sown courgettes in the greenhouse, where they should get off to a rapid start if I keep an eye on the watering.

When Martin and the lads returned from the pub, they said there was some grumbling from the encampment, but that generally order had been restored and the usual traders had been able to distribute their wares. They brought back carrots, onions, broccoli and beef, so I've started a stew simmering slowly by the fire. Martin had also picked up a large piece of pork belly and wants me to make crackling, which is a bit challenging but I think I might be able to work out how to do it for tomorrow. But the most exciting ingredient they found was yeast. Not dried yeast or fresh yeast, but a yeast culture that one of the WI members has been cultivating and sharing around. I'll have to keep it alive with a little sugar, while I decide how to use it.

And the rain and sun are encouraging the wild flowers and wild life outside. The garden is full of foxgloves, both pink and white, their tall majestic stems have shot up in the beds, round ponds and the borders of ditches. There are ducklings on the front pond again, but I'm afraid they won't live long as the magpies are swooping. But my broody hen is hot and cross and dashes from her nest to eat in a bad temper, when I check for freshly laid eggs, leaving her the five she has been sitting on for a week and a half now. Hens sit for twenty-one days, so her babies should be due around mid-summer and she will be a better mother than the careless duck.

Sunday, June 8
I wanted to go to church today, but I didn't want to

walk round the encampment on the village green. I'm sure it has settled down since Neil and the boys confronted them, but I still feel nervous. I was wondering how to get there, as we usually go through the village, when Gail came to tell me that there is another route across the river. An old rickety bridge has been made safe. It leads into the garden of the British Legion and from there we can walk straight to the church.

So we set off, but I made Martin and Tony come with us, just in case there was trouble. It was a shorter walk than round the village green and very pleasant, as we skirted the water meadows, crossed the quaking bridge, then walked alongside the Legion's bowling green, which is smoothly mown despite local difficulties. They must have an old-fashioned mower and roller, to keep it in such good condition.

The church looked very different to the last time I was there, as it has been accommodating some of the refugee families and in some ways was all the better for that.

As it was a glorious day, there were little children playing hide and seek amongst the yew trees and gravestones in the churchyard and there were sleeping bags rolled and put aside on many of the pews. Women were sitting at the table in the church room, drinking mugs of tea and a couple of men were tending to a barbecue outside. But none of them was irreverent and I noticed that several joined in the service, during which we sang 'Spirit of the Living God'. I think it must have been this last hymn which prompted Martin, on the way home, to sing 'spirit of the petrol pump' and Tony to rejoin with 'spirit of

the village pub'. Gail and I walked on ahead, leaving
them to their foolishness. I told her about the broody
hen and she wants to bring Alfie to see the chicks
when they hatch.

Monday, June 9

Summer has been here yesterday and today, but I
had to rush to bring in the sheets late this afternoon
when the sky darkened and fat raindrops started
falling for a few minutes. The linen was almost dry,
just right for the flat irons. I heat them by the fire, but
sometimes have to make sure they aren't dusted with
smuts before we iron white linen.

However, in contrast to the fresh bed linen and
scent of lavender water, which I use when ironing,
today there's also been the stench of the cesspit and
the reek of men covered in filth and sweat. We
suddenly realised that our drains were backing up,
which always means there is either a blockage or that
the tank is too full of solids for the liquid to drain off
through the soakaway. I suppose we knew it would
happen sooner or later and we would normally have
booked a tank emptying in the middle of winter, but
of course we can't book anything these powerless
days.

Martin and Stephen manfully tackled the
problem. First they prised up the heavy concrete
cover to the tank, which is situated in the hen run.
That appeared to have plenty of capacity, so then
they decided the problem must lie within the drains
leading to it, so they had to lift the manhole covers,
one by one, until they found the blockage. That had
to be dug out and carted away. I was reluctant for

them to use the wheelbarrow, which we use when we fetch goods from the village, but the buckets are used for water, so the barrow was the only option. And oh, how it smelt.

They've dug a pit over the back of the woods, as far away from the house as possible, to deposit the mess. Then they needed a good wash themselves, before I would let them back in the house. Luckily it's warm outside, so I gave them soap and buckets of hot water. A hose would have been better, but that's impossible without mains water. Eventually, they smelt reasonably clean, but I refused to let them bring their dirty clothes inside the house and will wash them outside tomorrow if the weather permits. Martin is threatening to dig a 'dunny' if it happens again.

Tuesday, June 10

A horse was neighing. No, I was dreaming and then I woke to the early light streaming through the window at 5.30. The sun was so bright I was wide awake and got up straight away, even though I'd slept badly and felt hot all night. I boiled water for tea and for washing, then went outside to open the henhouse. The hens were eager to be outside and pecked at their breakfast hungrily.

And then I saw tracks in the gravel. Not tyre tracks, but grooves, as if something had been dragged over the stones. And across the lawn a trail, where in some places the grass had been torn up. I couldn't understand what it was. It wasn't a vehicle, or badgers, which sometimes rip up the turf searching for grubs and worms. I followed the tracks and found they went right round the house, across the lawns and also up the drive as far as the road.

I then became concerned about the lamb and rushed to check that Sooty was safe in her bolted house. She was eager to be up and out too, so then I had to warm a bottle for her, which she consumed in minutes, butting my hand and tugging at the teat till it was quite empty. Sooty wanted to follow me back inside the house, but I can't have lamb droppings as well as mud and dust all over the floors, so I made her stay outside on the kitchen lawn and shut the back door.

As I boiled more water and made my breakfast, I wondered about the tracks and decided to look at them again. I walked across the grass and up the drive and then back across to the henhouse, with Sooty at my heel. And then I saw a pile of heavy linked chain by the garage. I couldn't remember such a chain being stored there before and asked Martin if he'd left it there. He was as mystified as me and so we don't know where it's come from and why there are tracks but we think the chain was dragged around the grounds. What does it mean?

The hens may have seen something as they peered out of the window of their house at first light, but they can't tell us what they saw, they can only lay fresh eggs. I collected four today.

Wednesday, June 11

Last night I'd made a kind of Chinese egg fried rice, using the belly pork I cooked on Sunday. I still had Chinese five-spice in the larder, which added a lot of flavour. And while we ate, we all speculated about the chain and the tracks.

Stephen must have been reliving the kind of horror movies I'd never see, as he delighted in saying maybe it was the march of the zombies. But then I had to stop him because he was scaring Jane, who has seen the same films and been terrified. I won't have him making up stupid stories when life is already difficult enough as it is.

Martin joined in at first, saying maybe it was an escaped convict, who'd been chained up in Reading gaol. So he got a fierce look and then I cuffed the back of his head to shut him up too. But that didn't stop Jane and Anna looking fearful and worried, so I then reassured them and said I was sure that there was a rational explanation. But I'm not sure there is one.

Martin and I looked at the tracks again today. Maybe they were made by a bike, but it's odd how the turf is gouged and torn. The chain is extremely heavy and must be at least three metres long. We've left it coiled up like a giant python by the garage, but I look at it every time I go out to check on the hens and wonder how it got there. I collected three eggs today and found that there are no more fresh eggs under the broody hen. She is so bad-tempered I think the other hens daren't approach her nest. But I still push her out for food and water and she rushes outside the house clucking, her feathers puffed up, quickly gulps her corn then races back again, to sit in a maternal daze.

Thursday, June 12

I found Jane crying in a corner of the garden today.

She quickly wiped away her tears, but her eyes were red and swollen. It's not true, is it, she said, what Stephen and Dad were saying. So I had to hold her, like the child she still is inside her twenty-year-old self, and tell her not to listen to them. Then, when she was calm, we went to stroke Sooty who was sensibly lying in deep shade, out of the hot sun, which has been shining with such strength since early morning. This little lamb is growing by the day and greets us with piercing bleats if she thinks we are about to prepare her bottle.

Jane knows she must eventually join the flock and be with her own kind, but it is such a pleasure to have this dear little creature reliant on us and so apparently affectionate when we are with her. We have become her family for now and must continue to protect and feed her until she has grown enough to be out in the field. And I know, from past experience, that even once she has bonded with her sheep family out in the pasture, she will still recognise us and run to greet us.

Once Jane felt better, I persuaded her to water all the seedlings we've planted out and to give the vegetable bed a good watering. It has been hot and dry since Saturday morning and although the soil is still moist deep down, the young plants need water. Martin should have done it early this morning, but he said he thought he should go into the village with Tony to check on the encampment. I hope it's all quiet. I don't want Jane upset again and I certainly don't want Anna being frightened. She needs calm and rest now her time is drawing near. She was told it could be early July, but babies arrive when they're ready, so it could be any time now.

At least I can be pretty sure when the broody's clutch of eggs will hatch. She made angry noises when I pushed her off today, but there were no more fresh eggs in her nest, just three laid elsewhere.

Friday, June 13
No! It's Friday the 13th and tonight there will be a full moon…

Saturday, June 14
Well despite Stephen's scaremongering and Martin's doom-laden predictions, even though it was Friday the 13th and the moon was meant to be full, the sky was cloudy, so we never saw the moon and nothing else either, come to that. I gave Stephen another clip round the ear for being so stupid and sloshed some of the dirty water from the laundry over him for his pains. That dampened his enthusiasm for scare stories.

And in the end, we found out what had gouged the grass and how the chain had been left in the grounds, from our neighbours. And it wasn't a convict, or a zombie or a wild animal. It was a horse. That's all it was. An escaped horse, looking for love. We heard the story today from Robin and Deirdre, when we met them at the pub market. They started telling us how they were woken in the night a couple of days ago by neighing. And I said how funny that was, because I'd dreamt about a horse neighing. That wasn't a dream, Robin said. It was a real horse. He said he'd jumped out of bed and looked out the bedroom window and there, in his paddock, talking to Benjie, their old piebald, was a large black and white horse, with a chain trailing from his bridle.

But how did it get there, I wondered. It's a stallion, Robin said. The one tethered on the little green up beyond the church. And I remembered seeing a large horse there last summer, tied to a stake in the grass, grazing in a wide circle around his tether. He must have broken free and gone looking for company, said Robin. Only there isn't much company about at the moment, so he stopped to make friends with Benjie. We led him back to where he belongs, but the long chain wasn't there. It's up by our garage, I told them, he must have dragged it all the way here, poor lonely horse.

So now Stephen is disappointed as well as damp. And I am disappointed in my hens. The Legbars haven't laid for two days and now I know why. They're either laying soft-shelled eggs or they're eating them, as I found the Rhode Island Red's eggs sticky with smears of yolk and bits of blue shell. I'll have to add grit to their rations.

Sunday, June 15

I walked to church with Gail and we again avoided the encampment on the green by crossing the river behind the Legion. Once there, when we came to the intercessions where prayers are said for people by name as well as regions of the country, I knew I only wanted to pray for one person. I know I should think of those in cities and towns who have suffered during this difficult powerless time and of course I want to pray for relatives and friends we cannot contact at present, but right now I only really want to pray for Anna.

It has been weighing on my mind that, with her time drawing near, we can offer her very little support and care. There is a doctor in the village and also an experienced nurse, but we don't have a phone to call for help and we cannot be sure the nearest hospital can cope with any kind of emergency. So as I sat in my pew, trying to concentrate on the prayers and the readings, I felt myself begin to panic, alarmed at the prospect of what could happen. Then I told myself that she is young, she is healthy, she should make it to full term and women all over the world give birth to babies every day without any kind of intervention.

I found it terribly hard to listen to the sermon, as I was mentally listing the preparations still to be made. Jane has helped Anna make clothes and terry nappies and the Moses basket is freshly lined. We don't know for sure when the baby will arrive. In normal times, regular checks and scans would give more accurate predictions, so all we know is that it will come when it's ready and that could be any day soon. So we must be ready too.

Monday, June 16

I decided this morning that I would spend the day getting ready for the birth. Anna could go into labour today, tomorrow or next month. I don't want to worry her, as she is bursting with health as well as her baby, but I will feel much better if we make preparations now.

My first baby, Stephen, was due in mid-January, so I bought Christmas presents early and packed my bag a month before. But he didn't turn up until the end of the first week in February and has continued to be a poor time-keeper ever since. And Jane was due on July 23 and when the day came, she popped out on time and is known for her punctuality.

So Anna and I sat together and talked about what she would need when the time comes. She won't have a lot of choice as there won't be gas and air, nor an epidural and certainly not a water birth. She asked if that might be possible, if the weather was warm, but after some discussion we decided that heating a large quantity of water, which might not be utterly pure, was out of the question, even though we still have an old blow-up paddling pool in the garage.

But Anna will have a clean bed and clean towels in a familiar environment. Rainwater is our cleanest source, so that will be boiled on the fire and I have put a plastic sheet and old towels under the bottom sheet, in case her waters break in bed. We packed the freshly laundered dry towels in a hamper in her bedroom, so they won't be used by mistake. And I have saved a fresh bar of soap too, wanting everything to be clean and new for the new life that will come soon.

Then, when I went to feed the hens this afternoon, I found the broody hen refused to leave her nest. She has gone into the dazed trance of imminent motherhood, so I left her to sit and dream of her chicks while I collected three eggs from the far corner of the henhouse.

Tuesday, June 17

I came indoors after hanging out the washing, to find Martin chipping away at the bricked-up bread oven at the back of the inglenook fireplace. I started to protest at the mess of broken bricks and the fact that he'd let the fire go out, when he said he was trying to see if he could open up the old oven.

I'd always assumed that it had been destroyed when another room was built on beyond the dining room, but he said there was a cavity behind the bricks so perhaps the oven still existed. This is really quite exciting, even though he has been chipping away for most of the day and I've not been able to relight the fire at all. I've had to use the hall fire to boil water, but as the weather has stayed dry, we've been able to use the barbecue outside as well to cook black pudding and eggs.

And the other exciting news was new potatoes! We are so starved of different foods and flavours, that even though we are all eating well and have nourishing meals, we are all so thrilled at the thought of tasting delicious new potatoes. We'll eat them tonight with some lamb chops and I'll spare a little of our precious butter for them and make a mint sauce as well. Stephen dug up the potatoes today, but we all agreed we shouldn't harvest many while they are so small, as we need the crop to feed us for some time. He thinks the next treat will be fresh peas.

Martin says he'll finish clearing out the oven tomorrow and then try to figure out how to make it work. It will be wonderful to have a working oven again, even a blackened, sooty one like this.

Wednesday, June 18

Today's been a good day for laundering linen, as we've had sun, cloud and a breeze, so the washing doesn't bake and stiffen, but dries relatively uncreased. And as the lavender is coming into flower, I dried some of the smaller things, the pillowcases, handkerchiefs and underwear, on the lavender bushes that edge the forecourt and the courtyard. They'll smell even sweeter than when they're dried on the line.

I know this compulsion to constantly launder is because of the baby's imminent arrival. With my own babies I felt the urge to 'nest', trying to complete every domestic task well before the big day, but with the prospect of a precious grandchild I feel as driven as if it was my own. All must be clean, all must be as near to perfect as possible, in this fraught and dangerous world we are now living in.

The linen is not as clean as I would really like because of the quality of the water. How did we ever take mains water for granted? The turn of a tap for fresh sparkling water seems like another life altogether. Since the mains stopped working, our cleanest source has been rainwater and even that can be cloudy when it comes from the water butts. When we have heavy rain we try to collect it in clean buckets and bowls, but there is a limit to how much we can store. The well is also a useful source of water, but it's murky and I insist we boil it first as it must be full of tiny bugs.

And out in the henhouse, the broody is also nesting. However, she is not rushing around madly cleaning and preparing, she is just quietly sitting in a stupor. I slid my hand underneath her this afternoon when I went in to collect the freshly laid eggs (three) and I pulled out a warm egg to listen for signs that the chicks will soon hatch. The first one I held to my ear was silent, but the second was cheeping. Perhaps tomorrow I will hear it start to peck through the shell, or maybe I will find it has hatched and is peeping out from under its mother's feathery bosom.

Thursday, June 19

Despite the heavy cloud today, it hasn't yet rained, so we've had to water some of the crops which baked under a hot sun yesterday. We're using dirty water for the watering, rather than fresh, although we still need to recycle water for the toilet cistern. Martin and Stephen don't worry about going in the cloakroom and flushing, they can go outside most of the time. And Jane and I don't mind either in daylight, but I can't insist that a heavily pregnant girl squats behind the bushes, so Anna still enjoys the luxury of our only flush toilet.

Today Jane and Anna wanted to hear the cheeping egg, so we all went down to the henhouse together and the girls waited while I crept inside to borrow an egg from the broody. She has started to murmur softly to her nearly hatched chicks. I slid my hand underneath her hot feathers and quietly slipped outside with the egg clutched in my hand. We took turns to listen and there it was – a tiny tap as well as a high pitched cheep.

I've heard it many times before and so has Jane, but it never fails to amaze us, this life inside the egg, talking to its mother and the world before it emerges.

I slipped back into the henhouse and gently replaced the egg beneath the sitting hen, who briefly came out of her muttering daze and pecked my hand. When I came out of the run, nursing the purple bruise on the back of my hand, Anna looked at me with a smile and wide eyes and said I wonder if the baby is talking inside me. It's certainly kicking, but maybe it's trying to talk to me and I can't hear it. But it can hear you, I told her, it will know your voice even before it's born.

It's at times like that, when we are laughing and marvelling at what is to come, that we forget how difficult life is now. But when I come indoors to stoke the fire and boil more water, I remember.

Friday, June 20

In my frenzy to make everything clean for the baby, I encouraged Jane to help me today in cleaning the carpets. Thank goodness most of the ground floor is brick and tile, which can be swept easily, but carpet has to be brushed or beaten. Oh, what I would give for a vacuum cleaner which dealt with dirt at the flick of a switch.

We have a very ancient carpet sweeper, which Jane pushed umpteen times over the fitted carpet in Anna and Stephen's bedroom. It collected quite a lot of dust and fluff, but the stair carpets we've had to brush by hand. It has made me realise how important specific brushes were to generations before electric hoovers. A regular dustpan brush just won't do the job correctly. Stiff bristles are what's needed.

So we brushed and swept all morning, and took

rugs outside to beat until finally we were satisfied that the baby will enter a relatively clean bedroom, if not house and certainly not world. The curtains are washed, the paintwork is polished, the bed linen has been laundered and there is a plentiful supply of clean sheets and towels in the airing cupboard.

Then we turned our attention to supper, for we have a treat tonight. Robin came down the lane saying he'd been trapping rabbits up the road. We don't have them here in our grounds and fields, which is fortunate for the garden as they eat their way through a veg patch in a single night. So we are having a casserole of rabbit with carrots and onions. I think sage dumplings will work well too, even though it is a fine summery day. And he brought another very special treat – strawberries! We don't have cream but we have sugar, though they are sweet enough just as they are after all the sun.

Out in the henhouse, where I collected four eggs, the broody doesn't care about cleanliness. She is still sitting and murmuring, but I swear I could hear peeping beneath her, louder than before. So I think the first chick may have hatched.

Saturday, June 21

This morning I woke at 4.30am to find the sun was already shining brightly and I realised that today is the longest day of the year. It's Midsummer's Day and we shall have more light than we've had ever since the power cut started. The house can still get too dark in the evenings to see to read or sew, of course, but outside, if it's not too cold tonight, we shall sit at the table in the garden until the sun goes down.

I agreed to go with Martin to the village today, to
see if the Saturday barter market is up and running
again. Martin had pheasants to take and Robin, our
neighbour, had more rabbits. Some of the younger
villagers were put off by the fur and feathers and
preferred the minced beef from the farm butcher. But
the older residents aren't scared of wild meat they
have to skin or pluck.

We collected asparagus and peas and were about
to go when we noticed some people dressed in white
sheets, moving amongst the tents in the encampment
on the village green. Mick, the publican, saw us
looking and said some of the incomers had daft ideas
about welcoming the sun today. It's not exactly
Stonehenge, he said, but they've been up Bonfire Hill
all night, waiting for the sun to rise. I expect half of
them fell asleep drunk, knowing this useless lot.

It was true there were quite a few figures slumped
in and out of tents, some in full sun, some in the
shade. But where are they getting the drink, I asked,
knowing that the pub had run out of alcohol long
ago. Oh they're making it themselves somewhere, he
said. End up killing themselves, they will, or go
blind.

We left then, as it wasn't a pleasant sight. I
wanted to get home and shell the fresh peas and
cook them with mint for supper. We're having
another rabbit tonight. I tossed the pea pods into the
hen run and the hens rushed towards their dinner.
Not the broody hen, of course. She is still sitting, but
I could just see a little pale yellow head poke out
briefly, then pop back under her brown feathers. So
one chick has emerged and more will follow.

Sunday, June 22

Last night we sat outside till ten, after eating rabbit
cooked with parsley and mustard, served with new
potatoes and peas. As the light slowly faded, bats
swooped overhead, then Jane squealed when she
saw a large toad crawling amongst the pots of herbs.
We all looked more closely and found what seemed
to be a family of toads living in and around the
garden shed. They must have thrived during the
mild, wet winter and will do a great job eating the
garden pests.

Everything in the garden is bursting with life
because the ground is still so damp from those
months of rain. And when we went to church today,
we found that various gardens which open for
charity every summer were still having an open day.
Although several owners have turned their flower
beds over to produce, the gardens were still
festooned with great flower-laden swags of pink and
white climbing roses and purple clematis,
clambering up cottage walls and over twisted apple
trees. And whereas in previous years the owners
would sell plants for their chosen charity, today they
were giving away surplus strawberries, peas, lettuce,
asparagus and radishes. Soon there will be broad
beans, cucumbers and beetroot, making me think we
haven't done that well with our vegetable beds,
which have carrots, cabbage and potatoes, but not
much else.

As we walked home, we noticed the elderflower
in full bloom in all the hedgerows and Jane asked if
we couldn't make something with the flower heads,
so tonight we shall have a dessert of elderflower

fritters to eat with strawberries. The hens have had the hulls from the berries, mixed with other scraps. The broody won't leave her nest yet and I think I saw two little faces peering out from under her feathers, late this afternoon.

Monday, June 23

Yesterday and today have been hot and sunny, yet here we are, trying to heat the bread oven. Martin thinks he's managed to restore it and now we're trying to work out how to use it. We think we have to heat it first by lighting a fire inside the oven itself.

The first time we tried, we closed the door and that soon made the fire go out. Now we're trying to get the inside of the oven really hot, but leaving the door open. It's hard to tell how hot it is and then we have to rake out the ashes. I was reluctant to waste much of our precious stores on testing the oven, but unless we try we'll never know if it works. So I've made some rolls with the yeast starter I've been feeding for over a week and we'll know soon if they work. I've left them to rise, covered over with a damp tea towel and when I've finished writing this I'll try baking them. Martin is heating the oven again now, with fragments of the Scots pine that came down last summer, as it burns very hot.

In the days when we had electricity, we never lit a fire in the summer unless it was suddenly very cold and rainy. But now we still have to keep the fire burning all the time to heat water and cook. It is sunny outside even though it's now gone six, yet here we are, stoking the fire and baking.

We're hoping for more supplies in the village this

week. It's been a while since the last delivery and our stocks are running low. We have plenty of meat and vegetables, but the staples are so useful if we are to make substantial meals. And I'm getting concerned about fresh water. It still hasn't rained and although the soil is quite damp deep down and everything is growing well, our crops could do with a good drop of rain. But most of all I want more fresh water for washing and for bathing Anna and her baby, when the time comes.

I took some well water out to the hens, as they don't care if it's murky and only kick soil into their drinking water anyway, when they scratch in their run. I carried a saucer in to the broody, as her chicks have hatched but she won't yet come out into the open. She hovers over them with her wings spread, like a great feathery umbrella, while she pecks at her food and sips her water. I've given her a very shallow dish of water so the chicks won't drown.

Tuesday, June 24

The bread rolls were dense but delicious. We all loved the crunch of the crust and the yeasty flavour of the crumb. I'm baking some more tonight, but it's too hot right now to be standing beside a blazing fire. The sun is at its height and we need water, so Martin and I are checking on our stocks. The two rainwater butts are about half full and the well still has plenty. But if this warm weather continues we could soon run low.

Martin suggested that he and Stephen should dig a couple of bore holes in the lower part of the garden and grounds, where the water table is high. They started digging this morning and if this is successful, that water will be used for the garden, mainly the vegetable beds. The soil is damp only a few inches beneath the surface, so they are hopeful that they will be able to tap into the ground water. Then the dirty water from washing can be used to keep the cistern flushing.

Jane is busy picking more elderflower. The bushes are full of the lacy caps this year and although elderberries would be useful too, she is determined to make cordial or wine with the flowers. I've been sterilising some old preserving jars and bottles in readiness.

And Anna is resting. She is feeling the weight of the baby in this heat and takes a long nap every afternoon. But she feels well and has been washing the elderflower heads to remove bits of leaf and insects. She has also been embroidering a blanket for the baby. The date and name will be added later.

But the broody has her babies. There are six chicks, four lemon yellow, two almost black. She hovered in the doorway of the henhouse today, with them cheeping under her wings. She may take them out by tomorrow, but for now I put food and water inside the house for them.

Wednesday, June 25

All this time, ever since the power cut began, we've stayed healthy. Through the wet and cold of winter we had little more than coughs and colds, but now, suddenly, we are all sick. We are all being sick, every one of us.

We feel wretched and I cannot think where this

has come from. The water we drink is boiled, even if it's rainwater. I cook meat carefully and it's always fresh. Could it have been the rabbit? I don't think so, as it was freshly caught and skinned. Maybe we picked up a bug with the sacraments in church on Sunday. But I don't think that's it either, as we've all fallen ill at the same time. It must be something we've eaten or drunk here.

I'm most concerned about Anna, who is also vomiting. She mustn't become weak and dehydrated. So I've given her the bottled water we kept by for emergencies. There was none in the rations that were delivered yesterday and until now I hadn't thought we'd ever need it. But now, she must recover quickly, just in case the baby comes early.

That's all I can manage for today. I've fed the hens and they are all fine and the chicks have come outside then been herded back again by their very protective mother.

Thursday, June 26

We are bruised and tired, but we are able to hold down food and drink again. I still have no idea why or how we became ill, but thank goodness we are no longer sick.

Martin thinks it was the bore holes that caused it. I think that's ridiculous, because the holes are nowhere near any source of foul water. And in fact, the so-called holes were more like mud baths. Martin and Stephen dug down as far as they could, but they never managed to collect a decent amount of water. They collected mud on their knees and feet, their clothes and their faces, but they couldn't seem to excavate enough mud to dip a bucket in a pool of water. They slung the wet mud over the veg patch, so at least it made a damp mulch for the plants and will have delivered a certain amount of moisture.

Stephen has been blaming himself for not properly boiling the water the last time he made tea for us all. He said he thought the water was hot enough, so I've stressed that all our water, even the rainwater, has to be boiled. It is boring, I know, but it's vital. And Jane thinks it's all her fault because she didn't wash the lettuce she picked the other day as it looked clean enough. It's nobody's fault, I said, but we all have to be more careful.

As we are all feeling rather delicate, we are only eating rice and scrambled eggs today. The hens are still laying well and I've collected four eggs. The chicks came out for a longer period with their mother and pecked at some green stuff she clucked over, telling them it was good to eat. I've changed the hens' water trough for a shallow plant saucer for now, as we once had a tiny chick drown in the drinking water. They stand on the edge, not knowing that a few inches of water is like a deep and dangerous swimming pool for a chick that's only a couple of days old.

Then, at 5pm, the rain began, so I've set out every bowl and container I can find, to collect fresh, safe water.

Friday, June 27
It rained yesterday, but not for long. We filtered the water we collected into empty bottles so we have fresh for when we need it. But at least the rain

refreshed the garden and we haven't needed to water again today, even though the sun has been shining all afternoon. Everything is growing quickly and we even have raspberries forming on the bushes.

Linda called in this morning and said Neil is going to do regular inspections of the sheep from now on, as the warm sun and rain create the humid conditions perfect for fly strike. I said I thought they would be okay since he treated them early last month, but Linda said the spray is not guaranteed protection and it's now seven weeks since they were treated. He will have to round them up in the pen to check the whole flock properly, so I may go along to help. He would normally be shearing soon, but it's going to be harder to do the job without electricity and it's easier to shear if the fleece is dry.

Then I asked Linda if she'd like to try the bread rolls I made. She thought they were really good and is going to give me some of her flour ration so we can bake more in the bread oven. Rolls are the easiest thing to cook in it, but I might try a small loaf next. I also thought I could add some herbs and I think I may even have poppy and sesame seeds somewhere at the back of the pantry. I've also realised that once the oven is really hot, it holds the heat for some time, certainly long enough to slow cook other foods. Martin wants me to make apple pies, but I've said I'll try pasties as I don't yet have fruit. Or I could maybe bake an egg and bacon pie, like my great-aunt used to make when I was young.

The rain was good for the hens too, as it dampened the soil in the hen run and encouraged the worms. I dug them up with a fork when I went in this afternoon, creating great excitement amongst the hens. I collected four eggs and the mother hen was teaching her youngsters to scratch in the soil for food.

Saturday, June 28

Heavy showers of rain today and it's also much colder, so I haven't minded staying inside cooking with the bread oven. Martin and Stephen went into the village with Tony and came back with minced beef, onions and carrots, so I can make a batch of pasties for supper and tomorrow.

I've been concerned during this warmer weather about keeping food fresh. The pantry is the coolest place, but I don't have a meat safe, like my granny used to have, so I feel I have to cook meat as soon as we get it. We've noticed more flies over the past week, so I hope Neil's sheep are still safe. He hasn't rounded them up today as the weather has changed. I expect he'll do it in a day or so when it's drier.

The cats have stayed indoors more today, which is a relief as they have been decimating the wildlife around here for the past week. I heard a commotion in the hedge a few days ago and found Tickles had climbed up to a nest and was sitting beside it on a branch, eating the fledglings straight from the nest as if it was a dinner plate. It was a horrific sight and I shooed her out, but I knew she would return later to finish her meal. And yesterday, just after lunch, Tom rushed into the kitchen and dropped a headless mouse at my feet. I told him to take it away, but I think he'd had his fill, so I had to pick it up by the tail and throw it into the hedge. I know it's in their nature and that we wanted the cats to keep the house mice away, but sometimes their murderous instincts are hard to stomach.

We've been able to collect more fresh water each time it rains, so we needn't water the garden for a day or so. The bore holes Martin and Stephen dug have filled with muddy water, so they are hauling some of that out to save for drier weather.

And I've been able to fork up more worms to make the hens happy, though I wasn't so happy to see one of them peck at a bold chick which tried to tackle one of the worms. So their mother shooed them out of trouble and found a worm for them herself.

Sunday, June 29

When Martin and I came back from church today, Stephen said he was worried about Anna. He said she was feeling uncomfortable and he thought she was getting contractions. I went upstairs to see her and found she was making the bed, not lying down.

She said Stephen was fussing for nothing and she and I both think the Braxton Hicks contractions are just getting a little more noticeable and more regular now. I asked her what she had been doing while we were out and she laughed and said she'd been sweeping the floor, then felt the contractions and stopped suddenly, holding her stomach, just as Stephen came in with a pile of kindling for the fire. He's just like his father, I said, getting worried for no reason. Best not to let him know next time, until the real thing.

Anna is looking and feeling really well, despite the sickness earlier in the week. I am very hopeful that she will have an easy birth, even though it is her first, and that the baby will be in good health. Then we sat and talked for a little while about the preparations we've made and how she feels about the forthcoming birth. She is sorry her own mother won't be here, but she has said she wants me to be present, especially if the village midwife or doctor can't attend.

Then we laughed a bit about how we saw the sheep getting on with lambing out in the open field this spring, without any assistance at all. It makes human beings seem like a load of weaklings, Anna said. Not only do the ewes give birth all alone, but their young are up and running about within a day.

This year's lambs are also now quite large. The oldest is more than three months old and the first of the young rams have already developed curled horns. I expect when Neil rounds them up for his inspections, he will pick out one or two for slaughter, as they would normally be going off to the abattoir by now.

Monday, June 30

Such an annoying day. It started fine and sunny, so Jane and I did the washing outside, put it all through the mangle and hung it on the line. Then at lunchtime, just when we needed a rest, huge black clouds covered the sky and within minutes there was a downpour. We managed to bring in most of the clothes before they were thoroughly soaked, but now they have to finish drying indoors. And it has carried on raining, with light showers and thundery bursts all afternoon.

As it is cooler, I haven't minded stoking the fire and the oven to cook. The bread oven is working out well, as long as I have really dry kindling to heat it, so Stephen is making a point of constantly bringing in more than we used to have just for the main fire.

I made the bread first, attempting a tin loaf, which has come out well with a good cracked crust. Then, as the oven was still hot, I'm roasting some of the lamb that Neil brought across this morning. He slaughtered one of the older ram lambs, before it became a nuisance, he said. I didn't ask for more details, as I don't want it to be one we gave a name to. I just want to think about it being a nice juicy hunk of fresh meat, which I'm cooking with rosemary and wild garlic. We'll have it with mint sauce and some new potatoes. We've been getting long-life milk in the rations recently, so I think I'll also make a custard tart, using our eggs, a little sugar and nutmeg. I'll bake the pastry case blind, with a weight of baking beans, then add the filling. It's not Martin's favourite, but I like it and so do the girls. I've still got whole nutmeg in the pantry, to grate over the top.

Neil said he had to give up sorting the sheep, because of the heavy rain. But he says the next day or so should be good. I asked how he knew and he just tapped his nose and said, shepherd's instinct. I think he's full of old wives' tales, or old shepherds' tales, but he does seem to understand natural signs. And without the aid of weather forecasts on TV, radio, online or in newspapers, we are reliant on people with a feel for the countryside to guide us.

Tuesday, July 1

Jane and I managed to finish drying yesterday's washing outside this morning, while it was warm and sunny. But the clouds started drifting across at lunchtime and I decided to bring it all inside, rather than risk a soaking.

Anna is restless and uncomfortable, but I don't think she is starting yet. She wanted to wash her hair, so Jane warmed water and washed it outside for her, on the garden table. We've no shampoo left, so it has to be done with soap or not at all. But I let her have a dash of vinegar for rinsing and her hair looks soft and lustrous after being brushed dry in the sun.

I wish my hair was half as thick and shiny. My highlights grew out long ago and I know it is lank and dull, so I tie it up in a knot most of the time and wear a scarf, looking for all the world like an old fishwife. And though my hands are clean, my fingers and palms are calloused. I've run out of hand cream and cuticle oil and a manicure seems another lifetime away. But at least my hands are strong and are capable of doing anything from digging the garden to washing linen, from kneading bread to feeding lambs and chickens.

Martin and Stephen went into the village this morning to see if this week's rations had arrived. They came back with bacon, cheese, more long-life milk, flour, rice, tea, cooking oil and butter. There was also a delivery of toilet paper, which was lucky, as we are running low and I think a pregnant lady should be spared the indignity of rummaging through a paperback book for a page to use. And to our great excitement, there was also dark chocolate!

We are all going to have one square each after supper.

With these extra supplies I feel I can afford to continue making bread, which we are all enjoying. We had fresh rolls this morning with boiled eggs as the hens are continuing to lay well. I collected another four eggs this afternoon and the chicks are thriving.

Wednesday, July 2

Such a glorious day and I was happily pegging out washing and thinking it might be warm enough to cook outside on the barbecue this evening, when Linda came rushing over from the caravan. She said the warm and wet conditions had brought out the flies and Neil was struggling to get the sheep rounded up. He wants to start shearing if he can, but needs some help.

Martin had just come in from splitting logs and said he and Stephen would go over to help. Linda said she wouldn't mind assisting, but several of the sheep look as if they've already got fly strike. I looked at Martin, as he can be terribly squeamish, unless it's a giant spider, and asked if he was sure he could cope. He crossly said of course he could cope and stomped off with Stephen.

I told Linda I was sure he'd be back before long, as he's never experienced fly strike before and won't even touch any dead creatures in the garden. She laughed and said she was with Martin on this one. She said she can cope with stillborn lambs, castrating rams and foot rot, but she draws the line at flies.

In the end, Martin lasted nearly two hours. He

came back looking rather green, saying he'd had enough and Neil had run out of pour-on. I told Martin to stoke the fire and put the kettle on and I went to the shed to see what I could find. We had a full can of Jeyes Fluid and I mixed up a strong solution to fill four old plastic plant sprayers. Then I grabbed my rubber gloves and went to join Neil.

By the time I got there, the sheep were sorted into three groups and Stephen was also looking rather grim, so I told him to go back to the house and help his father with the wood and keeping the fire going. There were only four sheep that definitely had fly strike and the other groups were lambs that won't be sheared this year and the ewes due for shearing. Neil was inspecting this last group more thoroughly in case they too had flies. Then we tackled the affected sheep. Neil held each one while I rubbed the Jeyes Fluid solution into the infected part, making all the maggots wriggle to the surface of the fleece and drop to the ground. Once they'd all been treated, we penned them up separately from the others, just to be sure they were clean.

Then we started shearing. Neil normally has a shearer visit in the summer with petrol driven equipment, but there is no way of contacting her or getting hold of the right kit in time. Neil was cursing himself for not having his own gear, so we had to cut the fleece away with dagging shears. I ran back to the house at one stage to fetch my dressmaking scissors, but there was no way we could speed up the process. We did about half the flock and then decided that was enough for one day.

When I got home, Martin said he didn't know how I could bear to touch the maggoty fleece. I laughed and said I would have collected the maggots for the hens, if they hadn't been contaminated with Jeyes Fluid.

Thursday, July 3

Today has been the hottest day so far and although I love the sun, I retreated to the house in the middle of the day to recover in the cool shade. Anna is resting and Jane is cooking and I have been helping to finish shearing the sheep.

They hate being turned on their backs during the process, but they must love being relieved of their thick winter coats now that the weather is so warm. As each ewe is released, the lambs find it hard to recognise their mothers, until they hear a familiar baa.

We found a few more odd patches of fly strike, but nothing as bad as the ones we dealt with yesterday. Linda says she can cope with it now and so I have done my shift and will leave the rest to her and Neil. They are actually getting fewer nicks than they usually suffer with the mechanical shears, so hopefully they will not get any flies bothering their injuries, which we sprayed with blue antiseptic.

Late this afternoon, Stephen said it was too hot to do any more work and he was going for a swim. I couldn't think what he meant, then he said he was going up the road, past the crossroads to the ponds. I knew where that was and they are more lakes than ponds, but there is a sign saying no swimming. Bugger that he said, on a day like this, I'm going in and no one's stopping me.

So I decided to join him. Jane said she would stay

with Anna and at the last minute Martin decided to come too. We were so hot by the time we'd walked the length of the lane and cold water always feels even colder when you're hot, but although it was icy at first, it was wonderful. Stephen and I swam the full length of the lake and back again, but Martin chickened out and lay in the sun on one of the landing stages that the anglers use to fish from.

Then we walked back in damp swimwear laughing at how we defied the notice and had swum in the open for the best swim we've ever had. I fed the hens and collected four eggs, then we sat and dried off in the evening sun.

Friday, July 4

Today could be the day, but it doesn't look like it will be. The doctor thought the 4th of July might be Anna's due date and there are still a few hours to go, but I don't think it is going to happen yet. Even with all the technical advances that have been made in obstetrics, there is still no guarantee that a baby will arrive when it's due.

It's not like chickens, which sit for twenty-one days and then the chicks pop out. A baby comes when it's ready and although Anna is prepared and is excited at the prospect of meeting her baby very soon, it will not come any sooner. Of course, if it was a planned Caesarean it could all be neatly fitted in around other commitments, but there is nothing planned about this birth, apart from the freshly lined Moses basket, the layette of tiny clothes and the clean bed.

Stephen has been pacing about, looking as if he is

already the expectant father, asking Anna every few hours how she is feeling. I told him she is feeling fine and all the better for not being pestered. Anna herself is calm, serene and happy. She likes to rest in the afternoon as she feels hot at night and her bump makes sleeping difficult, even with an extra pillow. But she is still keeping active, taking an interest in all our comings and goings.

So we may not have an Independence Day baby after all, but we shall soon have a healthy baby and that is all that matters.

Saturday, July 5

After the hot and steamy days at the end of the week, today is cooler and wetter. There have been fine showers of rain on and off all day, so I haven't attempted any laundry and we shall have to cook indoors tonight.

But despite the rain, we walked into the village for the Saturday market, taking a surplus of peas to swop for other produce and were pleased to find that strawberries were available again. And our farm butcher had a stack of hamburgers, saying he was only a day late for the 4th of July, so we took a dozen as they are easy to cook. We'll eat them tonight with a salad of freshly cut lettuce and dandelion leaves and I'll fry crispy onion rings, dipped in batter. I'm not sure my bread making skills are up to producing soft bap rolls, but I'll try all the same as the bread will soak up the juices from the meat.

As Martin, Jane and I walked back, we joked that we would make Stephen enter the village marathon, which was one of the main topics of conversation in the pub today. It always takes place in the first week in July and in previous years it has attracted serious athletes from all around the county. This year only local people will be competing, but as there is a large influx of strangers in the village there will still be competition for the outsider's cup. The race is not a full marathon but a course of some five miles over rough terrain, culminating in a splash through the shallowest part of the river and a scramble up a slippery riverbank. We decided he should get in training for next Friday, especially if he eats more than his fair share of burgers.

When we were home, Stephen said he would enter, but he needed barbecue sauce to go with the hamburgers. That's not an easy request to fulfil these days and we ran out of tomato ketchup and brown sauce long ago, so I investigated my almost depleted larder and created a concoction from an old tube of tomato puree, garlic paste, tabasco and smoked paprika. Then he said he would need a fried egg on top, to build up his strength for the ordeal. Thank goodness the hens laid well again today.

Sunday, July 6

Why won't some people heed warnings? Why oh why, just when we need calm and peace, do Stephen and Martin have to ignore my advice and end up casualties again?

Martin shouldn't have even gone into the attic, with his bad back and Stephen should never have gone up on the roof. I told them to leave the wasps alone and I told them I was sure we still had some powder hidden away in the shed or the garage. But oh no, they both had to go and 'investigate'. And the result is that Martin is hobbling about saying he's strained his back again and Stephen has hurt his other foot, the one that wasn't burnt by the boiling oil, but which only healed a short time ago.

It all started because Anna said she'd seen a few wasps in the corridor leading to her bedroom this morning. It is the time of year when they start being very active and we always seem to have a large number of nests in our old tiled roof, which faces the sun all day.

Anna wasn't too concerned, but I said we'd see if the nest was reachable, so we could dust it at dusk tonight. But Stephen became all protective and said he had to locate it right now and then Martin said it might be in the attic and before I could stop them they were off and minutes later were walking wounded. I told them before, not to do it and afterwards I told them off and said they weren't getting any of my sympathy. It's just like when the children were small and became stuck in the mud at a river in Devon. They were told not to venture into the mud, so why were they surprised I was cross when they were dragged out covered in stinking slime?

Still, at least Martin wasn't stung, as he reacts badly to wasp stings and we could do without anaphylactic shock on top of everything. I left him resting while I worked on the garden and Jane cooked supper, then I found the wasp powder. Later tonight, after dark, I'll go in the attic to find the nest and deal with it. I told the hens how annoying they all were when I fed them late this afternoon. They clucked sympathetically and gave me four eggs. It's so comforting to know that some things in life are utterly reliable.

Monday, July 7

So much has happened it is hard to know where to begin, as this has been the most momentous day. But the most important event of all has happened. Anna gave birth this afternoon. A girl, a healthy baby girl. I don't know how much she weighs, I just know she is perfect and Anna coped extremely well with a labour that started early this morning and she is now resting, with her baby tucked into the freshly lined basket beside her.

And now, although it is late and night has fallen, I can write this because we also have light! Everything is working again! As the baby emerged, the lights all over the house suddenly flickered and then, as she took her first cry, they all came on together in broad daylight. We must have left lights and appliances switched on all over the house and Martin rushed about to 'save electricity' as if it would disappear if we didn't conserve it immediately.

We have news on the radio and TV, we have a working fridge, I have an electric cooker again and, oh bliss, a washing machine! I keep thinking this might not last and of course, life is not quite back to normal yet as the mains water has not been restored. Apparently the treatment plants have to be checked and cleaned, so it will be a week or so before I can turn on a tap.

But for now, we have power and we have a new baby. We have survived all these months and so we can survive a little longer. Life may never be the same as it was before the long nights of the power cut, but it will be a life.

And as we ate supper with the lights on, we talked about the tiny new life upstairs and what she might be called. Martin said as she was born at such a momentous time, Dawn would be a good name, but he was shouted down. Then Stephen said he and Anna had already decided. She has a name – she is Hope.

EPILOGUE

Powerless – the year the lights went out began with a dream. A dream in which, faced with a long-term power cut, I responded by emptying the freezer to make a soup of frozen vegetables. When I woke, I thought it would be interesting to write a fictional blog based on such a calamity occurring in the country house where we had lived for twenty-one years, near a village, near farms, surrounded by woods and fields.

I thought about how we would heat the house, gathering kindling before the winter rains soaked the wood, how we would pick mushrooms and nuts, hunt for game and how we could survive on the wild food around us. I imagined being resourceful, resilient and positive, writing the entries each day, being faithful to the weather at the time.

Many of the incidents in *Powerless* were real, though many weren't. We did once find a deer dead on our doorstep, but no one was injured by an axe splitting logs. I really did rescue a fox cub from drowning in a ditch and I bottle-fed a sickly abandoned lamb one spring. But the real lamb died and only Sooty, the fictional lamb, lived on. And amongst the many incidents recorded in the blog, the disappearance of the hens, the hellebore circle, the toad-eating snake, the chain and the run-away horse, the fearsome cockerel and the hatching chicks, were all experienced by us. They didn't all happen in a few months, but they all happened at some time over the years.

During the winter we also experienced a four-day power cut which made me wonder if I should be careful what I wish for. But it gave me an opportunity to cook over the fire and test some of the theories incorporated in *Powerless*.

But eventually our time in that ancient house with its huge inglenook fireplaces, its uneven brick floors worn over centuries, its rough wattle and daub walls, its oak beams and its spiders and cobwebs, came to an end. It was time for us to move onto another adventure, which was documented in another less frequent blog. Entitled *A Moving Story*, it recorded the dismantling of a much loved house and the life we had lived there. We fed chickens, bred sheep, patted pigs, made hay and scared deer. We sat by blazing fires, mowed acres of lawn, pruned rambling roses, stacked logs and planted an avenue of trees, but finally it was time to leave and find a new way of life.

18195227R00181

Printed in Poland
by Amazon Fulfillment
Poland Sp. z o.o., Wrocław